FILIP AND MATEI FLORIAN
THE BĂIUȚ ALLEY LADS
Translated by Alistair Ian Blyth

Featured Artist
Ioan Atanasiu Delamare

University of Plymouth Press

20 ROMANIAN WRITERS SERIES

Filip and Matei Florian's *The Băiuţ Alley Lads* is the seventh title to be published in the series 20 Romanian Writers by the University of Plymouth Press. The series is one aspect of the University of Plymouth's ongoing commitment to introduce Romania's vibrant artistic culture to other nations. In addition to the literature, the University of Plymouth will be hosting a series of exhibitions and performances of Romania's visual and musical arts over the next five years. The following supplement features one of Romania's leading contemporary artists.

Featured Artist

IOAN ATANASIU DELAMARE

Ioan Atanasiu Delamare (born 1955) holds a PhD in Fine Art from the Nicolae Grigorescu Institute, Bucharest and has exhibited widely in Europe and the USA. His works, a reflection of a keen and lucid intelligence, depict wisps of unearthly dreamscapes, dancing with musical rhythms and gossamer colour. Atanasiu allows his hand to drift, piloted by the swell of inner thought and feeling, and leaving in its wake the visual language of his inner being. Like the Florian brothers, the resulting hallucinatory quality of the pieces challenges the imagination of the viewer, presenting a myriad of shifting interpretations. Atanasiu's themes revolve around the spiritual – his compositions depicting a beautifully strange and unsettling private universe.

Awards achieved include the Youth Award (1989) and the Graphic Award (1996) of the Union of Romanian Artists.

Liz Wells

UNDER WATER

THE BOAT

THE KYLE

THE BOTTLE

THE CAMEL

THE CHAIR

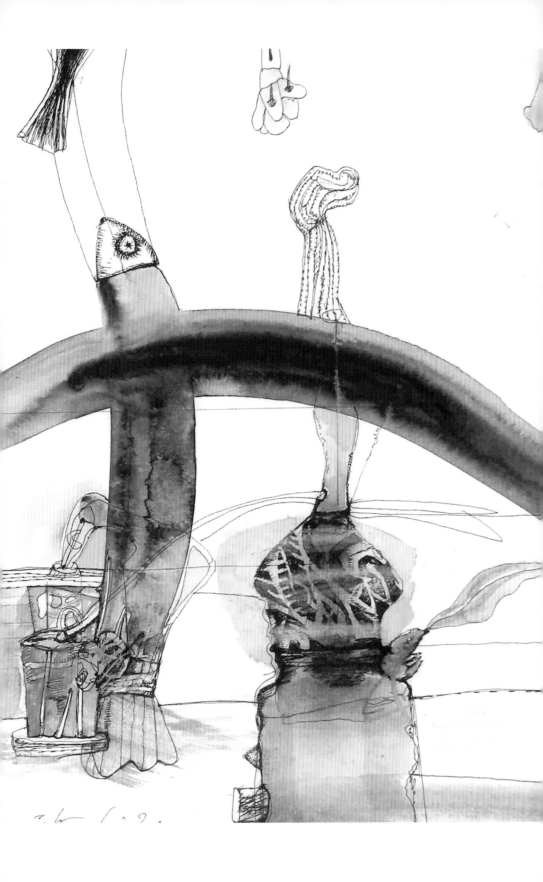

THE FISH

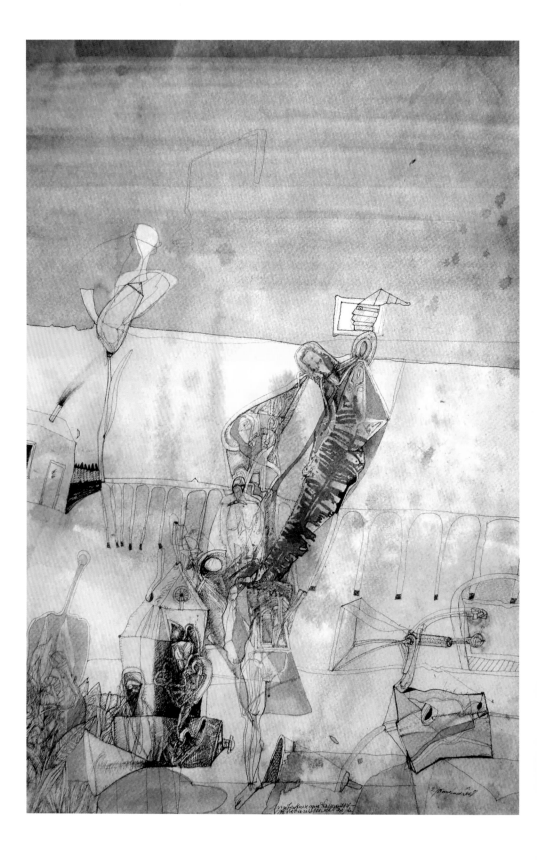

FILIP AND MATEI FLORIAN
THE BĂIUŢ ALLEY LADS

Translated by Alistair Ian Blyth

Contents

Alistair Ian Blyth

Introducing
Filip and Matei Florian

The autobiographical novel *Băiuțeii – The Băiuț Alley Lads* – is unique in this series of Romanian writers, not only in having two authors, but also in the fact that the authors are brothers, each a writer in his own right, each with his own highly individual and idiosyncratic style.

Filip Florian, born in Bucharest in 1968, spent his early career in journalism, both in newspapers and radio. He was a correspondent for radio stations Deutsche Welle and Free Europe. His first novel, *Little Fingers*, won success and literary prizes in his home country and has been published outside Romania, in Germany, Hungary, Poland, Slovenia and the United States. His third novel, *The Băiuț Alley Lads*, has been translated into Polish (*Starszy brat, młodszy brat*) with translations due in Spanish and Bulgarian. This is the first edition in English.

Matei Florian was born in Bucharest on 8 January 1979. Between 1998 and 2007, he was a reporter and subsequently editor for *Dilema veche* and *Dilemateca* magazines. At the Cultural Journalism Gala in 2008, his column *Audio and I'm Speechless* won the Music Criticism category. His short stories have appeared in various anthologies: *Povestiri erotice românești* (*Romanian Erotic Tales*), *Cartea cu bunici* (*The Book of Grandparents*), *Iubire 13* (*Love 13*), and *Kortárs román irodalmi antológia*. His solo literary debut was the novel *Și Hams Și Regretel* (*Both Hams And Regretel*). Matei Florian was awarded a writer's bursary by the Literarisches Colloquium Berlin in March 2009 and has given public readings from his work in Vienna, Leipzig, Berlin, Krakow and Warsaw.

Unlike other notable literary tandems, for example Ilf and Petrov, or brothers Arkady and Boris Strugatsky, where the two authorial voices are indistinguishable, coalescing into a single third-person narrative, Filip and Matei Florian have written a novel in which two separate and highly distinct voices alternate, chapter by chapter, entering into a dialogue. The dialogism of *The Băiuț Alley Lads* operates at multiple levels, simultaneously. There is the dialogue between the two authors, who comment on each other's recollections, adding nuances, supplying different perspectives, making rectifications, often with ironical nicety, and sometimes even intruding into the other's chapter with a parenthetical, mock-indignant interruption. Then there is the dialogue with the reader, whom each author separately addresses and tries to convince as to the veracity of his own particular account and perspective. There is the dialogue between the authors' present and younger selves, and the dialogue with their innermost conscience, bringing to light long buried, painful, but also hilariously embarrassing, episodes from childhood. In the case of Matei Florian, this dialogue takes the form of a chapter-long poetic letter addressed by 'big Matei' to the sleeping 'little Matei', who in a later chapter is described answering his future (and present) self in a dream.

There is also the dialogue between past, present and future generations of the same family: big Mircea, the mountaineering grandfather, whose time of dying coincides with the birth of little Mircea, the youngest of the three brothers, to whom he magically passes on his love of the mountains, a miraculous event described in a literal flight of fancy by Filip Florian. There is a dialogue with the historical past, in which Băiuț Alley – a small street in Bucharest, a mythical realm that lies between two valleys (Ialomitza Valley Street and Argeș Valley Street) – becomes a microcosm of the communist Romania of drab, uniform housing blocks, although the 'shades of this prison-house' (to quote Wordsworth) are often 'apparelled in celestial light' by the miracles and joys of childhood.

Since the fall of the communist regime in Romania and the return of freedom of speech, the five decades of totalitarian rule have, naturally and cathartically, dominated Romanian literature, in both fiction and non-fiction. Writers established during the communist period have been able to publish works either banned at the time or written for 'the desk drawer' without any hope of publication when the regime still seemed sempiternal, as well as new works looking back at an epoch that shaped their adult lives, often in painful or dramatic ways. However, the literary phenomenon of writing freely about the communist period also includes another, very different kind of author: writers who were still children or adolescents when the Ceaușescu regime collapsed and who look back at the period through the prism of childhood memories. One notable example is the book *O lume dispărută* (*A Vanished World*) by Paul Cenat, Ion Manolescu, Angelo Mitchievici, and Ioan Stanomir, in which the four authors compile an encyclopaedic compendium of growing up in communist Romania, an archaeology of the material reality of the period (the shortages, the shoddy goods), as well as an exploration of the social and, more indirectly, political reality of the time, whose darkness was perceived and interpreted differently through childhood eyes.

The realia of communist Romania in the 1970s and 1980s can be fleetingly glimpsed in *The Băiuț Alley Lads*: there are occasional references to the consumer products of the time, Cip sweets[1] and Drăgănești[2] trainers, for example, as well as cultural phenomena, such as *Rahan*[3] comics, popular singers and television programmes. But ultimately the aim of the book is not to recreate this lost and all too historical world, but rather to explore the imaginary worlds created in the mind of a child growing up, to recreate the miracles of childhood, which exist everywhere, regardless of whatever political regime adults have established. Nationalist-communist ideology is a strange and baffling grown-up world in the mind of the young Matei, who is introduced to the notion of the 'Homeland' in nursery school and presumes it must be embodied by the choleric Comrade Teacher Stănescu, until he discovers that it is in fact the peaked cap of the officer who has begun visiting his divorcée mother. In the end, the Homeland is, for the young boy, something all too concrete: a cap that he surreptitiously transforms into a potty by vengefully piddling in it.

In Filip Florian's narrative, Nicolae and Elena Ceaușescu appear as the principal characters in a game of nursery school make-believe, in which the author's younger self becomes the hero and centre of attention, playing the role of Nicolae alighting from the presidential aeroplane (a coal heap) to the cheers of his classmates. Thus, Nicolae Ceaușescu appears in the book only in a scene that is transformed into a childhood miracle, bathed in magical light, while elsewhere the dictator is an equally 'unreal' figure, a kind of superhero, mentioned in the childhood boasts and fantastical playground tales described by Matei.

Ultimately, *The Băiuț Alley Lads* could only have been written about that unique place called Băiuț Alley, consisting of Blocks D 13, D 14, C 37 and C 38, which stand in that area of Bucharest where the legendary Tudor Vladimirescu and his men once pitched their tents, during the Revolution of 1821; and it could only have been set in the last two decades of the Socialist Republic of Romania. But in its treatment of childhood, with all its joys and miracles, its flights of imagination, but also its nightmares, bogeymen, traumas and darker familial episodes, the novel transcends historical and geographical context to become a unique, dialogic *Bildungsroman*.

---

[1] Communist made Tic Tacs, complete with a shoddy dispenser.

[2] Nicknamed 'gumari' (gumsters), they were a cheap and durable trainer.

[3] Rahan is a prehistoric hero and inventor who anticipates modern inventions and wanders the earth, championing the downtrodden.

THE BĂIUȚ ALLEY LADS

I

A Few Things about Cristos

Coshutza always told me not to clout Cristos

I was riding in a trolleybus, hanging on the bar (in one of those demented moments when all you can say is that you're riding in a trolleybus hanging on the bar), when, all of a sudden, wham! I saw Coshutza. I saw him in the middle of the road, trailing his right foot through the dust, until he had swept the dust aside and the asphalt showed through, with that slightly cross-eyed gaze of his fastened on the toe of his training shoe, as if he were rooted to the spot. I saw him as he was on that long day when I reached the age of five and a half. Then I heard him – as if the trolleybus were a corner of Parva Alley, as if it would have been all the same to him if he were trailing his foot through the dust or riding in the trolleybus 19 years later. For, without raising his eyes from the toe of his right trainer, he repeated to me that terrifying prophecy: "I told you. I kept telling you, but you wouldn't listen. Now you're in for it."

We were hanging on the bar, Coshutza and I, and all I had to do was look at the other passengers' faces to realise that not one of them suspected anything, that they had no idea why Coshutza said those things to me then and that – let's be serious, it wasn't long until the university trolleybus stop – there was no way they could have heard them. Then I got off the trolleybus and, obviously, I forgot about it.

Now I'm trying to remember it all, to coax it out of Coshutza, but he, as chance would have it, has begun to fly from one corner to another. He's sticking his tongue out, yelling and spitting. And frankly it doesn't do him credit. Not that he was ever in the habit of doing it during all the years I knew him. I don't know who Coshutza is friends with nowadays, but I can't imagine that in the meantime that timid and rather taciturn boy can have changed so much as to start getting up to tricks like this. Cut it out already!

***

He knew very well why he said it to me. He knew because, on one of those evenings with flickering streetlamps, he had seen Cristos on top of the block of flats, ready to take flight. Coshutza swore that was how it was. He didn't have wings or a parachute. It was just him and his scary gang. In the blocks opposite the lights had come on and at every window and balcony there appeared a father, a mother or a grandfather, who were all yelling in unison at Cristos and the others not to do anything stupid like jumping, because they didn't believe in miracles, because no one has wings, and so on and so forth, daft things like that, said Coshutza. And Cristos obeyed them and didn't jump that evening. But Coshutza's cousin told him, and his cousin doesn't lie, that if Cristos and his gang didn't jump off the top of the block that time, it was only because they had done it before and they were too bored to do it again just to annoy some idiots. Then all of a sudden they jumped. They were in free fall for about two storeys and then, quite simply, instead of arms, they grew wings. The wings fluttered softly at first, then they beat harder, and all of them began to yell and whoop. They kept flapping their wings, he said, and gradually they rose higher and higher until no one could see them anymore, not even Coshutza's cousin, and somewhere, way up high in the sky, you could hear them shouting and cursing Dynamo supporters. Of the fact that they were cursing all Dynamo supporters there could be no doubt. It was something as clear as the light of day that whoever lived on Băiuț Alley, in the Camp Road district, was a Steaua supporter. Everyone apart from Filip and I. We'd never heard of anyone who didn't have a bone to pick with Dynamo. Not even the old duffers or Beardy Lame-man. And so, apart from the bit about flying, Coshutza's tale about the angels, or whatever the hell they were, who were chanting psalms of death to Dynamo, increased my grim fury all the more and made me want to kick and punch Cristos at the first opportunity I got. I didn't say anything about that to Coshutza, however, and he went on with the story, forgetting all about his cousin and telling me about how he had seen Cristos on the television news somewhere in the F.R.G., about how he was flying around and killing Nazis, about how after that he landed on the highest peak in the world, 12,826 metres, about how he met Lăcătuș and asked him for his autograph, about how Ceaușescu asked him to take him up there, on high, but Cristos didn't want to and so Elena called in the whole army and they started firing anti-tank guns and bazookas, with cannons and tanks, but nothing happened, because him you can kill only with Rahan's knife, after it's been left for two days and two nights in a jar of antelope's blood mixed with snake venom. That's what Coshutza told me and, to be honest, the only part of the whole story that interested me was the bit about the gang.

***

No, don't ask me about the evenings when I used to pluck up the courage, swallow my fear and my amazement and my despair that it had all come to an end and that Mother would never be coming outside again to sit down on the little bench from where she used to keep watch over the awkward games of a child who was not yet three, of a child who did not know that the street was a place full of strange beings that ran around, shot at each other and played football, beings no different from yourself and precisely for that reason so enchanted and mysterious (as if you were to believe that others were a kind of mirror image of yourself and all of a sudden you found out that it was not like that at all, because Migu is completely different to Pipitza, and then there is Doru and, especially, Cristos, and all of them are who they are and nothing more, each with a different mother and a different house, each ready to pick a fight for no reason, just to demonstrate their own unique existence on that street and on this earth).

And nothing will ever rid my mind of the day when time remained permanently suspended as a door shut – Flat 40, Florian – and the sun crept into the stairwell between the plant pots hanging in the windows and lingered there, lighting a green banister, a banister as green as a green lizard, the only creature that seemed to have life in all that bright, petrified stillness that was waiting for me to make a movement so that it could swallow me whole, once and for all.

Well, it was then that I understood what the Bogeymanman meant and that in your life the Bogeyman only looms in such rare and decisive moments; that only then do you have to be really strong; that only then does the world stir from its givenness enough to let you see it otherwise and, for an instant, long enough for a lizard to turn back into a banister, to experience the effulgent sensation that you are no longer the same as you were before, but rather you have grown older. (It seems that, apart from those moments, we are accompanied by a vast inertia, and if it ever disappears, then the Bogeyman appears. And I'd bet my life on it that he lives in that inertia very nicely thank you very much and only when someone rattles his nest does he deign to show his face.) Mother had remained behind the closed door. A flight of stairs awaited me, and beyond them, the street. I went out.

It took me a lot of fear and a lot of time before I learned the rules of the game. The first thing that I had to get used to was Cristos. To him and his older sister had fallen the task of heightening my fear, wrenching it out of shape, letting it burgeon until, quite simply, it vanished of itself. They sensed my fear, and they laughed.

There was no doubt about it: Cristos was the Bogeyman's revenge for having vanquished him that afternoon. I have no other way of explaining his insane appearances at dusk, wearing an eternal blue T-shirt, with a ferocious bull drawn on the chest. (I know there are words which, when used higgledy-piggledy, have the role of distancing you from the sentence you are reading. For example, 'to be foreordained'. But there is no way around it. And so I beg your forgiveness.) Cristos was foreordained to me, not because I alone was the target of his unmotivated attacks, but because none of the other children on the street seemed to realise what was really happening. It was as if his running towards me with that bull emblazoned on his chest, his bellows, his yells, my terror and my crying all used to detach themselves from the street and the people, from the gathering dusk and from everything else, and arrive in a place built purposely beforehand, sheltered from the eyes of mortals, where Cristos and I would trade punches. I'm lying shamelessly. In those days, perhaps because, as I have told you, Cristos was the place from where the Bogeyman bellowed, I used to suffer from the same impotent petrification that paralysed even my breathing (therefore it is proof of imposture on my part to pretend that I could have punched him). The only person who, smirking at me, let on that she knew what went on between Cristos and myself was his red-clad sister Luminitza. She played the role of witness, because in such matters there also had to be a witness, otherwise you risk going insane. Moreover, Luminitza used to perch on the fence by her entrance and watch the other children playing until the onset of evening. Then she would vanish for a moment and return with Cristos. She would point her eyes in my direction and

the street would gradually fade the din
ever more distant
the dogs still barking faintly
the street lamps would begin to flicker and
whirl and Cristos with them

25

I would see our fourth-floor window lit up
I would shout out "ma" and Fil I would feel the first thud
I would awake in my bed sweating the light was out
the comrade kindergarten teacher was making me tell my first story

***

I see you all like this: seated on chairs in a semicircle (a word I'll learn to say much later). Standing before you, I am the only one that can still hear the sparrows in the yard, because you are waiting for me to tell you the story. You look so daft when you're waiting: with your hands behind your backs, like the comrade told you, silent, gazing at me, who doesn't know how to tell stories. Who has never told a story in his life. I'm too little, you have to understand, and even if I were grown up, I still wouldn't be able to utter one word because you are all looking at me in silence. Look at you, Paul, about whom I wrote a poem in secondary school about a shoestring ("ha, ha, the shoestring is a worm," said Paul and his face lengthened to the floor) your mouth is half open, and at the corners of your lips have formed bubbles of spittle, which pop only to make way for fresh bubbles. Look at you, Ana-Maria, you have closed your eyes, you want to go to sleep or maybe this is how your mother has accustomed you to listen to stories, only when you close your eyes. Marianne, I swear to you that when I told you that story for the first time I didn't know that you would be killed running after a ball, because if I had known, believe me, I would have spun all the tales in the world for you, and, above all, I would have given you that stupid little black car from Germany which you asked to play with just for a little, do you remember? and I didn't want to lend you it in case you broke it and you called me a miser and later you died, but at the time I had no idea what miser meant, let alone that you would die and, you see, this is the last thing I would have said to you: be careful not to run after the ball, because for you a puddle will be a wretched open drain full of water, but in vain do I tell you all this, yet again, you are laughing now and you think it's a story like one of Coshutza's, a story without beginning or end, during which everyone grows bored and starts to make a racket, so that the comrade orders Coshutza back to his place, quick march! and with his head bowed – like at the beginning of the novel – Coshutza goes back to his stool (stay like that, Coshutza, please, I'll come back to you), and it's all too much, all of you are here, snot-nosed Angelica, yes, I see you, slobbering over that crust of bread, I see your revolting green snots eternally dripping like from a broken tap, I see you, Cornel and Diana, holding each other's little hands, not that I care one little bit, I see you Roxandra – boy, the story! That was the comrade, who doesn't know me (as if you can know a three-year-old tot) and yes, uh, once upon a time there was a kind of large darkness like a forest and in it there was a little boy, a hunter, a bull and a fox-x-x. Like that. And a fox-x-x. And the fox was walking along and when night came the bull hid in a hollow tree trunk and waited for the hunter and the hunter went to the tree and he didn't know about any bull because he thought he was all alone in the forest and tippy-toe the bull crept out of the tree and before the hunter could see him and get out his gun the bull picked up the hunter with his horns and put him inside the hollow tree trunk and put a boulder there so that he would never be able to get out again and so that the bull could stay in the forest all alone and drop litter and start fires everywhere but the bull didn't know that there was also a fox and a little boy and so he started to do all kinds of bad things and he told the hunter that he was going to die there in his forest and that no prince charming would ever come to save him and that he was a mighty ogre. And when night fell the bull dropped litter everywhere and went to bed with his older sister Luminitza because he thought that they were all alone but the little boy heard the hunter and with the fox he pushed the boulder away from the hollow tree trunk and when morning came they pulled the hunter out and he was tired and the ants had bitten him all over and the fox gave him some water from the tap until he felt better and he went to find the bull.

The bull thought he was dreaming. Do you know why? He thought he was dreaming because he thought he was alone with Luminitza but in front of him appeared the hunter from the tree trunk where he had put him and a fox with some flowers and a little boy. He tried to run away and to drop litter on the ground but he didn't succeed. It was all true. Then he ran away with Luminitza as far as the street and he hid. The hunter became ill because of the ants and he died after that. And the little boy and the fox buried him and after that his grave was covered in litter. Who knows who dropped the litter there?

The fox, they all said. Why, because he was a thief, the fox dropped the litter, because that's the way he was brought up, to snap off the bear's tail, to make fun of the storks and to play dead. Because in every story with animals, as everyone knows, there is always fox and the fox is always guilty. Because they didn't even listen to the story, because they didn't even take any notice of the bull, because you rarely meet a bull in a story, and when you do meet one, he is not guilty of absolutely anything. For all these reasons, the bull had to vanish.

***

You have to close your eyes. Like this. You have to let the wind start blowing, to hear how it comes back to life and goes around the street and the entrances to the blocks. Only like this, with your eyes closed, can you feel its whistling joy at going out for a walk among the plastic bags and at rattling the windows and darkening the sky. Only like this can you make things vanish and pack Cristos off to the country for one whole spring.

In one way or another, you have to stay like this for a long time (patiently to erase even the memory of the block across the way, of the exercise book and pen you're using to write all these things down in), so that Coshutza can appear to you once more. Only with your eyes closed can you see him once more, not on the stool where the comrade told him to sit back down, but perched on what we used to call back then the bunker (an abandoned concrete garage) dangling his legs in the air and giving me a reproachful look for the very first time.

No, you've got no right to clout Cristos.

At the time, he didn't know anything about Cristos's vesperal flights, he didn't even know about the Bogeyman or Luminitza, and, above all, he had no idea how a bull that had been staying in the country for ages could return to Băiuț Alley having turned into a lad like any other. What Coshutza felt was, I think, a kind of muffled jealousy because I had learned how to whistle and he hadn't, and this is one of the few things you can't do anything about. It was clear and the clearer it was the more it hurt him, because all he could do was to listen to me whistle and to respect me. He knew that all it would take would be a single shove and I would send him toppling off our bunker. He knew that, after the thud and his tears, everything between us would change forever.

It was not until Coshutza fell off the bunker that he yelled at me, amid his sobbing, that I would get what was coming to me, that his cousin, that he knew what, that I was shitting my pants. That if I laid a finger on Cristos, I'd be sorry.

Something told me that the ease with which Coshutza fell to the ground must somehow be equal to the ease of Cristos doing the same thing. I closed my eyes then and saw it more clearly than ever before: Cristos was no different than Coshutza, and Coshutza was an idiot. Coshutza must have sensed something, too. He knew that somewhere his final salvation, if he still had learned how to whistle, would be for that unknown lad from Băiuț Alley – Cristos the Saviour – not to get beaten up.

I'm going to beat him up, I would tell him. No, you're not allowed, he would tell me. And I had to take the trolleybus to the university in order to remember the day when I reached the age of five and a half.

***

On his return from the country Cristos was Cristi. He was a stupid peasant who couldn't remember anything (as if those dusks had been nothing but dreams of mine, the hallucinatory poem of a fearful child, standing petrified, refusing to go outside to play).

He tries to dribble the ball between my legs. It's a predictable feint. The ball bounces off my leg. Out. Header over here, header over here, shouts Cristos, waving his arms. Then it's a handball. Migu threw it in too high, and Cristos lifted up his arms. I pass, Pipitza shoots, 2-0. Migu and Pipitza start shoving each other. Tempers are fraying. The goalie threw the ball back in wrong. I had a clear field. 3-0. The goalie clutches his hands to his head in despair. The ball rolls under the Wartburg that belongs to Mr Florea from the ground floor. Go and get it, shouts Migu. Tempers are fraying. Cristos tries to dribble the ball between my legs again, but this time it isn't out. I pass to Bebe. 4-0. The ball is under the Wartburg again. Migu kicks the goalie in the behind. He's crying and doesn't want to play in goal any more. Half time.

He's back in goal, wearing the gloves. Cristos dribbles the ball past me and then falls in a heap. He's down. Red card, shouts Migu, but I ignore him. Cristos gets up, comes towards me, trips up again. He gets up, comes crashing down, I kick him in the face. I bust his nose. They are all standing stock still, looking at me. Cristos is groaning, bleeding. He can't get up. That's what you get for thinking you're Lăcătuș, I tell them. I turn my back. He's on his feet again. He's got a brick, says Pipitza. He misses, and now I'm really mad. He runs home, shouting for his mother and Luminitza. I catch up with him. I hit him. He runs inside the block and shuts the door. He was getting too big for himself, I tell them. We beat you 4–0. Luminitza and his mother have appeared. They're looking for me. I stick my tongue out at them and vanish behind the block. There's no way they can find me. I'm five and a half.

Coshutza is standing on Parva Street. All alone, in the middle of the road, trailing his right foot through the dust until he sweeps the dust aside and the asphalt shows through, with that slightly cross-eyed gaze of his fastened on the toe of his trainer, as if he had nothing else in the world to do except stand there and wait for me so that we could talk together. I clouted him. I made him bleed. Coshutza is looking at the ground, his eyes fastened on the toe of his right trainer. "I told you, I kept telling you, but you wouldn't listen. Now you're in for it." Have you got a stick? Leave it out. I haven't got a stick. Coshutza didn't have a stick and I was starting to feel afraid. Not of Cristos – he was bleeding and he couldn't even hit me with the brick – but of his mum and Luminitza. Maybe they'll wait for me outside my entrance until nightfall. What the hell am I going to do? Maybe they're hiding in those bushes behind Coshutza this very minute, ready to grab me. Where the hell can I run? Look at the way he's grinning. What's that you say I should do? Go to hell, that's what.

I sneaked towards Băiuț Alley, hiding behind the parked cars. I made my way around the back of the block, through the dark garden. Something inside me was pounding and racing like a train. If Migu and Pipitza are there I'll ask them where the two women are. There was no one. Just me. I was crawling along the ground, over the leaves, from one tree to another. Like an Indian. (If anyone had seen me, they would have crossed themselves: a solitary child, crawling along on his belly from one tree to another.) I found worms and ants. I found a red Cuban sweet. Then another. Some dope had lost them. I advanced, crawling, with two red Cuban sweets in my mouth. There they are. They're waiting for me. Not Luminitza and her fat mother. They had long since given up. They didn't have the patience. But Cristos was there, prowling around with a stick. He was ferocious, with a plaster on his nose, swearing and giving instructions. It was obvious that he would not have budged from the street corner even in a thousand years. There was also Cosmin from entrance D 14, Nicu from C 38, someone I didn't know, and Spook from the third form, whom I'd only ever seen messing around in the school playground. They all had sticks and they were all waiting for me. I clearly sensed that these were the last Cuban sweets I would ever eat in my life. I lay pressed to the ground and watched. They would not budge, and dusk was falling. I turned over onto my back and saw it very well. The sky looked like it was shrinking. It was like rippling water, suspended up there. It was changing colour. Then an aeroplane left a long white streak, and the streak reddened in the setting sun and slowly faded. The streak had almost disappeared, but I could still hear the noise of the aeroplane, or maybe I was imagining it and it was only the sound of the buses on Argeş Valley Street. It was growing dark and I was watching fishes in the sky when they twigged that I was there. I forgot about the sky and started running. They were letting out blood-curdling yells and whirling their sticks in the air, with Cristos at their head. I could feel him breathing down my neck, and the whoosh of air from his bat. I did a lap of the block. They hadn't tired, either. I did another. At the beginning of my third lap, I saw Filip with his satchel on his shoulder. It was all over. Spook was the first to throw away his stick and vanish.

The street lamps lit up one by one. It was the hour when, according to what Coshutza said, Cristos started to fly. But instead, Cristi was standing in front of me and begging forgiveness. The streak from the aeroplane was long gone. Not one shadow of a fish against the sky.

II

Pointy Shoes and Fleecy Socks

Well, what can I say? I don't remember much about it. In fact, I don't remember one jot. In the end, how many times had I not come home from school as dusk was falling, how many times had a jet aeroplane not been passing up in the sky, how many times had the buses not been rumbling at the depot, braying like donkeys, honking and revving before setting off on their route? What could have made me remember all these things? I'm not a chess player, or an elephant. I don't manifest any symptom of having a hypertrophied memory. If he says that that was the day I saved him from five kids who wanted to clobber him, and that I was his salvation, then that must be what happened. Believe him! By the sound of the whole escapade, it's clear that he has motives not to forget. It's a big thing, isn't it? To feel someone breathing down the back of your neck, whirling a stick and swearing that he's going to make mincemeat out of you. It's the kind of thing you never forget. All the same, I have reservations when I tell you to believe his story. For no other reason than there are certain details he has laid on a bit thick, much too thick. For example, the part about the football match, when he won 6-0, or something of the sort, and he beat the living daylights out of that clown Cristos (the one who came back from his holidays having turned into a stupid peasant called Cristi), when he kicked him in the snout and caused him a great big epistaxis (a nosebleed, in other words). True, he has been a good football player since he was little, albeit a bit of a ball-hogger (he has never been a one to pass, not even those short, simple passes, let alone those long, brilliant passes, as the commentators at cup matches call them), but he played well, I'll give him that, and that's why I do believe that his side scored six goals, or whatever, of which four were by him. But what seems far-fetched to me is the part about the punishment of that flying beetle, who used to jump off the top of the block with his gang after sunset. I am not denying that the lads grew wings and flew at will, everything is possible, and Camp Road has witnessed many things (I think you will have heard about the red Oltcit car abandoned for years in front of the Maternity Hospital, from whose steering wheel was born a miraculous baby girl, Mara

I think her name was, after the said steering wheel had carried a pregnancy for the full term, growing over the course of nine months, not all of a sudden, like the airbags you get nowadays, but swelling like a woman's belly, except that it had a hooter instead of a bellybutton; and you will definitely be familiar with the story about the flat on the fourth floor, it was in one of the D blocks, where the whole kitchen, walls, floor, ceiling and all, sprouted mushrooms because of the cold radiators and the steam from the cooker, until the tenant, I have the impression that she was a literary lady (would you believe it!) after using them in stews, schnitzels and pies, everything but mushroom jam, realised what a fortune she was sitting on, quit her job at the theatre, where she worked as a literary secretary, and got rich selling them in Moghioroș Market, until the police put a stop to it).

To return to the topic interrupted by the foregoing digression, I have to confess that my version of events differs: as far as clouting that insect with a child's face is concerned, Cristos, Cristi or whatever you want to call him, my brother did clout him, but I know that the circumstances were different. It was not like an Apache Indian out on the prairie, clouting the head of the tribe to usurp him, but rather it took place in the stairwell of our block. I was angry at the time and holding the fat tawny-haired kid with his arms pinned behind his back so that my brother could hit him. I might be confusing him with someone else, but it's still one thing to have kicked him in the middle of Băiuț Alley and quite another to punch him in the stairwell of the block, even if it still resulted in a nosebleed and snivelling. In any case, what I do recall is that the lad on the stairs did not run off shouting for his mother and some sister by the name of Luminitza. He kept whining: Grandma-a-a-a! Grandma-a-a-a! Ah, and there is another detail that arouses my suspicions … If he had found one Cuban sweet when he was crawling from one tree to another, red, yellow, the colour doesn't matter, I would have believed the whole thing with my eyes closed, but for him to have found two sweets and not to have kept one for me? Rather odd, isn't it?

To let it be clear how things stand, I'm Filip, i.e. the boy with the satchel on his shoulder, whom my brother claims was the only other Dynamo supporter in the whole neighbourhood apart from him (I have no idea why he brought Beardy Lame-man into it, especially given that he was a sensitive man: I saw him with my own eyes in the National Museum of Art during a school trip, in the fifth form, he was gazing motionless at a landscape with hayricks, as if he were light-headed from the scent of grass and had fallen asleep standing, like a horse). I am speaking (writing) in the past tense not because I used to support Dynamo and now don't: I still support the team and it would be the limit if I didn't support the Red Dogs any more, if I didn't love them any more, now that they've fallen on hard times and everyone snaps at their heels; the point of employing the past tense relates to other things, things that are no more, things that have expired, that have gone for good, that have turned to dust. For example, one of the things that come under this category is my hair, which has now well and truly been swallowed up by the earth. Of the fringe that came down to my eyebrows in primary school (limp, floppy and plastered to my forehead as it was), of the mullet tied up in a pony tail that hung over my shirt collar, of the long sideboards that masked my jug lugs, but made my chin look even pointier, of all these tonsorial endowments, which ultimately weren't really up to all that much, a magnificent bald pate has sprung up, not quite a Kojak, but not far off.

You will be wondering how it was I had long hair when every schoolboy in the land had a crew cut, at least all those between the Ialomitza Valley and the Doamna River, perhaps elsewhere too. I don't know. Some of you will know, but I'm not going to stake my life on it if I don't know for sure. Anyway, I eluded the barber thanks to Comrade Cîsu, the teacher who replaced Comrade Ulărescu (I should inform you that Comrade Cîsu, of whom I have a photograph in which I am standing next to her on the school steps, a group photograph, admittedly, with another 31 minuscule pioneers holding black and white tricolours, was a fairy godmother, slightly aging, without a magic wand, tall, thin, she would have made a good basketball player if she hadn't dedicated herself to small children, whereas Comrade Ulărescu, of whom I don't have any photographs, thank God, had been a harpy; I suspect that the roof of her mouth was black, but I cannot certify this as I never had occasion to ask her to stick her tongue out and say "aaaaaah", to examine her buccal cavity closely).

Comrade Cîsu did not allow just anyone to have long hair. It was a privilege I began to enjoy in the third form, in the second term, I think it was, after she had been chatting with a colleague who knew my Uncle Didi (a film-maker; at any hour of the day or night I can reel off for you all the titles of the films he wrote the screenplay for; to sceptics I am prepared to show his A.C.I.N. membership card), and she got it into her head, like a screw wedged fast, that I was going to appear in a film. I think that screw stimulated her imagination for a long period, in which she kept expecting to see herself in the darkness of a cinema auditorium (but not at the Favorit), all dressed up and coiffed (as is proper during an outing to the centre of Camp Road), with the rays of the projector caressing her chignon, so that the viewers in the seats behind would admire the gleam of lacquered curls, as she leaned on her husband's shoulder, her eyes moistening whenever her bespectacled little pupil appeared on the screen, seeking and discovering in his gestures some sign of her labours as a teacher, whispering to Mr Cîsu, but not until near the end, "look, dear, that boy is my pupil". In her imagination she probably also added a number of staffroom scenes, where the gall bladders of her colleagues will have suffered bitterly after the film's premiere, even if the tongues of the said teachers will have found the resources to congratulate her. In any case, her dream did not come true. My uncle (a great lover of cocker spaniels) did not for an instant think of launching me into a film career.

Towards the end of the fourth form, in a moment of tiredness, bad temper or who knows for what reason (ultimately, the menopause gives rise to so many different ailments) she called me up to the blackboard to solve a problem, she let me write a host of figures and arithmetical symbols and then, all of a sudden, as I was wielding the stick of chalk and my mind was full of multiplication and division, she said, listen, Florian, what is with that long hair? I want you to go and get it cut nicely for me. As short as short can be! And by tomorrow, otherwise you will be in trouble. From between her carmine-rouged lips there slid a sound similar to a bleat, but lacking the consonant B, whose emotional charge inspired nothing ovine, but rather pious indignation. Anyway, it is all in the past now. I hope with all my heart that Comrade Teacher Cîsu has vanquished the menopause and become a fairy godmother once more. And as for things that are no more, things that have expired, that have gone for good, that have turned to dust etc., because that was what we were talking about, I am of the opinion that they should not be dismissed lightly. The pointy black shoes (inasmuch as they were mine and no one else's, because I miss them very much, and they are not unimportant to me) are rotting somewhere in the lowermost depths of some rubbish pit, on some piece of waste ground, at the bottom of some lake (were it Cișmigiu!) in the roots of some linden tree planted by school children, in some attic, or in the shed used by the block's former cleaning ladies. Do you not feel pity? I do. Father had bought them for me on Lipscani Street one Sunday morning, when the shops seemed to be open especially for construction project workers, so that they could be useful to their families, if only to spend some money on them after being away from home the rest of the week. They cost 330 lei. I can tell you that exactly. Father did not hesitate because of the price, but because of their impetuous line, like that of a speedboat. He pressed his palm to my brow to check that I didn't have a fever. He asked me four times whether I was sure I liked the design, as if he didn't hear my answers or my pleas. Each time he asked he was amazed, very amazed, and he kept trying to explain to me that they were shoes for a dandy. He gradually understood how it is when you are making the transition from childhood to adolescence, but he could not suspect anything about the success Dan Anghel from entrance C had been having with the chicks since he got himself a pair of shoes exactly like these and nor could he imagine what pointy shoes meant to Nicoleta. They were impeccable, with pointed toecaps, a thick, very tall heel, and a transversal strap. True, they did not prove to be very comfortable. It was as if I was walking on stilts. They made quite a loud tapping noise and were slippery when dribbling a ball or running, but for kicking they were beyond compare: they launched the ball with pinpoint precision and it would reach dizzying speed, just like Nicoleta's lips when you walked her home after school and, without turning on the light in the basement of the block, you led her down the passageway to the box rooms, where it smelled of pickled peppers and damp potatoes.

My pointy black shoes made Alexandra Ştefănescu laugh in a way that set your teeth on edge. She was a slightly strabismic creature, who managed not to get nicknamed Wiry, even though her teeth, to stop them growing crooked, were for a long time girt with a metal retainer. She was the girl with whom, elbow to elbow, I used to break my glasses, throwing them at the blackboard from a long distance, to the cheers of my schoolmates with good eyesight and to the ire of my mother, who constantly had to take me from one optician to another to have new lenses mounted. It was a case of jealousy, I can say looking back on it now, but at the time her bitter pranks had a different meaning and weight, because, I must confess, it was her I loved, not Nicoleta Negoe, who kissed fierily amid the scent of pickles and other winter reserves. In any case, during a Romanian lesson once, not in the glory period of the pointy shoes, but later, Nicoleta stood up and asked Mrs Marinescu, a teacher on the verge of retirement, the organiser of the literary cenacle, to explain to her what the word wanker meant, because the boys kept saying it when they were quarrelling or fighting and her grandmother hadn't been able to decipher it for her. Sniggers resounded around the classroom. And what sniggers! Our gazes (including those slightly strabismic eyes) enveloped her, like silk a cocoon. And Marinescu sternly told her to sit down. I do not provide definitions of obscene words, my dear. Nicoleta reddened like a pickled pepper. The slightly strabismic eyes gleamed triumphantly and sought my presbyopic eyes. The comparison with the red pepper willy-nilly led my mind to pickles, the pickles inspired an image of the dark basement of my block, the darkness had the taste of a kiss, and that kiss, however sweet it might have been at the time, had acquired a bitter tang because of the insistence of those strabismic eyes.

But before the glory of the pointy shoes waned, a number of important events occurred.

Episode 1: in spite of the fact that we had not broken our glasses together for around a month and a half, Alexandra Ştefănescu invited me to her birthday party at the beginning of December and, just like that, as a favour, she told me I could bring my new friend Cezărică, a new boy from Galatzi, whom she couldn't stand and treated like a moron. At the party were a few of her schoolgirl friends and an insufferable cousin who spoke in a snooty voice and kept showing off to us about her Czechoslovakian bicycle. We ate cakes and meringues, we drank fizzy pop and played hide-and-seek until we got sick of it or at least until I got sick of it, at the exact moment when I opened the wardrobe in the bedroom of Mr and Mrs Ştefănescu and found her inside embracing Cezărică. I behaved reasonably, don't worry, I ran and tagged the left wall of the kitchen, one-two-three-Alexandra, one-two-three-Cezărică, as I could hardly have stood there like a pillar of stone and let them emerge from among the dresses, skirts and raincoats to tag me; I tagged Cezărică last, so that he would be it, and so I could try to convince her to climb into the wardrobe with me and hold me tight, tight, until I couldn't breathe. She showed me her elbow. It was small sharp and rosy. She stuck her tongue out at me. Did the cake have a fruit filling? Or was it chocolate? That I don't remember.

Episode 2: We are in the lunch break. It's cold outside. It's cold in the corridors. We are in our classroom on the first floor, with the lights on, because outside it is not only cold but also overcast. We are each amusing ourselves to suit our tastes and causing a break-time hubbub. Alexandra Ştefănescu is sitting at her desk, her mouth never stops, she keeps chattering away with her nose to the wind, in spite of the fact that, I repeat, it is cold, although the wind is not blowing. All of a sudden she notices my orange fleecy socks (brand new, smashing, pinched this very morning from dad's cupboard and, you should know, fleecy socks don't go by shoe size: the heel takes shape only after you wear them in) and she starts pointing at my natty attire: buffed and polished pointy black shoes, orange socks, and an ordinary school uniform on top. She laughs theatrically, tee, hee, hee, her head cocked to one side, and keeps shouting, what a peasant! What a peasant! I see red. Nothing I can do about it: I was born under the sign of the bull. I rush over to her to shut her up. I'm holding a Chinese pencil, fresh from the sharpener. She struggles, for she is not at all docile by nature (as I said, she managed not to get called Wiry, even though her teeth were cased in wire). By accident, the point of the pencil pricks her small rosy palm. A drop of blood as big as a penny appears, bulging like a soap bubble. She gives a short scream. A number of the boys jump up to catch hold of me, to show they're the cockerels in the farmyard. That puffed up Andy puffs out his feathers even more. He is the class first-aid person and he acts as if the victim is his property. He examines the wound with the air of a surgeon. He does not waste the opportunity to clasp her round the waist and massage her back. He runs to the white box with the Red Cross on the lid, comes back with an unopened phial of Rivanol and a bag of cotton wool. He pours out the liquid until her little pink hand and the blue cuff of her blouse turn yellow. He presses down with a huge pad and bandages the hand. All the while, he touches her, caresses her, whispers in her ear things which no one else hears, he props her up, he all but carries her up to the nurse's office himself. From the door, he pronounces the verdict, to all of us, but especially to me. Tetanus. How awful! It sounds worse than cholera. My knees are trembling and I am waiting to be put in manacles at any moment.

Episode 3: This is closely linked to the previous episode. Andy's diagnosis has not been confirmed. On the way to the nurse's office Alexandra slapped him so hard that he saw stars. On her return to the classroom, she ordered us all to leave her alone and she suggested to me that we should smash our glasses on the blackboard. I stuck my tongue out at her. I didn't show her my elbow, because it would have been too complicated for me to roll up my sleeves.

Episode 4: Ironically, my pointy shoe, the left one, did not give up the ghost during football or running. Probably it only got tired. But it finally broke when I was merely stepping off the pavement to cross Parva Alley one May afternoon when poplar down was floating through the air, as I was slowly wending my way home from school. In such situations you are never alone: either you are with someone else or you are surrounded by a whole crowd of disagreeable individuals. The misfortune never strikes you when you are in a secluded place, but right in the middle of the street. All of a sudden, you feel as if you are stark naked in front of a bunch of idiots. You get the picture, don't you? It was not the end of the school day only for me and, as if a dam had burst, a tumultuous stream of pupils was gushing through the gates, a stream which then thinned out, separating into streamlets depending on the geography of the neighbourhood and the final destination of each particle. As a result, when the heel of my pointy shoe broke off there was a sizeable, motley and raucous audience. I didn't have the inspiration to take my shoes off and walk the rest of the way in my stockinged feet (grey socks – I had given up orange ones once and for all). I examined the sole of my left shoe, from which protruded four stout nails (real spikes) and I hobbled on my way, holding the heel in my hand, for all to see, and with the strange sensation that my left foot was not touching the earth, that it was treading in mid-air. The nails screeched when they struck the asphalt. They had completely bent out of shape. I was subjected to cackling laughter, face-pulling, whistles and lame jokes. Happily, I did not espy any strabismic eyes, thank God, because, I swear, I wouldn't have done anything extreme, but I would have shouted, what are you looking at, Wiry? THE END (of the serial).

A little history and accounting would not go amiss at this point. In the time when my supposed film debut still seemed imminent to Comrade Teacher Cîsu, thus before I darkened the door of a barber's shop (what a time that was!) Matei (my brother, my co-author, as you will have realised by now) had not even been born. How sad! If only he could have seen me once in my life with long hair … Later, after the twilight of primary school, when I was already haunting the dawn of gymnasium school (dazzled by the gleam of my pointy shoes), my brother existed, he was suckling at the teat and from the bottle, he was munching dummies between his teeth until they disintegrated, he was mewling, he was bawling, he was making poo-poos and pee-pees, in his washable nappy, the disposable ones weren't around back then, he had already undergone an operation for pyloric stenosis (if he were to show you his belly, although I doubt that he would agree to it, you would see the scar, dating from the age of three weeks) he was gurgling in a gentle baritone, so that our grandfather consoled our mother saying, never mind, we'll make a priest out of him, he was laughing heartily and toothlessly, smacking his lips in his sleep, his food intake was gradually enlarging, now he was moving on to homemade sweet cheese, now on to soup made from mashed chicken and carrots, now on to grated apples and biscuits, you know the way, a boiled egg once a week, easy does it, a little bit of everything, so that he would have chubby cheeks, so that he would be podgy, when we dandled him of an evening, and so that he would be able to write nice stories for you today. He was born on the same day as international football star Adi Mutu (a detail unbeknownst to us at the time), and the needle on the maternity ward scale, when called upon to provide the first data about him, showed 4.3 kg, which is not bad. Today, when, thanks to the meticulousness of the *Sporting Gazette*, I now possess this key item of information about my brother, I can reveal to you, I can swear to you, that during the antenatal period at least, as a foetus, Matei was a footballer categorically superior to Mutu the Diamond (you will have to accept this degree of comparison, because it's a sports commentary we're talking about here). I am not in any position to comment on the way in which Mr Mutu, the maths teacher (the one who was later to inspire a passion for poetry and philosophy in his son) reacted to the movements of his son inside the womb of Mrs Mutu (the one who was to astonish London with her Romanian recipes, and later the grey city of Turin) but I know exactly how I reacted to the movements of my brother inside my mother's womb, because, I am ashamed to say, I still slept in her bed, taking advantage of the fact that Father was away working at the construction sites and showed up at home only once in a blue moon. Anyway, not quite at every bump, but at most of them, I used to say it's Dudu, it's Dudu Georgescu, because I was convinced he was bumping the inside of the womb with his head. Afterwards, to be precise, after he emerged from the huge belly he had been bumping for so long and arrived in Băiuţ Alley, a wee little thing all snugly wrapped up in a cotton nappy and a thick woollen blanket, given it was January.

I stopped sleeping in the same bed as Mother and went back to my own bed, which I had visited but rarely up until then, only when I was being punished or when Father was working in Bucharest. In fact, it was a period full of novelties: I tasted the milk that Mother sometimes squeezed into a little bottle with a tapering rubber pear on the neck, which had a little hole at the tip, and was left with the impression that babies must have dubious tastes if they are so keen on such a bitter liquid. I discovered something more tainted than the Bogeymanman, which made you cry all day and all night (it made him cry, not me) and which had a name like the breed of Lassie the dog, not collie, but colic. I had to do the shopping and chores a lot more than previously, which was a bit lousy. It was great to take my little brother for a walk in his pushchair and to have all the girls melt and say coochie-coochie-coo to the little tot and beg me to let them come with me. From the linguistic point of view, when he uttered his first words and afterwards, when he joined them up to form sentences, my brother had two, interrogative fixations: the question *where?* (he would follow you around the house, with a merry face, and drive you mad with that question of his: where? Where? Where what or where who was unclear. It was just where? Where?) And the question *this water you take?* (which he would ask anyone, anywhere, whenever he saw water, be it water flowing from a tap, a glass of water, water in a bathtub, a puddle on the street, the drip of a leaky pipe, droplets on the linoleum, a spring, a river, a pond, or rain pattering on the windowpane). From the ambulatory point of view, he was lazy, like all baby boys, and his first sally on his own two legs, not leaning against any object, but walking freely, occurred on precisely his first birthday, before the guests arrived. We were all present to witness it, in my Father's room. He let go of a shelf of the bookcase and set out venturesomely across the room, holding his hands out in front of himself. He did quite well at first. We were mute with emotion and delight (and love, let it be clear!). Then he rushed to reach his destination and hit his forehead on a shelf of the other bookcase, a plank with sharp edges, painted yellow, which split his head, so that during the ceremony to cut a tuft of his hair and let him choose from the three symbolic objects laid on the tray, he had a huge blood-red bump above one eye (whether he likes it or not, it will be impossible for him to hide the scar if you wish to look at it). As for my premonitions, when I called him Dudu, Dudu Georgescu, he confirmed my clairvoyance. He gave good headers.

Before nearing the moment "when time remained permanently

suspended as a door shut – Flat 40, Florian – and the sun crept into the stairwell between the plant pots hanging in the windows and lingered there, lighting a green banister, a banister as green as a green lizard," i.e. before being allowed to go out on his own, to make contact with the street, with Băiuț Alley, with the children there, Migu, Pipitza, Doru and, above all, Cristos (as he lists them), plenty of other stories have been recorded, in which he is in the foreground, stories that have been laid up in the family's golden store (our family possesses such a store, the same as the Radio Broadcasting Company boasts about its library of golden oldies). Before divulging a few of them to you, I am, however, obliged to make a correction, a rectification, otherwise it would mean I was lying to you when I promised that I would introduce a little history. On the door of our flat was inscribed neither the number nor our surname and I guarantee you that Mother would never accept to titivate with such inscriptions an object meant to protect you more from drafts and neighbours than thieves. So, at one point, Matei contracted a urinary infection, which, because of its olfactory side, early on earned him the nickname Stinky Skunk and transformed his botty into a pincushion because of the injections. Then, a record unequalled by any predecessor or any younger member of the family, he broke three mirrors, all Venetian, within the space of less than six months. With a small, black, massy ball from a game of skittles he hit the mirror of a wardrobe that had once belonged to Mother's Great-grandmother. Then, with a humble jumping jack, he hit the mirror of the dressing table with the marble top. Finally, the glass pane and mirror of a rosewood vitrine fell victim to him (or rather to the lead soldier he had hurled). It is interesting that the all too familiar standard bathroom mirror fitted in all the blocks in Camp Road, which costs but 11 lei at any glazier's shop, never held any attraction for him. As for the imaginary characters that accompanied his solitary games, they were called laffie (read "lassie", with adult eyes), Kindo, and a duo called Tim and Ştam.

III

The Incredible Adventures of Ştim and Ştam

Ştim and Ştam appeared in a mustard jar, the morning after I dreamed of hairpin bends and devils. Were it necessary to invent a realm from which they might appear – grave, translucent blobs, faceless and ageless, with no distinguishing features other than their existence – then that jar which Mother used to rinse out once the mustard had finished, to use it thereafter as a thick, ugly, durable tumbler, that jar upon which I fastened my still sleepy gaze, was by far the most appropriate.

What I have learned, however (I didn't need to read it in a book; all I needed to do was pay a little attention), was that when miracles take place, even a minor miracle like this one, it is not enough to take into account only one aspect. To make you see that I'm not just playing the fool or leading you by the nose or pulling your leg, for the sake of the pleasure that carries away all grown-ups as soon as they start to write, I insist on informing you that I am fully aware of how improbable it is for two characters to appear, as if by magic, in a mustard jar. True, it would have been much simpler for it to have happened like that, but it would have been somehow embarrassing for me, because

1. I would be tossing the truth out of the window and
2. I would never be able to look you in the eye again (not to mention Filip, who, you can be sure of it, would never want to have anything more to do with me after that). And so, at least for his sake, if not for your sake, and, ultimately, for my own sake, I am going to attempt to clarify, with all the delicacy demanded when telling the tale of a miracle, how it was that Ştim and Ştam materialised at eight o'clock one gloomy Sunday morning, probably in October.

So, Ştim and Ştam sprang into being one gloomy morning, the day after the night when I had that dream about hairpin bends and devils, which has pursued me (like a magical spell) to this day. That dream, which I described in a poem a while ago, went like this:

or then as if down a wooden chute
a slow-motion dream slide as if down
a cochlea upholstered with darkness lit by
neon lights I was descending by hairpin bends towards
the inside-out dusk
(I don't know why it looked like a) membrane (anyway)
through which pulsated the breath of a huge
being hidden beyond the edges
of the chasm where there was still smouldering
the ash of a John fire (John was a kind of saint
to whom I used to write poems) where
the writhing tongues of the devils still gave off light.

You're perfectly entitled not to like it. In the end, I don't even like it myself, but I was much younger when I wrote it (this might be an excuse) and back then poetry was, to my mind, loftier than prose (now it merely seems mendacious: for example, why the hell didn't I add that the neon lights were flickering dimly, like in the bathroom, so that I could feel how the terror was coming to birth like a diffuse and obscure threat? And why did I say "beyond the edges of the chasm" when in the dream there was quite obviously a glade with sparse grass at the edge of the chasm?). Anyhow, I don't think there is much point in dwelling on this dream. All I know is that I woke up groggy (I've already told you that), with the flickering of those neon lights and the writhing devils in my mind. I took a book with pictures and not too many words, *Snow White*, and went into the kitchen. Mother was toasting bread on the hob. I don't know how to describe it, but that scent and the burning light bulb (it was very gloomy outside) made the kitchen seem like the first and the last place on earth, the only place whose existence you could not doubt, as if God had created, before everything else, not light, water and dry land, but that kitchen of ours in Camp Road and Mother inside it, toasting bread, and then summoning me from sleep with a storybook in my hand. I don't know what was the point of that book being there. I did not so much as glance at it. I knew it by heart, but, I feel obliged to repeat, when you are dealing with a miracle, even the unimportant details have a meaning of their own. Filip was not at home. Maybe it wasn't even Sunday. But as for the jar of mustard (into which my eyes pierced without me feeling the slightest disquiet) and as for the morning and the scent of toast, you should have no doubt. I might pretend that I heard the sound, diminished by the windowpane, of horses' hooves clopping on the asphalt, as a cart passed by, and the gypsies hollering "any old i-i-i-iron", but something tells me that I would be superimposing different images, and superimposed images are the last thing I need now.

I was not expecting anything. The dream had slackened to a slow throb – on this point the poem does not lie (there was a gigantic being whose breath I could still feel pulsating). I was sitting on a chair, at the table, staring into space, until that space completely engrossed me, enough for me to realise that what I was looking at was the mustard inside a jar. I don't know whether you have ever been curious enough to observe what goes on inside a jar of this sort, but I can tell you that, at first, all that will strike you is something that might be named yellowness. If the mustard has been started, then all the better: the teaspoon excavates tunnels, paths, channels. From this point on it is very easy to lose yourself in them, just as they are, yellowed and moist. And in the same way that a miracle (unfortunately or fortunately) always has a logical explanation, I don't think it would be hard for someone to ask the question, "what good are all these tunnels and intersections and pathways if there is no one to live in them?" I think that must be what I wondered, too. And so, as a natural combination between the answer to a logical question and a miracle with the scent of toasted bread, and without Mother, who had her back turned, even suspecting what was happening in the kitchen of Flat 40, on this earth there appeared two inseparable friends, my trusty childhood companions, Știm and Știam. I didn't whoop for joy and nor did I whoop in terror. The light bulb did not flicker like the neon strip in the bathroom. The window did not burst open in a gust of wind. And the dogs did not so much as let out a whimper when, from inside the jar of mustard, there resounded, for the first time in Camp Road, and perhaps for the first time in the whole universe (I have no way of knowing), the following conversation:

"How are you, Știm?"

"All right, Știam."

"How's Missus Știm?"

"All right. What about Missus Știam?"

"All right. Bye, Știm."

"Bye, Știam."

Please believe me that I did not so much as blink when I heard them talking. It was something that I had learned not long before: you quickly get used to miracles. Especially when you're that age.

The problem is always older brothers. Not that they have anything against our miracles, not that they frown on them, or anything like that, but they just can't seem to be able to understand them. And if they are 11 years older, then all you can do is slow down and spell everything out for them, nice and clearly, in order to avoid any future surprises. Be that as it may, I should like to make a pause at this point. A detour. A digression. A divagation. A deviation from the subject in hand. What we are wont to call a parenthesis. Anyway, I shall make the following points, seven in number:

- Younger brothers possess their own distinct and inviolable reality
- Beyond the indisputable merit of having been able to watch Mother's belly growing (with you inside) of having taken you out in the pushchair, of having listened to you gurgling like a priest, and so on and so forth (the list could go on for several pages), older brothers have no right to insinuate that your memories (sparse and vague though they might be) are, in fact, false
- When this nevertheless does occur, full responsibility must be taken for such an assertion, in order to allay all suspicion. As a result, ambiguities of the "I don't remember much about it" (see Chapter Two, Pointy Shoes and Fleecy Socks, line one) type will no longer co-exist on the same page as a confident assertion like "he has laid it on a bit thick" (lines 18-19)
- Objections, reservations and misgivings would be much easier to accept if, only for an instant, we, the younger ones, were given the right to decide what is true and false with regard to certain events in the childhood lives of the older ones (e.g. Filip + Alexandra Ştefănescu; Filip + Comrade Ulărescu)

In conclusion:
- Younger brothers are envious of older brothers
- Younger brothers and older brothers are never equals
- All this comes down to Ştim and Ştam

How the hell could it not all come down to them? What guarantee do I have, as a younger brother, that Filip is not mixing everything up again, the way he has already (a 4-0 as clear as the light of day confounded with a dubious 6-0, as I hope you will recall) when, immediately before this chapter, Chapter 3, he completely forgets the initial *sh* and turns my dear Ştim into a common or garden Englishman or American or Australian, conceived by a mother and a father and christened Tim, like millions of other Tims, in a church with godparents and the whole works. How am I to defend myself when he will say (and, at a pinch, he will call upon Mother as a witness) that it was not they, Ştim and Ştam, who were the ones I could hear talking, but rather myself? What am I to do when that *but rather* will turn into an *undoubtedly*? I repeat: you quickly get used to miracles. And, to prove to you that I am not just saying it, to prove to you that my pants are not on fire, I shall narrate how this conviction arose:

It was enough for night to fall, between the blocks, among the leafless trees and the dogs like any other dogs, straying from the field where there were once houses, perhaps there are still – such things count for but little here and now – straying along one of the Băiuţ paths and barking at some smoke, as suffocating as only a tractor tyre doused in petrol can emit, barking at us, at Migu, Pipitza, Doru and me, who were gathered around the fire, sweating for joy, our faces lit by the enormous flames. Dogs will bark at anything at nightfall. At the moon, for example. Anyway, it was enough for night to fall and for the moon to appear finally to make us afraid. Fire looks different in the dark. It takes on a life of its own and mocks you. If Radu had been with us, he would have said, "Damn it, this blaze will spread over the whole prairie." But he wasn't. There was no one but us and a fire that was threatening to catch hold of some leafless trees, and then the prairie, the blocks, the street; a fire that could no longer be put out by four winkles straining to piddle, let alone with spit or stones; a fire which, as we discovered, loves it when you fan it with bits of cardboard, that would not even dream of dying, but on the contrary puffs itself up even more, like a fat Bogeyman, and drives all the fathers outside in their slippers, drives them out of their minds. Around about then is the time to make a run for it as fast as you can: only a dope and a sissy would think that so many men driven out of doors at night, egged on by their wives, making their way towards a flaming tractor tyre, could come in peace. All the children in the world who have ever shouted, "you can't catch me!" know that they are the ones being sought, as if in the men's minds there were a magical connection between cause and effect or, more accurately, a ritualistic gesture that might produce the annihilation of the effect (the extinguishing of the fire without water) through maltreatment of the cause (kicks in the behind, clipped lugs, nose and hair-yanking, chestnuts and fists). They might have miracles of their own, but, to be honest, I have never seen this one happen. We were running twice as fast, Pipitza and I. We somehow ended up running in the direction of the field: if the men didn't kill us, like they were promising, yelling blasphemies and blue murder, the maddened dogs would have torn us to pieces; maybe that was our salvation, besides the stairwell of the block where we hid.

Leave us there for a little bit, we're all right, we're safe, because now I want to tell you something with my grown-up voice: miracles reveal themselves from their apparent cochlea (the one you have passed without noticing or trodden on a thousand times) only at strange moments, when the sky darkens with rain and reverberates in you with its dust, gusts and floating ruled exercise books, when your heart (and Pipitza's) is thudding on the staircase of a ten-storey block, after you have dreamed of hairpin bends and devils and you have been lost in contemplation of a jar of mustard. It is entirely possible that in those moments the reality with which you are accustomed to look at things shatters, a breach yawns open, a fissure through which you can see (feel, understand) things that are *other*. Or else the same things all of a sudden become other. This is why it is much simpler when you are a child: the habit of seeing things in a single way is not as ingrained, you have not yet learned anything about inertia, and so there is nothing more natural than to emerge from the staircase of a block (if you will allow me to return to the story) where you have been hiding for the eternity of a few minutes, with your heart pounding even in your toes, and to say to Pipitza, "Hey, the moon's followed us like a dog. What are we going to do? It'll give us away!"

No, it had not followed us into the block, in any case it wouldn't have fit, as we both agreed, but it was waiting for us docilely outside, even though we were some three hundred metres from the spot where it had first come out, so that it could have a look at the fire. There were two explanations for this: 1) it knew that Pipitza had fetched the petrol and that I had lit the match, and now it was doggedly determined that we should be punished; 2) it was bored to death up there in the sky, and it liked us and our tyre and just wanted to make friends with us. "It's a shit," said Pipitza. He was more convinced of the first explanation. "It's a roly-poly dog," said I, whence it is obvious that I inclined towards the second. And so we put it to the test, so that we could find out which of us was right: I ran in a zigzag, then back again, we crawled along on our bellies, we walked on all fours, we crouched on the ground and we told it "shoo": whatever we did, it followed us everywhere. It was fast, too. It was a roly-poly dog. But Pipitza was also right: it was still a moon. He knew as well as I knew that it was not always like that, like a blotchy ball, that sometimes it was stumpy, sometimes it vanished, sometimes it was like a fingernail. "Then again," he went on, "a dog would have come inside the block if we'd called it, wouldn't it?" And finally, above all, it didn't have a tail to wag. It was, of course, a moon. A friendly moon that ran after you whatever you did. It was, although I had no idea what such a thing was at the time, a miracle. The first.

I shall tell you (a prophetic consequence) that the moon is full of Ştims and Ştams waiting to be discovered. It's full of shits, of roly-poly dogs, of moons that keep following you. It's full of flying Cristoses. Of Kindo Laffies that peel off the T-shirts on which they were printed. Of fourth floors full of ghosts that follow you out on to the street in the middle of the day, that follow you and Bebe, that hit you in the face and throw you to the asphalt, to the amazement of all the gawpers that don't live on the fourth floor and, as a result, can't see anything or, even less so, understand that only an iron hand can save you in such situations. Of crosses carved into the wood in the gardens behind the blocks, crosses that turn red in the bark of the tree whenever danger threatens, for example when Beardy Lame-man is about to chase you away with buckets of cold water for having the nerve to look for snails under his balcony window. Of miracles that herald something you can't avoid. Of dreams in which you see Mother gliding upside down along the corridor, past cupboards and doors, coming towards you, and of kindergarten comrades who say "he's sleeping like an angel, let's not wake him up," and then the mothers go away, we wake up, and the dream blurs into reality if no one says that it is impossible given that the comrades said what they said, the mothers went away, and people can't walk upside down. Of hollow tree trunks which the ants seek all their lives because once they get there they gain wings and can fly. Of African masks beneath which you discover sweets, photographs, toy cars. Of children that grow up and forget everything. Of children that grow up and don't quite forget everything, but don't want to know about anything any more, that find explanations for things, like the moon is a satellite, ghosts don't exist, pixies even less so, it was a human hand, Mother's or Filip's, that hid the surprises there, as if we didn't know how things really are.

My honest opinion is that you shouldn't take any notice of people like that (they're backbiters, cowards). The best thing to do is to pause for a moment, take a deep breath, perhaps splashing your face with a little cold water will also work wonders, and if the whim has left you, it may be that some things will take compassion on you and go back to being how you left them. And it may be that you grow so accustomed to them that you'll no longer call them miracles or wonders. The moon follows you around. Full stop. If that doesn't convince you, well, then I'm sorry.

Or: Ştim and Ştam converse. Anywhere, any length of time, about anything at all. In fact, no, not about anything. Call them dimwits, dullards, dopes, but more than "How are you, Ştim?" "All right, Ştam" and the rest of the news, always the same, about each of their families, they never dared to utter (or else it seemed pointless to them). What can you expect from two amorphous beings who appeared out of the blue in a jar of mustard? As far as I was concerned, it was nice just knowing they were there. And I think that they felt, in their own faceless way, the same. Think about what it must be like to be conserved all that time in a jar of mustard, like a genie in a lamp, let's say, and then one fine day a kid from Camp Road comes and calls you to his side. What do you say to him? That his world is wonderful and that you like it at kindergarten, too? Come on, take us with you to play football! Nonsense. What makes you think that spirits like them will have come here just to discover football or how amazing Cuban sweets taste? If I had expected, even only once, them to accompany me wherever I went, like vassals or chattels, they would probably have seen to their own business and not deigned to break away from their world or come to visit every now and then. Without me showing off about it, the only reason they did come was because they liked me. I wasn't their god, inventor or master. At the most, I was their discoverer (but even this is wrong, because it was they who allowed themselves to be discovered). I was, what else can I say, nothing more than their human friend. Does that not seem like a lot to you? Let's be serious; I'm not asking you to envy or accept me, but I haven't heard of many people who can boast a friendship of this kind. I should also mention that they were phlegmatic and good-natured, family men in a certain sense, boring in a tasteful kind of way, because, and let's keep this strictly between ourselves, when you have been born into a world of certitudes, you cannot be any different. They appeared when I called them. On rare occasions they might be detained by some business on the other side. They would always apologise if they were late. They were well brought up, polite, however strange that might seem to someone with a low opinion of mustard. They never brought their wives with them, but they talked about them. The wives were all right, as you have already found out, and they themselves were all right. Most of all they liked to come when I was taking a bath. They would talk on the 'phone then. They always got it mixed up with the shower head. I never asked them about it, but it would seem that the telephone was their main attraction here, on earth, from which we can draw the conclusion that in certain worlds such things don't exist. Nor were they adverse to cartoons. They would stay with me when I was tidying up my room. They cheered me up. Because what can be more cheerless than tidying up? They got on well with Mother and with Filip, without ever saying "how do you do, missus?" or "how was your day at school?" But they felt comfortable around them. I never heard them complain. When it came to speaking, I did that for them: yes, I spoke on their behalf, but how the hell could I do otherwise when they were so stubborn or reserved, whatever you want to call it, and did not want to cause a whole carry-on with linguists knocking at the door wanting to research the phenomenon of squeaky or grave disembodied voices that went from one room to another without you being able to pinpoint where they were coming from.

They had a phobia about miracles. They could not understand why something as normal as their presence here, among us, had to be viewed with such curiosity, fear and mistrust. I think that this was also the reason why they liked Filip and Mother so much. They didn't ask any questions. They accepted or pretended to accept their existence as something natural, unquestionable. Not that I insisted on goading them to talk. It wasn't a feature of our relationship. And besides, it took me no more than two seconds to understand what telepathy means (that was how they communicated). To make myself clear, I was a kind of receiver that would pick up a question from one of them, a kind of thought, let's say, and then, as agreed, I would say it out loud along with the other's answer (how are you Ştim all right Ştam). When you find yourself in a place, on earth, in this case, you are required to abide by certain rules. If these rules say that in order to speak you have to use words and if your name is Ştim and Ştam and you can't be bothered, or you haven't the time or inclination to learn such rules, the best thing is to have a Matei to help you across the barriers, to ease your way, to translate, to make contact, to establish the connecion, to be your guide within the borders of a world seemingly at war. It wasn't at all hard for me and I did it with pleasure. I didn't feel like a pioneer, an explorer. I repeat: I didn't ask myself any questions about it; everything was perfect. It was not until later, I think it was after we moved to the Dristor district – either because I didn't like the neighbourhood, which was dusty, dirty, new, or because some muddled theory entered my head, one that ended with a "why?" – that they stopped coming to see me and probably hid away in the mustard jars of other countries, continents or worlds. That was the way it had to be. I have no further explanation. Wherever they are now, I am convinced that they and their wives are all right. And I don't know what you think, but this thought is enough for me. Bye Ştim. Bye Ştam.

IV

A Few Miracles from the Biographies of Older Brothers

So, at the end of Chapter Two, before the last full stop, I wrote Tim instead of Știm. And, I must confess, it was no mere typing error. Quite simply, that insufferable letter, a ș, a capital Ș, must have wagged its tail so fast that it leapt out of my memory, like a fish leaping out of the water, a bleak, let's say. It went splish, splash or splosh, and I mangled the name of a nice pixie and made Matei sad. I am terribly sorry, especially given that Matei, with his curly locks, his chubby pre-school cheeks, the scar on his forehead from his first birthday, and his voice that made Grandfather think he was seminary college material, so often used to take his friends for boat trips in the bathtub, referee their water polo matches, which they would play using my ping-pong balls, and submerge himself while tightly pinching his nose to cheer them up and so they could time how long he was able to hold his breath. He used to allow them to use the shower head to make their 'phone calls, embroil them in not at all bloody battles between plastic soldiers, make use of their auto-mechanic skills to dismantle his toy cars, and invite them to listen to disks with children's stories on Father's record player (I think they must have lost their wits after *Prince Charming, the Mare's Son*, from the way they used to squeal when the ogre cried, "Ho, ho, ho! Now I've got you, my beauties!").

The bad part is that I never got to see Știm and Ștam, perhaps because I wear glasses, perhaps for some other reason. Around the house, I would hear Matei talking and, I won't deny it, I used to think he was talking to himself. Given that there were so many things happening in Băiuț Alley, in the basements and stairwells of the blocks, in the classrooms and corridors at school, it never crossed my mind to spy on what was going on in our Flat 40 and thereby discover those two minuscule beings whose voices were identical to Matei's. And to continue being honest, the miracle of the presence of Știm and Ștam passed unobserved, like a bluebottle flying through my window as I slept and then out again. It is shameful for a miracle to happen under your nose without you noticing it. It is pitiful. But that's what happened. The pixies managed to dodge Mother and myself, even though my brother claims they felt comfortable around us. They also dodged Father during his short, infrequent and sleepy appearances, when he came back from the construction site, and, stranger still, they also managed to elude Stoicescu, the block superintendant (he had a lizard face and was a captain in the secret police), who didn't put them down on the list of tenants required to pay maintenance bills. And even if I have truncated the name of the affable Ştim, I hope, laying aside remorse and pique, that at least you will keep your eyes peeled and never put your trust in the letters ş and ţ, because those little tails of theirs can get you into a scrape. As for the theory articulated by Matei in the previous chapter ("The problem is always down to older brothers") my opinion is exactly the reverse. And, to demonstrate that the problem is always down to younger brothers, I too shall list a number of points, also seven in number:

- For a while, younger brothers are convinced that there is only one reality, even though there are two kinds of brother, younger and older
- Younger brothers do not suspect that older brothers have, in the past, done all kinds of things shoulder to shoulder with angels and pixies of their own
- Clocks tick independently of the will of brothers
- Each age has its miracles, each miracle has its witnesses, each witness has a brother (or was on the way to having one)

Consequently:
- Brothers can write a book together, but they cannot meet the same angels and pixies at the same time
- Even when they grow up, younger brothers remain younger than older brothers
- Younger brothers do not forget the kicks in the backside they received from older brothers

Ultimately, there is a part of older brothers' biographies to which younger brothers only have access via stories. It is a slice of childhood, but it looks like a slice of cake and younger brothers imagine it drizzled with syrup and glazed with chocolate, full of walnuts and raisins. Are older brothers privileged? Hmph! They know what they know about the part of their biographies that is unknown to younger brothers and they also know what they know about all the known parts of the biographies of younger brothers. Because they have witnessed the whole childhood of younger brothers, piece by piece, older brothers cannot imagine any of the separate parts as being a brioche or a cheese pasty. And if they venture to have memories, however imprecise they might be (confusing a 4-0 with a 6-0, albeit without bringing into question the victors or their superiority on the pitch, i.e. on Băiuț Alley) you have seen for yourselves what they get for their pains. They are treated like old fuddy-duddies with a screw loose. In Chapter Three, 'The Incredible Adventures of Știm and Ștam' it is set down in black and white that 'they just can't seem to be able to understand them' and 'if they are 11 years older, then all you can do is slow down and spell everything out for them, nice and clearly, in order to avoid any future surprises'. What remains for me, Filip, hidden up to now behind the mask of *older brothers*, to do? To think with nostalgia about how I used to kick *younger brothers* backsides. To immerse myself in my own miracles and swim around in them calmly, among fishes with tails less slippery than the letter.

Miracle A (a). In the depths there are no lobsters with pincers and whiskers or little fishes in all the colours of the rainbow. There is no undulating seaweed, or mermaids, or treasure scattered over the sand. The bottom is miry and is trying to swallow up my feet. The water is like mud or yellow soil and is everywhere, to the left, to the right, overhead, a water that grips me, clenches me, presses against my puffed-out cheeks, makes my arms turn limp, pulls my head downwards as I struggle upwards. And I am drowning. I think I cry out, but I do not cry out, because my mouth is closed or else I had it closed a short time ago, when I was still paddling my arms and legs and there was not as much water and it was not as black, like pitch, when it still seemed to me like mud or yellow if not russet soil. Then I am looking at a little fluffy cloud, like a toy donkey made of felt (and my cough was like a donkey's braying). I am stretched out on the grass and Father is kneeling beside me. He is as white as the little cloud, how strange! His clothes are dry and his eyes wet. He has bluish-white lips and an unlit cigarette, a stub, between his lips. Next to Father is Nicu, the boy who sells us worms and sometimes fishes with us. His clothes are sopping wet and his eyes are dry. He pulled me to the surface, not from the midst of my miracles (where, in writing this chapter, I set out to swim calmly), but from a pit in the bed of the Danube where I had fallen aged four, as I was paddling near the shore.

Miracle A (b). I know for a fact that we left the house where I was born (which, being a house, was not in Camp Road, where there are only blocks of flats) and we set off on a visit to my cousin Strutzi. It must have been very late because Mother was carrying me in her arms (and Mother carried me in her arms only when I was dozing off, and I used to doze off only when it was very late). We were alone in the yard, by the gate, and all of a sudden I saw the moon above the house fronts, gables and lamp posts, above the trees and the rooftops, a huge, full moon, in the middle of which another mother was holding in her arms another child, in fact, she was holding him in her lap and rocking him gently, a sleeping baby. It was the Mother of God and the Holy Child! They were gazing down on us from the sky with such affection, and Mother and I gazed at them too, for a long, long time, until I fell asleep. Mother always used to say that I was dreaming, and she still says it today, now that I am bald and no longer five years old, and even if she gazes at any moon with the joy of a blind man seeing the light. Maybe I did dream it, but I know for a fact that I saw it.

Miracle A (c) (comprising sub-miracles *a', b', c', d', e', f', g'* and *h'*, all of them having taken place in the town of Turnu-Severin, where Father was posted after university, where Mother found a job, and where for 29 months we trained for life in a block of flats in Camp Road):

a'. Together with my pixie (whose name I shall not divulge, because he was single, not double, like Ştim and Ştam, but because it sounds too much like the name of a fizzy drink from the present day) and watched over from the shadows by my guardian angel (whose name I shall not tell you because I myself never discovered it) we lit a fire in the big room, on a jute mat, using a pile of newspapers, two books with nasty stories and a roll of toilet paper. Fortunately, I did not for one moment intend it to be a campfire, with leaping flames, but just a little one, like out on the prairie, so that the palefaces or hostile tribes would not find me by following the plume of smoke. Afterwards, the remains of the mat I stuffed into the laundry basket, and the ash and cinders I swept under my bed, in my little room. Mother did not speak to me for five days. Not so much as a word. For five days!

b'. On the Sunday I accidentally discovered what a huge mistake it is, if you live in Block H 3, to walk along the Cerna Valley when the bumblebees are buzzing, when the rays of the sun are streaming through the alder leaves and sprinkling the river with glittering points, when you are passing through a herd of horses and your heart is beating for joy and fear, as if each horse were both a prince and an ogre, when Mother and Father are kissing, when you are poking anthills with a stick, when you are chomping pink Serbian chewing gum that looks like a filter cigarette, and then step barefoot into water as cold as ice and jump back out as quick as a flash, astonished and horrified, hearing the laughter of your parents. Well, after all these things, when you arrive back home (here comes the mistake) you find a lake of poo and pee flooding the whole of the flat, almost up to the knees, a textbook inundation caused by a blocked pipe on the first floor (as the grown-ups explain), a situation which you call an inundisement and, thanks to Mother's linguistic joy, you turn it once more into laughter.

c'. When the kindergarten was closed and Romana was on her holidays, in other words when we were not holding hands or descending from the coal heap in the yard to the cheers and ovations of the others and to the smiles of the teachers, playing the roles of Nicolae and Elena Ceaușescu alighting from the presidential aeroplane, my parents used to lock me inside the house. One day, let's say it was a Thursday, when, unlike on Friday, there are no three evil hours and no fast, Father came back from the factory to fetch a file he had forgotten and found me in front of the block. I hadn't broken the lock on the door or opened it with a skeleton key. I had quite simply gone out of the kitchen window, our little kitchen with the gas cylinder, on the second floor. It hadn't been my idea, I admit. Cerasela had taught me to knot two sheets and waited for me on the canopy outside the entrance to the block (it was the first time I abseiled, a prophetic moment, because I later did my army service in the alpine corps). After that, I entered the stairwell, also via a window, and then went outside; it was true, there was no way back into the kitchen. It was lucky Father showed up, because, apart from him walloping me until I was numb, like after eight injections of moldamin, he had the door keys in his pocket.

d'. In summer the heat in Severin is so intense, so muggy, that you seek shelter in the shade wherever you can. We were sheltering between some bushes in the cemetery. We had spread out a blanket on a big slab of stone (on which someone had carved some letters and numbers). We had laid out our things in our little house and were busy cooking dinner in a rusty tin can (in which some candles had been left burning). I fetched four worms. I snapped them in pieces and left them to simmer in the stew. The girls mashed up some rose petals, marigold buds, and iris leaves. They sprinkled in some gravel and dust and stirred the pot, so that the stew wouldn't burn and stick to the bottom. And when it was ready, they served the food on the plates (pieces of newspaper, torn into roundish shapes). After that, given that we were playing mummies and daddies anyway, we had to take off all our clothes and sit around the house watching television. We hung our clothes up on the rack, a wooden cross (on which someone had carved some letters and numbers), but something wasn't quite right, because the mammy and baby didn't have willies. So we looked for two twigs and positioned them in the right spot, so that Cerasela and Lori could both have a willy, like normal people.

e'. We moved from Block H 3 to Block H 4 at night, so that all the neighbours wouldn't be able to gawp at our belongings. We lugged one lot of bundles and packets less than a hundred metres (which was why there was no point hiring a van) and had to go back and do it all over again: we descended from the second floor, crossed the expanse of beaten earth, and climbed to the third floor, to an identical flat (but with south-facing windows). The brickwork of the blocks had been left unplastered and the balconies without railings. A woman was shaking out some rags from the fourth floor and laughing at the jokes of some men below, as if they were tickling her (this happened on our seventh trip or maybe the ninth). Then, on the eighth or maybe the tenth trip, she slipped – she was too busy tittering at the men and wasn't paying attention – let out a terrible scream, didn't even try to flap her arms (who knows, maybe she would have managed to fly), and on landing, very close to Father and me, did the splits, with a yell that certainly wasn't one of victory. I make this comparison because later, in Camp Road, whenever I saw Nadia Comaneci perform a perfect landing, and Cristian Țopescu, the commentator, would yell like he was out of his mind, I used to think of that woman doing the splits and her yell.

f. The sunny lighting of H 4 did not agree with me, and nor did the altitude do me any good (even though it was only one floor higher), or the new view (which contained a beige Pobeda, parked sideways). Even if my new room was the same as the old one, I no longer had any appetite for games of Red Indians, or abseiling, or anything else. When they locked me inside the house (as I have already told you) I merely glued myself to a chair and did not budge. I was so afraid of evil spirits, with their bulging eyes, claws, leering faces and grinning mouths, that I used to wait for hours hoping that the burglars would come. Because the burglars rid you of the spirits. The burglars never came, and I, who did not budge from the spot, who looked at the bathroom door as the farthest and most frightening place in the world, piddled up against the wall a number of times. I was hardly going to wet myself.

g'. The beige car would set off through the puddles, spraying droplets like a motorboat. It would set off through the snow, leaving two furrows in its wake. But it would always return, rumbling, to the same spot, so that I could see it from the window, parked sideways. Then there was that business with Fane from the sixth floor, who always used to slap me across the back of my neck and say that I had a head like a watermelon, who after every cup match used to chase me and catch me, twist my arms behind my back and tweak my ears (and what jug lugs they were!) until it stung so badly that I would start to cry and, while I cried, he would think that I was admitting that Nelu Oblemenko was better than Lucescu, who back then wasn't a manager, but a right-fielder who could make curving passes, a doting father who without a doubt used to bring little Răzvan, the future goalie, whole mountains of that pink Serbian chewing gum that looked like filter cigarettes. And one Wednesday, during a break in the league games, because Rapid had beaten Știința in the final and for 40 days it is not well to disturb the dead, Fane lent me his catapult. He told me I couldn't hit the Pobeda. And the Pobeda was no longer sideways, because I wasn't up in the big room or the small room, but outside, on the beaten earth, in a position from where the Pobeda could be seen parked head on. And of course I was able to hit it. I hit it with my first shot. I smashed the windscreen to smithereens, showering the bonnet with tiny blue shards (like the scales of a bream). And Fane chased me, caught me, and twisted my arms behind my back until the sergeant major and his wife came (his wife was a nurse; she was the one who had given me moldamin shots when I had a cold). They were shouting, as red as boiled lobsters, he in pyjamas, she in a dressing gown. In the end, all the people came outside and Fane told them that I supported Dynamo. Later, Father arrived (he supported Steagu). Afterwards, he went away again, not straight away, but two days later. He went to Bucharest to buy a Pobeda windscreen with the money he had been saving up for our holiday in Sarmizegetusa.

h'. H 3 and H 4.

Pause in the miracles (timeout): This is so that I can have a respite in which to reiterate that Miracle A, with all its dense points and sub-points, took place before life in Camp Road and was, in effect, a preliminary miracle.

Miracle B. Harun al Rashid had been away in the wars for quite some time. He loved his country and wanted to defend it. But he also loved his wife, and so, even though she was guarded from bad men by the eunuchs, Harun al Rashid, without her knowledge, had also arranged for his trusty djinns to keep watch over her, so that nothing untoward would happen. And do you know what happened? Those eunuchs weren't really eunuchs. They were just pretending to be eunuchs. But in fact they could do all kinds of things and, given that the woman had a longing for what it was that Harun al Rashid used to do to her in peacetime, she came to an agreement with the eunuchs to do the same things to her, or in any case to do them together.

It was a good job the djinns were there. They were terribly annoyed at what they saw going on in the lady's boudoir and crawled underneath the palace (down to the very foundations, I think) and began to shake it with all their might, to punish the wife of Harun al Rashid and those eunuchs who had lied about being eunuchs.

And then, as I was reading in *One Thousand and One Nights* about the annoyance of the djinns and about how they shook the palace, the block in Băiuț Alley really did begin to shake, in spite of it not being a palace. The walls and the furniture were booming. The lampshade was swaying back and forth, as if I had climbed up on a stool and given it a swing. The toys, exercise books, books, and pencils were bouncing up and down on the shelves and desk. The lamp was leaping on the bedside table. And I myself, however hard I tried to sit still, kept bumping towards the edge of the bed. But most dreadful of all was the din, the rattling of the panes in the window frames, the jerking of the doors, the thuds, followed by a very loud thud. There was an uproar echoing from somewhere else. Objects that were sick of jumping up and down were now falling onto the floor. Those djinns were really running riot. However loyal they might have been to Harun al Rashid, they were much too like the evil spirits from the Crihala Forest for my liking. And now they had invaded Camp Road.

As a child of nine (and thus more inoffensive than the eunuchs), I couldn't understand what it was I had done wrong. I grabbed the blanket and leapt to my feet. In the corridor I bumped into Father, who was tottering along in only his underpants, without his glasses, having been shaken out of his sleep. Then Mother appeared. She came out of the bathroom, dripping wet, wrapped in a towel. I was trying to tell them about the djinns (so that they would understand what was happening). I was stuttering, trembling, getting my words mixed up. We were being tossed about, like on a ship in a storm. Mother was clutching me to her breast and stroking my hair. All of a sudden she understood what I meant by the djinns and told me it was an earthquake. It was an earthquake, a big earthquake, and when I found out, I calmed down. Father was now fully awake. He dragged us under the lintel of a door (Father knew very well what you have to do when there is an earthquake). He steadied us with his arms and there we stood, pressed up against each other, for a long, long time, until all the objects had come to rest, until all the banging, thudding, rattling and booming had stopped. The electricity was off and the only light was from the moon (a large, reddish moon). People were beginning to scurry about, streaming out of the blocks like ants from an anthill, screaming and running. Nobody must have told them that it had been an earthquake and not the fury of the djinns smiting Camp Road. Later, we discovered by candlelight what the loudest of all those crashing noises had been: it was the television screen, bursting like the Pobeda windscreen hit by the catapult. Before I fell asleep, Mother told me a story about how a host of gnomes fled out of a mushroom with white spots and ran through the flowers and blades of grass in the forest glade, screaming happily, just like the people outside.

Miracle C. I was sitting on a sledge. I was holding the rein and whispering, "go, Kita, go!" And she heaved with her elongated little body, a body slightly darker than honey, until the sledge began to budge. That was the hard part. After that she ran like mad, with her mouth open and her tongue lolling to one side in the breeze. I could hear our hearts ticking, like two kitchen clocks. I could sense how they gradually merged until they ticked in unison. Between the Ialomitza and the Argeș Valley, who has ever possessed such a dog? No one, I tell you, no one.

Miracle D. Block D 13, with four entrances, four floors, and 40 flats. We lived in the last flat on the last floor of the last entrance, on the north side.

Miracle E. The Spanish teacher was sitting cross-legged. The skirt of the Spanish teacher had ridden up on either side. I was standing by the Spanish teacher's desk and watching her mark my composition in red ink. The Spanish teacher's left thigh was bared. The day was sunny. The Spanish teacher's high-heeled shoe was twitching gently up and down. All kinds of red marks were throbbing against the blue ink of my composition. The Spanish teacher's left thigh darkened to a milky-coffee brown whenever a cloud crossed the sun. I would have liked to write a long, long composition, with lots of mistakes, because the Spanish teacher's left thigh had fallen asleep. It was obvious it had fallen asleep from the way it was breathing, and I wouldn't have woken it for anything in the world.

Pause in the miracles (another timeout). Let me catch my breath and point out that all these miracles were recorded in calendars prior to the day, hour, minute and second of Matei's birth. This is so that I can think about whether it's worth continuing.

Miracle F. The lads from Anfield Road. My God! And my heart had been tut-tutting since early that morning. At first my heart felt as big as a triangle of processed cheese. After chemistry and geography, it was as big as a plum. After all my lessons, it was as big as a radish. At lunch, it was as big as a cherry. In the afternoon, it was as big as a clove of garlic. In the evening, side by side with another Dynamo supporter (Matei), it was too tiny even to quiver in expectation at such a big match. It was a heart as big as a peppercorn. Evening turned to night. Mother and Matei went to bed. In Flat 40 the buzzing silence before battle had descended and my heart had shrunk to the size of a flea, because the armies (each marshalled under white and red banners) were not to clash at dawn but in half an hour, on the whistle of a man in black shorts and jersey, not at the signal of trumpeters and buglers. And how can the silence not have buzzed during those moments, how can it not have crackled like an electrical transformer, when the moustache of Ian Rush was already bristling in a changing room, when the pupils of Kenny Dalglish's eyes were sizzling and sparkling like hot coals, when Whelan was snuffling softly, and the palms of Țețe Moraru, in the other changing room, were expanding before his very eyes, the same as the Mosquito's thatch of hair and Gigi Mulțescu's craving to do the victory samba. The seconds dragged by lazily. Altogether there were still more than a thousand of them to go. I gave up counting and switched to the other channel. There, a girl with black hair in a ponytail and a blond young man were deeply in love and they had got engaged and war had broken out and the two teams must have been emerging to warm up and he had to go to the front for Mother Russia and she was so beautiful and anxious and he gave her a little basket of hazelnuts because she was his little squirrel and in the bottom of the basket under the hazelnuts was hidden a love letter, but she didn't know and she ran after the truck in which he, in uniform, lost amid a torrent of other uniforms, was leaving for the Front and the anthem *"You'll Never Walk Alone"* intoned by tens of thousands of voices, must have been droning above the wharfs of the port, wafting out to sea, and he had a brother, a pianist, who was also courting the girl with the black hair in a ponytail, a brother who had not been called to arms, because the Red Army also needed a little music (not just cannon fodder) and some pen-pushers exhausted by so many retreats from the advancing Germans, and by so many human lives lost, sent them, her and the pianist brother, an official letter, informing them that he was dead and she wept and she wept until she married the pianist and who knows how Liverpool F.C. must have been attacking and she got pregnant and the pianist hit the bottle and started hitting her and one fine day the girl found the love letter hidden in the basket of hazelnuts and she read it and she wept and she wept, all the more so because in the meantime she had received another letter from him and he hadn't died and was fighting heroically and who knows how Dynamo's defence was holding and the pianist treated her like a cad and she gave birth to a baby boy and he, being away at the Front when this happened, threw himself in front of the enemy bullets while carrying out a noble mission and he saved his comrades and he died and who knows how history would have turned out if that (cursed) tuft of grass hadn't altered the trajectory of Augustin Oneață's kick when from the middle of the pitch he set off alone, streaked through the scattered defenders like a fireball and tricked Grobbelaar, but the ball hit the goalpost and before he gave up the ghost he saw a gentle light filtering through the leaves of the birch trees, a light that grew brighter and brighter, a dream of his wedding to the girl with the black hair in a ponytail, they were so radiant together, he wearing a tail coat, she a dress like frothy milk, they were shining together to the strains of Orthodox hymns, and who knows how it would have turned out if it had not been for that insipid goal by Souness and that drunkard, the brutal, philandering, poker-playing pianist, got what was coming to him in the end and when peace was declared the girl went off to wait for her lover amid a stream of happy soldiers, at a railway station, not knowing that he had joined the army of the angels (the pen-pushers had not informed her of his demise the second time or else the pianist had kept it secret from her, I don't remember) and a strapping young infantryman snatched the child from her arms and lifted him towards the heavens and uttered some memorable words about the future and after that the words *konets fil'ma* rolled across the screen, in Cyrillic letters, and I, an impassioned Dynamo supporter, discovered that I had been watching *The Cranes Fly* and not the semi-final of the European Champions' Cup. Augustin Oneață's miss and Souness's bland goal haunt me today thanks to television repeats, and the whimper I seemed to hear that night, near the end of the film, is finally explicable. It was Știm and Știam, who were probably crying along with me.

V

Brothers Can Write a Novel Together

To: Matei Florian,
Băiuț Alley, no. 1,
Block D 13,
Entrance D,
4th Floor,
Flat 40,
Sector 6,
Bucharest.

Sender: Matei Florian,
1st Floor,
Sector 5,
Bucharest.

> My Dear Matei,
> a few things need to be left to one side – the I that
> becomes you when I write, the you
> that is going to become me 20 years from now, time
> is so stupid: whether then or some other time, best of all
> is now: sleep, Matei, Mama
> has left the lamp with the green shade lit, the Bogeyman
> Man lurked and lay in wait for you there, in
> the dark corner of Dad's room (eternally the same,
> dark, for ever and ever
> amen) he won't be able to
> do anything if dad ever comes back turns the light on asks for sand-
> wiches reads goes away
> again, always to a different place, what
> matters is here and now the way
> he's waiting for your ears to start ringing in all this darkness and
> above all silence so that

he can peel himself away from his hiding place, a
man with phosphorescent eyes who floats in a black,
invisible sack, a
chunk of mobile darkness, better
we wallop him across his chops, stupid Bogeyman
Man, shoo, get out of this letter
in which Matei is sleeping
in which the cranes are still flying through the dining room
in which Augustin Oneață hits the goalpost without
anyone noticing
in which England is so far away lost in the fog
and the floodlights, it couldn't
be otherwise, we can't imagine it any other way, it's
clear that
his grimacing mug is the last thing we're in the mood for now, for
him to come in and disturb us and petrify us, scram
monster, it's
bad enough me showing up here unshaven
pen in hand in Chapter Five, ready
to wake you up, Matei, or even worse to scare you, hey you,
Bogeyman Man,
what do you think you're doing here, get lost, leave us alone, it's
needful for me to do this, to get rid of
that pest, so that we can be alone
with each other, me
here and you there, together
as if this were the way it has always been,
as if this were the most natural thing in the world
(a little Matei and a big Matei
chatting wordlessly
in a book in which it's late, it's night)
like this, quite simply, without me
being a magician or any clair-
voyant bunkum like that, without
there being any need for anyone else apart
from Filip and 'the whimper I seemed
to hear that night,

near the end of the film,' that whimper which seems
to me to be in need of explanation, for Ştim
and Ştam who were perhaps crying (although
I never remember them crying) and for this
need, perhaps
a ridiculous one,
to have done with the damned past,
to abandon the story for a few pages,
to rest like a pestle in a mortar inside the present where
everything abates where
I can remember that the most beautiful little house in
the world is under the blanket where
I can cup my hands over my ears and listen to
the train passing within as if rattling softly over a bridge
towards the ribcage and that thing Mother
calls the abdomen where
at last I can write to you I
can banish the Bogeyman I can explain some things to you
about
these crafty letters
the only ones that can
draw us closer together
more than any photograph or memory, it is
enough for you to believe, not to
mock them not to debauch them not to take
the words
in vain, these letters which
have to endure a
cruel detour, to wander in the wilderness to
creep up on you, words
you can only read
like this,
in a dream, over
which I stumble, with which I have to make a reckoning, in
which I rediscover myself in you, it's a wretched business me
having to appear on tiptoe like
an affable burglar like a

loving thief who
makes a bow who
says good evening who
empties himself in order to fill himself with you who
pounces on you to nest within you who
steals you away who
has the unimaginable cheek, the unheard-of temerity to
claim to be you, do you hear that, and then
he goes away again,
with boundless love, with grovelling humility,
back into the book, Chapter Five, where
I becomes you again, and I won't stick my nose in
and spoil someone else's broth
and all this
so that I can touch you and shout: you existed! damn
and blast its hide, you have to forgive me somehow, to
to clasp me tight and call me we, at least so that
people will
sigh applaud shout
encore, how lovely, at least for the sake of
our older brother,
Filip, for the sake of
the sadness that should have overwhelmed him
when Kita died, that dog
which you and I never did get the chance to stroke
which for us
never meant anything more than
a black and white photo, and perhaps also
those large letters in green felt-tipped pen that
Mother read to us long ago
'today Kita died,' then
the day and the month and the year in smaller letters
just as green, or perhaps for the sake of
his enchantments,
the intentional ones: when he used to turn girls into boys with a
twig that wasn't even magic,
and the unintentional ones: when he brought a terrible earthquake

into the world just by reading it in a book,
as if
Uca were to tell you a story about birds and they would
begin,
all of a sudden, to
fly like crazy all around Flat 40 to
bump against the windowpanes and walls later to
find the open window and
hide, perhaps
in the poplars in the school yard, among
the sparrows and collared doves of Camp Road
as if
it were night in a book and we
really were talking in one of your dreams
one of your dreams about a big Matei who
is mumbling something about
a letter, a novel, about forgiveness and other
such nonsense, the kind of things
you would have to be mad to dream about as long
as you have Laffie Kindo and I don't know what else
other labyrinths with fish where
you little ones
always find something to do, you
always get along just fine, and
in the morning you go to kindergarten and so
on and so forth, important stuff not
fiddlesticks tommyrot pangs of conscience more
or less improbable which
have no
business in the dreams of a man in his right wits, let
alone
in those of a child, you see, for
all these things you have to forgive me, I am
the liar who gnaws the bone I am
John the madman who fires the cannon I am
a grown-up who barks and snaps I am
ready to be put in a cage

I invent dreams for you which
you never dreamed, I
take you from where you are and
bring you somewhere else, here, I
say to myself that as long
as your stories still swarm inside me it
means that
I'm not such a bastard after all, that
I still have chances of survival I can still be saved
I can still find you tucked away inside me we can still
talk, without
me realising that
I don't deserve it that
I didn't ask your permission that
only you can give me permission to
find you to confine you in stories or letters, what
can I say: thanks
little man, here I am pretending
to be polite – Mister Little Matei…
would you please give Big Matei permission to play with you?
to go outside to play?
you can also watch the Dynamo-Liverpool return match in which
that dunderhead Alexandru Nicolae slips and
that moustached Rush puts
a goal past Moraru and then laughs and runs around, and
the screen splits into four
for the replay, to make
it even more unbearable,
so that you can't watch, so that
this is what sadness despair unhappiness
betrayal must mean, so that
you lock yourself in the bathroom and
burst into tears, so that
I can write about it, if it doesn't upset you too much,
and continue with the story,
can I borrow some special
feelings from you so that I'll look more clever?

will you tell me what you'll be doing tomorrow, what you
did yesterday and so
on so that
my big brother who is also your big
brother won't contradict me?
will you be so kind as to let me go on using you for a little longer,
long enough for my head not to ache because of
me being so polite to you?
honestly, Matei, if
it were up to me, it would
be enough for me to know you are there,
that you are all right, healthy, surrounded by the toy
soldiers you lead into unbelievable battles, I would
let you beat me without any remorse, I could
not care less
about anyone or anything else, but
it's good to know that
grown-ups have an invisible Bogeyman man who
keeps them on a leash, some
more so than others, one of those
miserly ogres that doesn't even have
the courage to show himself, let alone let you know who it is
you're fighting,
but I think
that you have to have some gumption
on that score, we all too readily forget the nice
things, the important things, we all too readily
fret and worry when
we don't find you, we all too readily
succumb to the feeling that we ought
to beg your forgiveness, all too readily we want
our soldiers to
conquer other worlds in
which we'll
feel better, we'll
be alone, with no
Bogeyman around or other scary grown-

ups (just us and
all our Mateis
big and little
from beginning to end
thank you very much and with no business
being in a story that doesn't even need to be written,
but just to be soothed), you understand me, when it comes
down to it, even if the monster doesn't vanish,
the stories and the letters can still
continue and bring us
closer together, me and you and
Filip and everybody, sleep Matei, I think that
our brother is about to
turn off the television, I think that
it's the end of that film and it's
late.
And there's really no more point whimpering now, Matei.

VI
Bits and Pieces, People, Big and Little

Little Matei must be overjoyed!

I think he must be biting into a piece of apple pie, drinking some squash, reading and rereading the letter from big Matei, eating fistfuls of Pufarin rice-puffs, sucking a Mentosan lozenge, crunching a boiled sweet and thinking of all those things set down so curiously on paper, things such as he has never come across in any of his storybooks. I am in no doubt that the curly-headed addressee is in possession of the text we have just perused together (I, in my capacity as brother of the Mateis, and you, in the capacity of reader): in such a personal, private matter, no bureaucratic errors will have crept in, because the epistle did not go by the usual channels; it didn't require an envelope, stamp, or postmark. It is certain that it was not a postman, but a different kind of messenger, who took it to the place where it was destined to alight, among the toy soldiers and cars, or on top of the Rahan comics. And how wonderful it would be if little Matei, after finding out about what life will be like 20 years later, were to reply to big Matei! Which is to say, if, all of a sudden, some sheets of paper (ruled, plain or squared), with clumsy big letters, with crayon drawings (little houses, pine trees or stick men), were to arrive and prove that both *the one* and *the other* are (and are not) the same, that *then* communicates (and sometimes even blends into) *now*, that time is like the water of a river, flowing in one direction, but along which you can travel both up and down. Perhaps it was not in vain that the chubby-cheeked little Matei broke the family mirrors with that little black skittles ball. He probably intuited that the silvered glass, in spite of its shining Venetian splendour, ignored the past and was unable to decipher the future. We might suspect that this saddened him. He was afraid that the mirrors would bind him to the present, to the apex of the present moment, to each hour, minute and second, that they would prevent him from communicating with older Mateis. And so he smashed them to smithereens. Falling asleep before that match which inflamed all the blocks (imperilling their earthquake-proofing) and before that film about the flying cranes which caressed the neighbourhood like a gentle breeze (cooling it), he tossed and turned in bed, he snored and breathed through his open mouth (due to polyps), he dreamed – what can he have dreamed?

I suppose he must have dreamed of white and red angels, because Dynamo were playing in the semi-final of the European Champions' Cup, in the very den of Liverpool F.C., and the flight of the cranes, invoked by the film's title, proved to be merely a metaphor, a trick intended to pull the wool over the eyes of the Muscovite censors, because in reality it was the fluttering of wings more delicate, more tender and fainter than those of migratory birds, a fluttering that arose in the big room of Flat 40 (entrance D 13) and then poured through the open window out over Camp Road. If little Matei's letter were ever to arrive, if it were to turn up one fine day on the table, under the pillow or among the T-shirts of big Matei, I hope it would also contain the little, the very little, story of that dream.

I miss that little boy who used to reveal himself in his sleep so much! He was my little brother, you know…

***

As far as I am concerned, I do not venture to send a letter to little Filip. I am afraid of disappointing him, of troubling him. The kid that once bore my name, with his preternaturally pointy chin, his fine, limp hair (but still hair, you do understand?) would have been bewildered to see himself today, bald and bearded. However much he might try to calm himself and resign himself to the thought that two and a half decades (reckoning from when Matei emerged weighing four kilos three hundred ounces from Mother's belly) causes a multitude of changes, he still would not have been able to suppress his astonishment and he would not have been content to recognise in the new physiognomy (mine, but also, in a way, his) only the jug lugs and the spectacles on the nose. In the end, on the evening when Mother was frying potatoes, not suspecting that a stork would make its nest in her belly and hatch Matei, little Filip wrote on a paper napkin, in the kitchen, that he wanted to become an *argitect* or a *gebul*. What became of it? Not a lot. The only person in our family ever to lean over a drawing board, with a passion, was an aunt who, as a pupil at music school, had spent her entire childhood bent over a harp. On the other hand it would be easy for me to pull your leg and say that I, big Filip, fulfilled the other half of the wish. No one will guess what a *gebul* is, and so I can calmly boast such a profession.

Reading that note as the potatoes sizzled in the pan, a note which may have been preserved in some draw full of paper and scraps, Mother was not able to understand what occupation was meant. And she asked me to translate it. In fact, she asked little Filip, who at the time was still learning how to tame the letters of the alphabet. But you can observe what is, rather unjustly, going on here: his memories are always mine, not the other way round, and his ideals are, as a rule, my failures, whereas my thoughts never entered his head. Endowed with an identical birth certificate, the same DNA and a single guardian angel, only we know the significance of that word not contained in any dictionary or any directory of the professions. I'll not play any longer. I'll not go on fooling you. Now I shall reveal to you, the same as he did to Mother in the kitchen, that *gebul* meant *volleyball player*. At the end of this minor outburst of schizophrenia (convinced as I am that splitting in two resembles a washing machine – it cleanses a man, but wrings him out like a rag, to the very last droplet), I admit that I, the only Filip, have never had any dealings with this occupation.

I was a goalkeeper. For Steaua. For the juniors. A complicated business, because back then, in the fifth form, in the days when the terraces didn't refer to sundry sexual acts in their chants or question the paternity of sundry people connected with the game (referees, players, coaches, managers, federation officials etc. etc.), when they (and I) used to make themselves hoarse singing 'Long live Romania/Long live the flag/Steaua's got no tomorrow/Just like Aldo Moro' and 'Spring is on the way/Steaua's going to pay/Iordănescu's in the trees/Playing football with the fleas,' I found myself going to the Ghencea Stadium cattle market, mingling with the beasts that grazed there and kicked footballs around with their hoofs. Even though my blood was seething with white and red Dynamo microbes (to match the leucocytes and erythrocytes), I entered of my own free will the malodorous milieu at the end of the no. 41 tramline, a place flanked by numerous cemeteries, overrun with grassy, slaggy training grounds, infested with viruses, bacilli and hunched streptococci, all of them red and blue. The naked truth is as follows: I placed my dives, reflexes, clears, goal kicks, skinned knees and bruised elbows in the service of the enemy. It was terrible. My soul was being roasted over the coals and, I swear, when I went to bed there was a smell in my room like the burnt heart of a red dog.[1] Something would weigh on my chest. It wasn't the quilt. It wasn't Fifi, the cat. But it weighed so heavily that it took my breath away. It must have been the remonstrating eyes of the lads fastening on me in the dark, from the poster on the wall in which they were marshalled in three neat rows on the freshly cut grass of the Dynamo stadium, one sunny day, with gaffer Angelo Niculescu in the middle, Lucescu crouching, leaning his right hand on the turf, so that it would be clear who wore the captain's ribbon on his arm, with Dinu gazing into the distance, towards the Emergency Hospital across the way or towards wars with the Germanic tribes, with Dudu Georgescu somewhere near the edge, tall and with wig-like blond hair. I have all kinds of excuses and justifications. I can explain how it all happened, how a staunch Dynamo supporter could commit such a dreadful sin.

A. The problem of friendship and loneliness
a) In the fifth form, every day was 24 hours long; *b)* of those 24 hours, around a quarter melted away with street football, dodgeball, kick-ball tennis, mule, twentyone, Cuban, and so on; *c)* street football, dodgeball, mule and so on and so on, were played in front of the block and in the school yard; *d)* in front of the block and in the school yard it was swarming with friends and acquaintances; *e)* friends and acquaintances, in Camp Road, were, in their vast majority, Steaua supporters; *f)* Steaua supporters, given that it was only a quarter of an hour's walk, went to the Steaua grounds; *g)* as a Dynamo supporter crazy for football and for having friends, in order not to be left by myself, I went to the Steaua grounds, too.

B. The problem of public transport, money and time
a) From Băiuț Alley to the Dynamo grounds on Stephen the Great Boulevard was a long journey, involving two separate buses and one tram; *b)* on the buses and the trams it smelled of sweat and farts; *c)* the smell of sweat and farts lasted one hour there and one hour back; *d)* one hour there + one hour back = two hours; *e)* two hours + one hour at the I.T.B.[2] stops (where you could feel your ears growing longer the amount of time you had to wait for the four buses and two trams) = three hours; *f)* three hours travelling time for a single training session with the Dynamo juniors is no joke; *g)* time was scarce in the fifth form, because lessons started at noon and the morning was short; *h)* in the morning, for some reason, your lugs stung more badly when the I.T.B. ticket inspectors tweaked them; *i)* in order not to get my lugs tweaked, I had to buy a ticket; *j)* one I.T.B. ticket was cheap, six were expensive; *k)* expensive means more money; *l)* I didn't have money; *m)* and

nor was I allowed, as a lad in the fifth form, to go into town every day; *n)* there were daily training sessions for juniors not only at Dynamo but also at Steaua, in my neighbourhood; *o)* as a kid mad for Dynamo, I went to Steaua to play football.

C. The younger brother problem
a) In the fifth form, in the winter holidays, Matei was born; *b)* Matei was a baby; *c)* when a baby appeared in a flat in Camp Road, hundreds of chores used to appear with him; *d)* these chores were usually done by mothers, fathers and grandparents; *e)* Father was away at the construction sites; one grandmother I had never even met, the other visited once a year, bringing frankfurters from Leonida[3] and brass crucifixes; *f)* the frankfurters were tasty, the crucifixes nice, and the chores fell upon me, alone at home with Mother; *g)* if I went outside for street football, dodgeball, mule and so on and so on, it was called playing; *h)* I couldn't play all the time if Mother was knackered and had so many things to do; *i)* if I went to training sessions, it was called having a serious occupation, and so the chores could wait; *j)* as a kid crazy for Mother and for Matei, in order to get out of doing the chores and to have a childhood, I went to Steaua.

These were the circumstances in which the villainy was committed. Despise me, vilify me, deride me, mock me, look at me askance, do whatever you like. All that I ask is that you look at my deeds with detachment. It was a long time ago, after all. I was a traitor, it is true, but in the end I was only a kid. I trained at Steaua. It's not as if I joined Iliescu's party. In any case, my career at the Ghencea grounds was short and uninteresting. The trainer made me run until I was blue in the face, not even around the pitch, but around the outside of the stands, to make it longer. Whereas for strikers, midfielders and defenders this would have had a smattering of logic, for a goalkeeper it seemed to me idiotic. I hadn't gone there to become a marathon runner, but the trainer, with his wino eyes and titchy brain, wouldn't discuss it with the likes of me. He liked to see me turn scarlet, soaked with sweat, gasping as though on the verge of an asthma attack, my legs wobbling and my soul turned to mush. It was as if he guessed I was a Dynamo supporter.

Finally, after he had warmed us up, he would split us into two, three or four teams, toss us some scuffed, laced footballs, and leave us to play. It was like in ping-pong, the winners remained at the table, and the losers went and stood behind the nets to wait their turn. He would stand on the sidelines and eat sunflower seeds. Sometimes, rarely, he would swear at one of us or clout us across the back of the neck. You never knew whether he approved of what you were doing and, however much I dived and rolled between the goalposts, however many balls I saved, however many shoves, punches and kicks I caught, he never picked me for any championship matches. If Father had, like the other fathers, visited him, bearing demijohns and carrier bags, fat envelopes and gas cylinders, bottles and crates, maybe I, too, could have played in goal at the official matches. But Father just wouldn't give it a rest, with all his construction sites, especially now that Matei had been born. And Matei was a baby, and with all babies all kinds of household chores crop up. Three months after that, I stopped visiting the trainer, although I dreamed of inscribing on the bonnet of his car, 'Down with Steaua'.

***

There is now a need for clarification, for explanations, otherwise the story will become deceptive. There are in this text little things, whether spoken or assumed, which seem like trifling details, but which are not at all, and without their elucidation the whole cannot be whole. For example, the apple pie that little Matei bit into was not merely a slice of pie dusted with icing sugar. It was a symbol. First of all, because Mother had never in her life made pies, and whenever we asked her to, she would just give us money to go to the pastry shop. Secondly, because the apple pie in question, a smashing one, was Auntie Lucica's speciality. But Auntie Lucica, the sister of an aunt by marriage, is one and the same person as Uca. And Uca was, for Matei, more than two grandmothers put together, more than seven. She was an earthly guardian angel. The beautiful gentlewoman (in a photograph of her from her youth she looked like Liz Taylor, and when I told her this, in her bedsit next to the Frigocom,[4] she blushed and pecked me on the cheek) had had a crippled marriage after her husband, a lawyer, had a riding accident a few years after the wedding. They had excised a piece of his cranial calotte and replaced it with a metal plate. She had tended him like a nurse and endured a long widowhood. The communists took everything away from her. They had reduced her to the role of an archivist in a damp, unheated ministry basement, where, among the spider webs, mouse droppings, cockroaches and slugs, squashed rats used to turn up under the files. She used to lend money to her sisters even if she had a tiny pension and never got anything back. She liked to go to the cinema and to travel by bus. When Mother had to go back to work after her maternity leave, Uca agreed to look after Matei, more from compassion and to fill her time than for the money she received. Then, before Mother could find a permanent nanny, as they had agreed, a short circuit occurred. Her heart blossomed (like lilac in autumn, as that moustached journalist from *Free Romania* would say; this was her favourite paper, especially the obituaries). She did not want to leave. In time, she even refused to accept any more money. She would scold Mother for not giving the child proper meals, for not doing the ironing and sewing. She took offence when, in the park, an older boy wouldn't give Pușița his wooden sword. Also in the park, she asked another boy to give Pușița his toy truck. Pușița was Matei, as you will have realised. And the boys in the park were bad and badly brought up.

In the food shop on Ialomitza Valley Street, Uca asked for a bag of biscuits, she knitted vests, bobble hats and booties (she knitted me a long white and red scarf, which I could wrap twice around my neck and it would still reach to my waist), she got up at the crack of dawn, queued in the market and brought us the first strawberries every year, you used to lick even your fingers after eating her *zakuska*, she cried when I put a Jean Moscopol album on the record player, she was not crazy for me, but I was dear to her. One day, talking to Mother (it was definitely a day without rain or fog) Auntie Lucica said that without Matei she would have died and not known what love was. And she thanked her. She was 70. When she was 80, and we no longer lived in Camp Road and Pușița was in lycée, I saw Uca bending down to tie his shoelaces. God rest her soul!

Then, at the beginning of the chapter, it is written that big Matei's epistle to little Matei must have found its way among the toy soldiers and cars or on top of the *Rahan*[5] comics. This was no mere throwaway item, inasmuch as my brother, of pre-school age at the time, a snot-nosed kid, a pipsqueak, a wee bairn, a nipper, whatever you want to call him, used to withdraw into his room for hours at a time and direct major troop movements, wage imaginary wars talking to himself, gaze at you in amazement when you opened the door and, discountenanced, ask you to close it again. His toy cars were auxiliary pieces. They did not count for much in the assaults along the highways of the carpet, in the hasty retreats under the blanket (where the folds and wrinkles formed caves and tunnels) or in the rallies on the heights of the bookcase. The main role was played by the soldiers. And not because that is the way it is in battles, but because Matei imparted to them tiny souls, one soul for each, and then he treated them like his comrades, like little men with their own different personalities, reactions and feelings. As far as the *Rahan* comics were concerned, given that he didn't have a clue about the publisher's communist agenda, my brother was agog for them. He adored that blond savage, who was unfailingly courageous, righteous, valorous, freshly shaven, agile, skilled in the use of weapons, and courteous with the cavewomen. Matei suffered unspeakably when that exemplary *homo sapiens*, indignant at the habits of the caveman exploiters, was hit by a poisoned arrow and collapsed lifeless at the edge of a swamp. It was then that I saw that even for a kindergarten kid, a week can be leaden grey. It was a good job that in the Stone Age it sometimes rained torrentially. The raindrops were so dense, large and penetrating that they were able to cleanse the venom from the wound and chase away the bacteria that were planning an infection. Rahan got better, tended by a breathtaking brunette, who was heedless of the fact that umbrellas and raincoats had yet to be invented. The girl, in her leopard-pelt bathing costume, kindled a fire, brewed herbal potions, moved lithely and healingly amid the stalactites and stalagmites. Matei cheered up. Life went on.

Another lacuna concerns our architect aunt. In spite of the episodes with the harp and the drawing board, she did not have any vocation to stoop before other people. She was prevented from this by her character, principles and back pain. As a little girl, she used to throw her dolly on the floor, scream 'give it!' and shake her cot until she got it. She used to goad stray dogs with sticks. She refused to flatter anyone. In front of adults she used to demand her rights whenever she felt she had been tricked or ignored. She emigrated to Germany in 1978, and when she came back to visit the first time (together with her ex-husband and his German girlfriend) she whipped up a storm. On Băiuț Alley, among the Dacia 1100s and 1300s, the Skodas, the Trabants, the Fiat 650s and 800s, the Moskviches, the Wartburgs and the Pobedas, a huge brick-red BMW with a Frankfurt number plate came and parked. For a few days I was famous. After all, there was a direct link between myself and that limousine, which had something of a holy relic about it, given the way that everybody kept processing around it and touching it. And I chewed Doublemint gum until my jaws were numb.

Then there is an anthropological and, in a way, ethical problem: how could Steaua supporters have had no tomorrow, like Aldo Moro? The man was born on 23 September 1916, in Maglie, in the south-east of the Puglia region. He was a jurist, a member of the '46 commission that drew up Italy's first post-war constitution, a minister of Foreign Affairs and Education in '55, appointed Secretary of the Christian Democrats four years later and president of the party a bit later, five times Prime Minister, a family man, a man of responsibilities, a proponent of collaboration with those socialist scoundrels in the cabinets he headed, kidnapped by the Red Brigade at the beginning of '78 and, after all negotiations failed, murdered on 9 May of the same year. So, how could the illustrious statesman, slaughtered like a chicken for the pot, have had any connexion with those peasants from Ghencea? Honestly, as a Dynamo supporter, I am of the opinion that even 'f**k Steaua' is better than 'Steaua's got no tomorrow just like Aldo Moro'.

Describing my nocturnal roastings (when in my bedroom it smelled like the charred heart of a red dog), a name appears in passing: Fifi. It is followed by the explanation: the cat. But we can't just leave things at that. About Fifi, dear Fifi, there are so many things to be said! She was a stray. She couldn't have curled up on my chest in the fifth form, because she had already settled into the monastic life at some point in the third form. She was scrawny, no matter how much she ate. She didn't live to see the days of Whiskas, Kitekat and absorbent cat litter. She slept wherever she liked (especially on our pillows). She did her pee-pees and poo-poos in the bathroom, in the drain in the floor. She ran around like a mad thing. She didn't walk around with her nose up (like a prim miss) and she threw herself into the furnace of love with that dustbin tomcat (who, for her sake, mauled the other dustbin tomcats) and after days and nights spent in the block basement and in the bushes, she returned to the fourth floor, starving, frozen, ruffled, drubbed, and with her belly about to swell. In the summer, we went to the mountains, she, Mother and I, in the car of an uncle with the soul of an accountant. It was hot, very hot. As usual, I was nauseous. We stopped at Ţigăneşti Monastery, to interrupt for a while the mystical trance of Great-grandmother. My uncle remembered, out of the blue, that he had been an officer in charge of supplies, that he had kept a tally of mess tins, boots, caps, epaulettes, and Linemann spades, and it occurred to him that in all the boscage of the barracks inventory there figured not one cat. And so he had taken the decision to leave Fifi there with Great-grandmother, to let her take the veil. I protested. I bawled. I said anything that came into my

THE BĂIUŢ ALLEY LADS

head. I refused to get back in the car. They talked down to me. In my throat a bitter lump had appeared, which kept growing and growing. Fifi remained behind in the grass, tabby and frightened. I squashed my nose up against the rear window. I smeared it with tears and snot. In the end, the only thing I could do was to throw up on Uncle's coat. A spew full of grief and hatred. Mother kept her silence.

It would be fitting for the friends and acquaintances from Camp Road mentioned in passing under point *A (The problem of friends and loneliness)* sub-points *d* and *e*, to be transformed from notions into characters, to be given faces. Or at least for some of them. This has already happened in the case of Luigi, firstly in the '90s, in a short story published in a literary gazette by a very, very young Filip, a Filip who still had a fair amount of hair. For some reason or other, the Filip of that time wrote in the third person, and his qualities and deeds were imputed to a vaguely outlined character named Andrei M. I shall let you read it, in order to find out a few things about Luigi.

The Shit

Or when he had gone with a friend from the next block, one afternoon. He wasn't even ten yet. He was bored. The street was deserted. They had gone to the kindergarten, where his friend's brother was in the big group. Then they ate biscuits for something to do, until they reached the schoolyard, where they got sick of that floury, insipid taste and thought of throwing them away. They were on the weed-filled patch of waste ground under the windows of the biology labs. They stepped around the puddles without taking any notice of them. They were talking about a war film that was showing in the cinema by the market. It was his friend (Luigi they called him) that trod in the dog shit.

Although Luigi is the kind of name gypsies like to give their children, he wasn't a gypsy. It was more a case of his mother having had a crush on some Italian singer when she was pregnant or when she christened him. It made a loud squelch. It had dirtied his trainers. He used to worship trainers, that boy. Hey, he would say, to feel the ball against your foot properly, you have to play wearing trainers. Anyway, he was swearing at the bullock-sized monster that must have been caught short there. Back then, they were too childish to tolerate being laughed at, and so they started throwing stones in the puddles. They splashed each other from head to toe. They looked like

20 ROMANIAN WRITERS | 83

pigs that had been wallowing. The idea came to the main character, Andrei M., who, as I said, was a child back then. I mean, what would it be like if we smeared the biscuits with this mud and made sandwiches with them. In the schoolyard, the children had come outside. It was the after-lessons day-care period. The boys were running around after a deflated ball. The girls were playing 'land, o, land, we want soldiers!'[6] The teachers were not to be seen, but it was impossible for them not to be around somewhere, in a sunny spot, knitting and pondering what they were going to put on the menu at home that week. He knew all this very well. The after-lessons day-care period was in his blood. He didn't even need to look behind him, towards the school. From the shouts and squeals alone he could describe everything that was happening. It was the hour when the parents began to arrive. He always had to wait until five or six. But this day had been an exception. His mother had got off work early and taken him home. He knew them all. They were his comrades. Serious people, with whom he used to catapult bread pellets at lunchtime and loosen the screws in the girls' folding beds when the tutor went out into the corridor to have a smoke. He was smearing the biscuits in a leisurely, unhurried way, as if he were tickling something inside them. With a twig he took some of the dog's digestive residues and spread them carefully, little by little, until it looked like the cacao cream of a Eugenia sandwich biscuit. A woman who was passing, along the path between the puddles, had screamed, 'What the devil are they up to there?' She had even tried to chase them. A thoroughbred housewife, large, fat, with shopping bags. She hadn't managed to catch them. She had quickly tired because of her varicose veins. They could hear her swearing and cursing more than a hundred metres behind them. They were on the football pitch by now, nibbling the clean biscuits and offering the others left and right with great largesse, as if it were the most natural thing in the world. They kept stopping to chat with boys they knew, about daft things. Only two boys sampled them, and in any case that had been a quarter of an hour before. There wasn't any great appetite. In any case, how can a taste do any harm when it's a matter of healthy stomachs? One chubby boy wolfed one down and then pelted away after the football that was whizzing past at that very moment. He made no comment. Nor did he even have time to do so. His bottom was pumping like a widow's and he kept trying to shoot at the goal. The other, a nondescript lad – in spite of his efforts all he could remember about him was a squashed face – commented, gave advice, and so they let him sit down next to them and ingest three cream biscuits. He even lauded the taste, albeit briefly, until they heard the woman's shrieks once more: 'What are you doing? You little bugger! Throw them away this instant!' Lord, the way things can turn out sometimes! The fat woman who had chased them was the boy's mother. They scampered like rabbits over the fence around the sports fields. The truth is that man borrows certain features from the species of the national fauna, be they wild, be they domesticated. The boy with the squashed face, for example, had been blessed with the traits of a mule. He went up to the fence and cadged some more biscuits from them. And they gave him them. What else could they do? Refuse him them? He swallowed them almost without chewing them, while his mother tried desperately to lay her hands on him. She was screaming, 'Throw them away, you stupid ox! They've got shit on them! Throw them away when I tell you, you fool, you idiot, damn it, boy! Throw them away or I'll kill you!' He was chomping away, smiling at them, with complicity. They were hanging from the wire mesh of the fence, watching. The football match had finished. The woman was panting. She was as red as a pepper. 'Ooh, argh... you little bugger, wait 'til I get my hands on you! Spit it out, you moron! Don't swallow it!'

The tutor had shown up by then. He was approaching briskly, scratching behind his ear and puffing on the cigarette wedged in the corner of his mouth. One of the lady teachers had put down her knitting and was standing rooted to the spot, with her hands on her hips. What she could, or could not, make out only she knew. The others carried on knitting, two loops front, two back, two front, two back.

Luigi then vanished from the stories. He rested for about a decade and a half between the covers of a file and in my memory. He emerged about two years ago, when he became the main character in another little text, signed by a now bald Filip, gnawed by rheumatism, a smoker's cough, gastritis and nostalgia. It is pleasant and amusing to quote yourself. It is as if you are putting on a shirt you have washed and starched yourself, on which you have sewn new buttons with your own hand. Here is the little text in question:

Luigi Pătrașcu and I, Pioneers
I could tell you about how the rays of sunlight, as slender as noodles, were seeping through the leafage of the poplars in the yard, were trickling down

the school walls, over the grey, knobbly plaster (which Luigi Pătraşcu knew very well was not a *calcio-vecchio*, but rather spatter-work made using a broom), then slopping through the open windows of the classroom and (given that they were like noodles, and from noodles drip hot soup) spattering beads of sweat over the pupils' brows, under Comrade Teacher Ulărescu's armpits and perhaps her back, at the bottom, where her blouse was rucked up over the waistband of her skirt. As for the flies, with their buzzing and acrobatics above the teacher's and the pupils' desks, there are a number of things that readily spring to mind and which I shall tell you. The fact that they were buzzing and tapping against the windowpanes was nothing out of the ordinary, but they were overdoing it, they were doing it in a brazen way and at inopportune moments, for example when one of those tinkling voices, with a blue dress and white hair bows, was reciting something from the literature textbook, gathering together roses, industriousness, weevils (with the stress on the *vils*), wheat fields, the Party and pine-garlanded mountain tops. It was then that a large bluish-black fly dizzily dropped down the Comrade Teacher's cleavage and started buzzing around down there, growing even dizzier, I thought, because the rays of sunlight, I must remind you, were like noodles and what was dripping from them was like soup. How I rejoiced! Comrade Ulărescu did not shriek, but her lips (with tomato-red lipstick) emitted a kind of whistling noise hard to imitate and, you will understand, even harder to replicate in writing, a whistle in any case classed in grammar as an interjection. And she, Ulărescu, leapt from her chair in front of the blackboard and began to shake her whole body, against the backdrop of chalked additions and subtractions, until she pulled her blouse out of the waistband of her skirt and fluttered it a few times, long enough for the bluebottle to fly out and for me to be convinced, on seeing the colour, that Luigi Pătraşcu had known what he was talking about when he said the comrade's bra was pink.

Later, as if the rays of sunlight, the flies and the bra hadn't been enough for one morning, the whole of 2 D was overwhelmed by huge excitement, like an insufferable breeze, which instead of cooling caused feverish frissons. Comrade teacher Ulărescu had returned to her seat. She had calmed down. Her features had set once more into the expression of a stuffed owl. She was calling us to stand up one by one and listening to our proposals for the 10 free places in the first rank of pioneers. When it finally was my turn (I was sitting at the back of the class), I pronounced the name Luigi Pătraşcu, because, in my opinion, although he spoke haltingly, slurring his syllables, and still had to use his fingers when he counted, to him it was fitting for the trumpets to play and the flag the flutter. The comrade asked me to list a part of my classmate's qualities and merits, to describe his qualities. It is true that I remained speechless for a time. I kept shifting from one foot to another (oh, what Drăgășani[7] trainers I had!). 'Stop fidgeting!' she snapped. And I managed to mumble, 'He's an industrious pupil'. I could hardly have told her all the things Pătrașcu knew! She agreed, 'Hmm, hmm, it might be a motive…' But shortly thereafter, when it was his turn to stand up, he sniffed and recommended me. The teacher's eyes did not sparkle with the gentleness of a doe, as the poet once wrote, but rather they bulged, as I have already told you, like an owl's. Her palm descended on the register with an admonishing smack, convinced (the palm, not comrade teacher Ulărescu) that we had made a deal with each other so that we could both get onto the list. And she rejected me.

At the Military Academy it was a first-rate festive occasion. The white shirts on the platform in front of the statue! The scarlet cravats with the tricolour border! The belts with the large buckles, the ones with the national emblem on them! We, the many, the very many, the ones who did not enjoy the privilege of having been made front-ranking pioneers, were gazing up at them, the front-rankers. We were also gazing wide-eyed at the stone heroes and the war veterans. You wouldn't have said that they had fought the same fight. We, the ones lower down the class at school, were down there, on the terraced plateau in front of the Military Academy. We were singing from the bottom of our hearts, 'Ta-ra-ta-ta, the bu-u-u-u-ugles have sounded,' and they were answering, from up there, 'I pledge my troth/My undying oath/As a pionee-e-e-e-er.' Luigi Pătrașcu was somewhere among them. I couldn't pick him out among so many, but I knew that he knew all about the lingerie of the teaching staff, why Dobrin hadn't been picked for the Mexico match, how to sneak into the Favorit Cinema without a ticket, and why Dan Spătaru[8] sung through his nose.

As far as I was concerned, it was there in our classroom that I had become a second-rank pioneer, while the flies were buzzing and tapping against the windowpanes as usual. It was beautiful. I think it would have been even more beautiful if Comrade Teacher Ulărescu had at least run a quick iron over the flag beforehand.

Having blown the dust off two old texts and reproduced them here, on rereading them I ascertain to my amazement that the portrait of Luigi is incomplete. A number of details are missing: he was bowlegged, he used to pinch apples from the market stalls with thievish dexterity, to toast sunflower seeds and share them with the whole street, and to try and imitate Gigi Mulțescu's dribbling skills (without the master's sparkle). He didn't hate the coach with the wino eyes and titchy brain, he was crazy for films with Germans and for Daniela Roșu, and he had a house full of paintings, where it smelled of garlic and pickles.

For the Cuban to appear, it was necessary to build C 37, a block as big as a village, with ten storeys, six entrances and two hundred and sixty-four flats. While it was under construction, there were fierce battles between the armies of the D blocks to conquer the foundations. We used to build redoubts from rocks and clods of earth, arm ourselves with sticks, catapults, blowpipes with paper darts, maces, spears, shields and siege ladders. We fought blindly. In the evenings, when we abandoned the pit full of concrete and iron casings and edgings, teams of scouts would slip behind the enemy lines and destroy the casemates under cover of darkness. In the mornings, at school, a kind of armistice held, but afterwards we would become enemies once more and start all over again. During a lengthy siege, in which we held out only by the skin of our teeth, Bogdan Guță got his head broken, which is to say a little hole appeared in his forehead, from which the blood spurted like a miniature fountain. Guță, nicknamed Puță (Todger), fell to his knees, boggled his eyes and fainted. The little hole in his forehead straight away grew to the size of a plum, someone (not me) ripped his T-shirt into strips and bandaged him, someone else (not me) hoisted the white flag. Technically speaking, it wasn't surrender, but rather a forced cessation of hostilities, during which the aggressors turned as white as sheets and trembled like leaves. When he arrived, in pyjamas and slippers, Mr Guță walloped his son, to warm himself up, and then laid hands on two lads, the first he managed to catch (ironically, one of them was from our army) and gave them a good hiding. Later, there was a court case. And Mr Guță had to pay two thousand lei for the tooth he had knocked out of Gigi Monkey's head. Anyway, Gigi Monkey used the money to buy himself a pair of Lee jeans, a Red Flame leather football, and a radio, with the result that for a while we all wanted Mr Guță to punch us in the mouth.

C 37 wasn't an ordinary block, however. Not even from the very first.

The cranes, bulldozers, concrete mixers and labourers rumbled, roared, and cursed from its heights louder than elsewhere. The blood that had trickled into its foundations, from our wounds and scratches (incurred during the fratricidal fighting between the D blocks) was not a sacrifice sufficient to ensure the solidity of the walls. More was needed.

One day, while Mother was hanging out the washing on the balcony, a truck went rattling past, the truck was full of panels, the panels began to slide and fly off the back, one hit a woman as it flew, it squashed her on the pavement and severed her carotid. She was young. She was screaming horribly. She died before the ambulance could arrive. In fact, C 37 is not an ordinary block even today. There is, it seems, a connection between this block and Al Qaeda, and the thread sets out from Parva Alley, right next to General School No. 57, traversing the country and the continent it crosses the Atlantic, it stretches all the way to the shore of North America, winds its way around Long Island and the Statue of Liberty, meanders the streets and boulevards, slips through the exhausting New York traffic, and reaches the Twin Towers. It was in the newspapers and on the television. I saw it with my own eyes Troc's father, on the news, on various channels, explaining all kinds of things about an Arab who had rented a flat on the first entrance, pretended he liked young women, old Mercedes cars and small-time wheeling and dealing, but scarpered when the Romanian Intelligence Service got wind that he was caught up in big-time villainies and was one of Bin Laden's men. Presented on television as the block superintendant and with his full name, Agop Kirkorian, Troc's father looked old, emotional and vaguely culpable. You would never have thought that he had once been a stiff, bespectacled officer who forbade his son to keep up his football (although he played fantastically and had won over the coach with the wino eyes and titchy brain) and made him keep his nose in his books (where, to be honest, he wasn't that great at dribbling or shooting). In the fifth form, when he was a major and stern, we used to call him Agop, and Troc, whose name was Silviu, we called Oagăru (Jäger).

Troc lived on the first floor of the first entrance and was in class I. Also in C 37, also on the first entrance, but on the third floor, lived the Cuban. That lad (also in class I, also with an officer father, but a unit commander, a lieutenant-colonel) used to walk around in a size 84 tracksuit and size 21 rubber boots. He used to wipe his nose on his sleeve or the back of his hand. He would lend his legs to whomever had a ball. He used to play leapfrog, piggyback, hide-and-seek, shove ha'penny, twirly-whirly, snap and many, many others. He didn't get on with the girls and used to rise at the crack of dawn to go to training sessions with the Steaua juniors. When he used to come and call on me, if I wasn't at home, Mother would always entrust him with Matei, so that he could take him out in the pushchair. The Cuban was convinced that my brother was highly intelligent, because Matei would point his finger at his forehead and knew what sound a cow makes.

[At this point in the narrative, Matei, in his capacity as co-author, has asked me to record the following: 'I wonder how they, memories, might illumine some corner of your mind so that out of the blue you could see yourself as a baby in your pushchair smiling at the blocks, the buses and above all the blonde noggins endlessly burbling over your words (words at least strange, if not magical) like coochie coochie coo, like riki tiki tiki tomba, like la-looie ba-looie ba-looie? I would really like to know, because, you see, what is gnawing away at me is the idea that I wasn't a baby like other babies and nevertheless, no matter how hard I try, the way things seem to me, I don't have the slightest shred of evidence that any of the things I have been told were indeed true'].

The ping-pong on the table in the Cuban's dining room was smashing, especially when it was raining outside and we used to pick out books from the B.P.T.[9] series to stack up for the net. One afternoon, I grew bored of it after about 10 sets (I think I must have been losing) and wanted to go home, but he hid my boots when I was about to leave and laughed all the while I was looking for them. It was not until I found my footwear in the larder, behind a sack of carrots, that he calmed down and begged me to stay. From a drawer he produced some rumpled magazines, not with photographs, but with drawings of naked birds in all kinds of positions. I stayed to have a look. How could I have missed an opportunity like that? I was terrified by the idea that from the blanket box under the sofa bed, from the balcony, or out of a cupboard, his mother might pop out (she was a shift manager at the Lilypad laundry) or his brother (a polytechnic student, former jockey and owner of the said magazines) or his father (the paunchy lieutenant-colonel).

All of a sudden it is winter and a few street lamps have lit up, the schoolyard is white and deserted, a gust of frozen wind is blowing, snowflakes are falling. You can play two-man football when the Cuban can shoot from any angle, with the inside of his foot, with his laces, with his toecap, with the outside of his foot, and I am saving everything that comes at me, I am rolling through the snow, diving at the base of the goalposts, floating beneath the crossbar, boxing, yelling, shouting, rubbing the corners of my mouth with my sopping gloves, pulling up my waterlogged trousers, which keep drooping and baring my belly, deflecting every ball, and he is bursting, yelling, shouting (unlike me, not for joy, but in frustration) he is kicking more and more furiously, and in the end he tricks me and scores a goal. We are yelling, shouting (he for joy, I in despair now). It would be nice if I could tell you that one of us pulled a wafer biscuit from his pocket to share with the other. I would be lying. We left the schoolyard with our arms around each other's necks, talking about a girl from class J who was going out with an African.

Then, the camp in Breaza had everything you could ask for during a spring holiday: cheeping birds, girls' skirts, macaroni, marmalade and potato stew, fresh shoots of grass, maths lessons with Stănescu, my tutor (in D) and his teacher (in I), toothpaste on the doorknobs, an excursion to the huge cross on the mountaintop, during which we kept shoving each other in such a way that we would break our fall with our palms on the girls' wee breasts, cow clart, stray dogs, blossoming apple trees, pillow fights in the dormitories, discos from seven to nine p.m., games, the homeland wants you! (who? Nicoleta-a-a-a!) hawks and doves, blindman's buff and lots more, and, in addition, probably the jewel of that camp, a long veranda on the ground floor where we would jump down at night (without Stănescu suspecting anything) a veranda on which I arranged the first kiss in the Cuban's life, convincing Nicoleta to have a little pity or at least show him what she knew.

P.S. 1: I forgot one of the chants from the fifth form: 'Steaua, you're no good with goals/But just for shovelling coals.'
P.S. 2: I didn't know that *Rahan* comics were printed by the communists either.
P.S. 3: Later on, the Cuban was nicknamed the Badger.
P.S. 4: The Badger is now a football coach; when he was a player, during the '94 World Cup, in the penalty shoot out with Sweden, I locked myself in the bathroom; I heard he missed.

VII
Pitch Black with a Whiff of Cheese

I think something nasty must be happening with my noggin. Otherwise I can't explain why it's started itching me (not on the outside, but on the inside, which is even nastier because if it had been on the outside I could have put it down to dandruff or head lice or something, but dandruff is too easy an explanation, and in any case, let's be honest, it would be no great bother if I went down in the lift and asked the old codger from the shop round the back for a nifty shampoo to give this hair flour its marching orders, at least for a week. As for head lice, thank God, since the time I stopped associating with Paul, who always used to donate a couple to me – he had a hatchery for them in his hair; it must have been 20 years ago – I haven't managed to incubate so much as a single louse egg. It seems that God has been protecting me or maybe He said to Himself that I suffered enough back then because of that instrument of torture with myriad sharp teeth, which reeked unbearably of vinegar and was called (how stupid!) a comb, or when the curls that refused to let themselves be untangled fell to the merciless scissors so that my pointy head remained bared, or when that stinky lotion deigned to scorch my scalp in search of the enemy and an entire nursery school group, small, medium or large, not to mention the whole of Băiuţ Alley, would understand very well what ailed me and shun me without remorse, like I had been struck down with the plague. I hope with all my soul that He won't be piqued at the fact that I have invoked Him so frequently at the beginning of this chapter and I also hope that I won't have offended Him so mightily that He will bless me with a brand new dose, the cutting-edge in parasitic bugs, just when I am reaching an age verging on the respectable. For no other motive than I wouldn't want my future wife to give me the boot for such an unworthy reason.).

What is certain is that this itch (as if someone were grating their fingernails across the *calcio-vecchio* granulation of a wall that remains forever imprinted in my mind) is worryingly reminiscent of that feeling which people are all too eager to label 'pangs of conscience'. Undoubtedly, each individual has been endowed with the inalienable right to name his inner itches in whatever way he pleases, and so don't expect me to blow my top if one of you gets the urge to point your finger at me on the street and say, 'Ah, there's the bloke who has the pangs of conscience but won't admit it'. Maybe I'll get a little upset, but, on my word of honour, I won't let my chagrin show in any way. The bad part, with itches of this kind, is that they're never content to stay in one place. For example, a few times up to now, I've had the ever more acute feeling that this damned itch (now it's a kind of buzzing) has begun to slide droning down my throat (where it came to rest for a little and turned into a lump) but now, in exactly the moment of writing, it has planted itself (this time smouldering) slap bang in the middle of my chest. You have to understand that, however much I would like various things to remain tucked out of sight at least until the Last Judgement, if not forever, however much I would wish (and I have wished it like a madman) them to remain far from the guilt-inducing eyes of Mother and Filip, however much I might try to shirk and dissemble that it will pass, this itch is becoming unbearable and more than ever I need (like any normal human being, I expect) to scratch it voluptuously and at length. I don't know whether it's a good solution, because in some cases, as you know full well, what can happen is that precisely the scratching will give you eczema or something worse, but, what with one thing and another (and given I don't trust doctors) I can't glimpse any other way out. And because it is not a matter of dandruff or head lice, things I would be able to get rid of using the familiar methods, I can't think of anything else except to rummage around in writing, to knock together a few stories, to rake up secrets, in the hope that, once and for all, this insufferable itch will reveal itself and, after a public unmasking, be so kind as to get lost. It is my duty (I've no idea why it should be my duty, but there's nothing I can do about it; it seems that I, too, am in possession of something like a code of honour or common decency or some such twaddle) to warn you that scratching an inner itch almost always results in confessions and that these confessions wouldn't be a problem if they didn't bring with them all kinds of dubious epithets of the 'disturbing', 'shocking', 'vicious', 'violent' variety, which, apart from agreeing with the substantive 'confession' in gender, number and case, also offers you an immeasurable quantity of chills down the spine, so that you will feel like scarpering, dropping everything as fast as you can say 'fish' and getting out of this book for good.

But now you have grown to suspect me of having pangs of conscience, I wouldn't for the life of me want to be tarred as a common criminal who doesn't know how to treat his readers with respect. As for Mother and Filip, however much I might look for a saving solution, I can't glimpse even the tiniest escape hatch down which to make my getaway before I break their hearts. I only have to think of how Filip believes at the beginning of chapter six, that little Matei 'must be biting into a piece of apple pie, drinking some squash, reading and rereading the letter from big Matei, eating fistfuls of Pufarin rice-puffs, sucking a Mentosan lozenge, crunching on a boiled sweet and thinking of all those things set down so curiously on paper, things such as he has never come across in any of his storybooks', and I become as embarrassed as a wee bairn catching Father Christmas up the chimney.

I don't know what you would do if you were shrunk down inside a book that exuded such a hieratic state of joy, let alone such a paradisiacal languor, in the realm of so many wonders (which, by the mere fact of being listed, offer the taste-buds luxurious pampering), I don't know whether you would go into a huff because of the absence of a box of Cip[10] sweets or whether you would merely view this omission (as I do) as an instance of tender concern for the friability of milk teeth. I don't know whether you would hide your tears like any self-respecting adult and, above all, I have no way of knowing whether you would feel something resembling a tingle, or rather an itch, worming its way deep inside you. But I really can't imagine what a tongue-tied soul must lie buried within me if I can't explain to Filip why it was that I looked at him in amazement when he opened the door and why I asked him, in embarrassment, to close it again, when I used to take refuge in my room for hours at a time, when I used to 'direct major troop movements' and 'wage imaginary wars' talking to myself. How am I to tell him that this cursed itch alone obliges me to reveal all that carnage bedecked with terror and blood, with fear and agony, which I would have wished to keep locked up in the darkest corner of my memory? What he will think – let us now for the first time leave the door wide open – about the nocturnal darkness which, at two o'clock on Sunday afternoon, steals from behind the drawn curtains like a cat (an unreal, translucent, threatening cat) like a lynx and stealthily envelops them, the green foot-soldiers, as yet inert, as yet ridiculously small, the soldiers that seem to scan the endless expanses of the featureless tundra, without yet being able to say whether they are alive or dead, as long as God Himself has not yet decided on any move, He has commanded nothing except that night should close in, and closed in it has (like a cat, perhaps, or a lynx), a fog might just as easily descend, a kind of unseen blanket covers them like the roof of a cave, then it withdraws as if it had never been invented, everything reverts to tundra and is as motionless as in the moments before the genesis, except that here there is no need for any word, it is enough for there to be a hand, an arm, for a hand to open and the thumb and forefinger to grip the general, to swivel him back and forth, to accustom him to the diffuse light, to the lay of the land, to himself, to allow him to understand his purpose in that strange place, to teach him to see, it will be his destiny, the sole purpose for which his presence there is tolerated, here are the binoculars, here is the general, lads, we're in a devilish fix, night is drawing in, and we're out on the open plain, if those villainous Indians decide to attack, then we're done for, I order you to form columns, we're heading towards the edge of the cliff, I know the way like none other, I have been victorious in thousands of battles, careful, lads, we have to keep our eyes peeled, we all know what that bitch's whelp Joe Lemonade is capable of, that paleface traitor who has taken up with those shitty Indians so that they can gobble us up alive, Jack, take aim, shoot anything that moves, at your orders, boss, Bill, stop snivelling, you're making yourself a laughing stock, I want discipline, I want us to destroy them to the last man, behind a huge rock that's the spitting image of a book there are lurking the two red feathers of an Indian with a bow and arrows, a steady hand holds the reins of his horse, another hand helps him dismount, the Indian is stealing (like a cat, perhaps, or a lynx) behind the rocks, he's taking aim, whizz, an imaginary arrow is hurtling towards Bill, the other arrow, the real one, remains frozen in the preternaturally taut bowstring, a groan, aargh, an almost inhuman cry, and Bill is mown down, shoved seemingly by the same hand, he agonises, he cries out for water, Frank, water, I've been hit, an arrow, Frank gives him water, even though he is kneeling and holding a rifle to his shoulder, the general is looking through the binoculars like a madman, in vain, a knife flashes in the pitch black of night and buries itself between the frail shoulder blades of another soldier, a nameless soldier, a soldier without a story, and with a final effort he manages to toss a grenade, boooom, the tundra shakes, the rocks echo back, boooom, an Indian camouflaged behind a hill that is like a wrinkle in the pillowcase is thrown up into the air, from the knife he is still holding you can tell that he was the one who killed the grenade-thrower, he deserves his fate, doesn't he, the blast of the explosion has thrown him right next to Frank, but Frank proves to be a coward, he runs away, he deserts, he's out of ammunition, click, click, he can't riddle the shrapnel-riddled body of the knife-wielding Indian with bullets, there are no fine tales to tell about cowards, the Indian's feet tread on Frank's throat, and the knife savagely rips open his chest, the blood spurts like a fountain, Frank goes to a better world, he is tossed over the edge of the cliff, the torrents of the river cleanse his wounds, he appears once again, he quickly returns, a hand lifts him in his flight back to the battlefield, he is just as ferocious, but now he has a different name, even the general seems to know his name, hey, Private Bob, where have you been hiding? There is no time for introductions, Private Bob empties his magazine, bang, bang, bang, into the head of the knife-wielding Indian, this is for my brother Frank, you cretin! The Indian finally dies, he remains motionless in the middle of the tundra, he will be revenged, Joe Lemonade shows up, on a horse, with a lasso, which he seems to be whirling, but in fact it's an optical illusion, you would think that Joe is fused to the horse, but there's nothing he can do about that, Joe seeks out the general, I'll catch you with my lasso, I'll take you prisoner and throw you to the coyotes, no one crosses Joe Lemonade's gulley alive, your men killed Inchuchuna, now it's your turn to be killed, Joe keeps his word, the thumb and index finger of a hand help him to wreak havoc, from behind a rock, from the heights, a mounted Indian shoots arrow after arrow, the general's radio operator has no time to call for reinforcements, a blood bath heralds the dawn, which presently appears, as the curtains are drawn back, the tundra is drowned in the blood of the minuscule plastic corpses, on which a pack of invisible coyotes is feeding. 'The soldiers' guts have no taste,' a voice manages to say, from the upper reaches of the universe, and the rest is silence.

If it weren't for the curse of certitude that perfidiously whispers in my ear that nothing, even when followed by a full stop, can mean anything more than nothing as long as you have heaps of things to rake up, to narrate, to bring to light, then everything would be all right, I would be able to sleep soundly, dreamlessly, without open doors, without itches, and in my insensate state – believe me, I'm capable of it – I would snore for hours. The bad part is that there has yet to be invented an infallible method that would allow you to get rid of certitudes by kicking them up the backside, after which you could go quietly to bed. I only have to think of how many times Mother's nail file used to vanish, without her, in her motherly innocence, ever having any inkling of the stealthy footsteps, the diabolical grin, the trembling and depraved hand that would swipe the nail file as if a sacred object from her shelf in the bathroom (the same hand that mercilessly smote hordes of little plastic men) and I feel faint and my knees sag. I only have to picture how Filip's blue eyes darkened on discovering that Rahan was in the strange habit of emerging from the pages of his French comic, making sure that no one was looking and then, on tiptoes, more like the lowest form of thief than a blond savage, '...courageous, righteous, valorous, freshly shaven, agile, skilled in the use of weapons, and courteous with the cavewomen,' stealing (like a cat, perhaps, or a lynx) into the bathroom of Flat 40 in Băiuț Alley, where his hand expert at pilfering would always hit upon that nail file on the shelf, and then, saturated with a ferocity verging on senility, returning to the bedroom where he had materialised, alone, menacing, proud, to give voice to that shout which always heralded a major battle (Raha-a-a-a-an!) and, with a monstrous hatred, unbearable to witness for any living creature endowed with reason, rushing to the shelf littered with innocent and delicate creatures (little girls with frocks and dresses, with chubby cheeks and doe-like eyes, with long, quivering eyelashes, which even the terrifying sight of the looming nail file could not prevent from blinking innocently, perhaps for the very last time; all those creatures, Transylvanian Miss, Oana, Luana and Sînziana,[11] doomed to perish at the hands of the crazed Rahan, armed with a nail file that only his blind bloodlust could make him mistake for a knife) seizing them by their short, curly, long or silky, blonde or brunette hair and their delicate shoulders, ah! how easily dismembered, by their chubby and all of a sudden useless legs, circling them dizzyingly as if in a dance of death, smiting them on their little chins with his fist, hurling them so that they would fly, briefly, dizzyingly, until they hit the ceiling, a wall, the floor, casting himself upon them, roaring for the umpteenth time his infamous name, Raha-a-a-a-an! and, in a final release, plunging his terrible weapon up to the hilt, once, twice, a thousand times, until there was not a single spot on the plastic body that was not an open wound; I only have to picture how Filip will be filled with horror on reading this diabolical deed on the part of Rahan – a deed which, I am convinced, his French publishers, however socialist they might have been, would never have dared to imagine – and I feel utterly condemned, submerged in pitch blackness with a whiff of cheese.

Perhaps it will seem strange to you, but that Rahan of Flat 40 was I. And how the hell could it not seem strange to you, when even I make the sign of the cross on discovering that the doll slayer of chapter seven is one and the same person as the Matei of chapter six who 'suffered unspeakably when that exemplary homo sapiens [exemplary? *Matei's note*] indignant at the habits of the caveman exploiters, was hit by a poisoned arrow and collapsed lifeless at the edge of a swamp.' How could such a villain suffer, let alone unspeakably? Not even I can explain how such a thing was possible, but I swear to you, by all I hold dear, suffer he did. There's not much point going into details of a technical nature (in broad strokes, Filip renders the atmosphere of the comic strip) but I feel the need to intervene with a rectification, you know, the part about how the raindrops were dense, large and penetrating, and then the bit about the breathtaking brunette (as far as this point is concerned, I'm certainly not going to poke my nose in; each to his own taste, and anyway I was too little to dwell on details of this kind) washed the venom out of his wound, and all the rest of it, but it has to be said, no offence intended, that Rahan was by himself when he woke up and the whole business with the poisoned arrow and his death proved to be nothing more than a nightmare induced by some poisonous mushrooms he had eaten in the previous issue.

It wouldn't be any big deal, but I don't want you to get the idea that Rahan could be slain by just any milksop with a few poisoned arrows in his quiver. It is true that I did suffer, even unspeakably (how was I supposed to know that Rahan wasn't dead?) and that that suffering was, in a way, educational, or maybe I'm getting things mixed up, and it was Mother wondering what had happened to her nail file or Filip hearing my screams and drawing the wrong conclusions, because, although I am at a loss to explain it, guests ceased, as if by magic, giving me dolls and Rahan was fated to do battle with the bluebottles instead. An innocent occupation! And it was not so much a case of the mistaken notion, as regrettable as any mistaken notion, that between bluebottles and pterodactyls there is no notable difference (the mind of a six-year-old Rahan is capable at any time of confusing the Jurassic with the communist period) as much as a case of the deep-seated awareness that every creature is doomed, sooner or later, to extinction (see the dinosaurs) and that the bluebottles, merely because of their anachronistic buzzing, a throwback to prehistoric times, could be no exception.

As far as they were concerned, everything was decided: the end had come. As you can imagine (any room with open windows during the summertime can stand as witness) Rahan had slim chances of success. However many wings he sliced off with a razor blade (a strictly scientific experiment which demonstrated, if further proof were needed, the huge adaptability of those creatures, which, at a pinch, have nothing against changing into beetles), however many legs he pulled off (with infinite care, so that flight would become more difficult for them, but not impossible), however many muscular pterodactyls were constrained to live with a pin thrust in their abdomens and later end up as food for the spiders lurking behind the radiator, however many sub-aquatic voyages they were forced to make in the transparent capsule of a submarine in the form of a glass, not to mention the countless specimens that served for medical research in a strictly surgical sense, let alone those used as wallpaper in the most unexpected of places (curtains, mirrors, windowpanes, cupboards, dressers, books) and not taking into account the cohort of those that gave up the ghost in the plastic dungeons of vitamin C tubes, the fearless blond hero had to admit that although he was unvanquished (his heroic nature by definition excluded the possibility of any defeat), he was, at least, vastly outnumbered. This does not mean that the battle did not continue for a good few years, during which time things became clearer somewhat, as Rahan went back to becoming Matei and the pterodactyls, naturally, reverted to being bluebottles. As a sundry item I can also tell you that today the war is over, with the bluebottles having won a victory by default, and that no one and nothing in this world will convince me to wreak revenge on them now. The only pleasure I still permit myself is to deal a formidable flick to the head of those flies that buzz too loudly. This kind of palliative has a mildly tranquilising effect, and moreover it has the great advantage of causing only minor lesions.

On the other hand, I would very much like to know what kind of mean and cowardly spirit impels me to ascribe so many villainies to Rahan alone. When will things be clear enough in my mind to allow me fully to accept, with courage and dignity, like my brother Filip, that for certain actions responsibility must be shouldered? After all, even something as grave as betraying Dynamo for the sake of Steaua can be explained, justified, excused. The main thing is not to lose heart or run away, but to remain calm and confront the facts, no matter how villainous, with solid arguments, with points and sub-points, so that the guilt of having made a pact with the devil will be erased, forgotten, so that it will cease to niggle and haunt you. And so, all in all, nothing remains except for me to abandon Rahan to his dolls and pterodactyls and to dash outside. Let none of you believe that I'm giving myself a chance, that I want to scarper out of the way of Mother and Filip and crouch behind Florea's Wartburg, and to hide there until nightfall and the end of the chapter. No, I have sworn to you that I'm not going to dodge anyone, and if I say that I'm going to Migu's and Pipitza's doorbell on the second floor, then you can be sure that this is exactly what I'll do. Maybe they want to come outside, too, eh?

How can I be so daft? Of course they'll want to come out. When was it ever the case that they didn't want to go outside? Hmm? Migu, even if he had homework, still used to go out. Pipitza doesn't count, because he's still in kindergarten. He'll come out anyway. What can you do in the house except scrap with your brother? He-e-e-y (this is Migu), you scrap with your brother, but I don't scrap with you, that's 'cause I smash you. I mean, Pitiza couldn't take on his brother Migu, 'cause he'd box his lugs until the sun went down. That's what he thinks (Pipitza isn't talking to Migu; Pipitza is putting his shoes on and talking to me) I could beat him any day of the week. I could beat him in my sleep if I wanted, apart from all his bragging he's soft as clart.

Ha! Pipitza makes a move like one from a Bruce Lee film he saw on video. Migu's not overly impressed. Knock it off. That's all he says. He's seen the film, too. I wait for them to put their shoes on. I'm first! Pipitza says and tears off down the stairs. He jumps on the banister and slides down it. He falls with a terrible crash. He jumps back onto the banister, tumbles onto the stairs, picks himself up, and starts swearing, while his brother laughs fit to burst. He calls him stupid. He shows him how to slide down a banister the proper way. Migu's an artiste. He slides fast, first on his belly, then on his bottom. Want a round of applause? Big deal, mutters his brother. In any case, I got there first. I was second! The second's the best! Stop! I said. I'm not stupid enough to go sliding down banisters. What if he broke his arm? What would he say then, eh? He's saying that I'm stupid and I don't know how to slide down a banister. Maybe I'll clout him. Pipitza sticks his tongue out at me. He's fast. Now I'm really annoyed. He jumps over the fence, tries to dodge me, left and right he goes, but I catch hold of his T-shirt. He's tugging like mad to get away. Caught you! He calms down. I calm down and let him go. What, does he think I'm going to chase after stupid people like him? Leave him be, 'cause he's in the huff, says Migu. Huffy, puffy! Pipitza's acting all big. He's doing a belly dance to the tune of huffy puffy. He's trying to annoy me. Just watch me box his lugs, says Migu. I don't chase after stupid people, I say. Pipitza's bored with it already. Truce, hey, truce. Let's play dodgeball or something. But he won't go and get the ball. Stop! he says. I say it and Migu says it. It's obvious: no one's going to go. It's too quiet on Băiuţ Alley. All the wimps are at home playing with their dollies. Or with their toy soldiers, I say. Wimps! And I spit with incredible accuracy in the left eye of a fairy drawn in chalk. Now Migu spits and now Pipitza. It's a real spit-at-the-fairy world championship here in Sector 6. And the winner of the gold medal is ... Matei Florian of Bucharest! Well skin my todger! Migu is disqualified. You can't talk like that at a world championship. The silver medal goes to Pipitza Nicuşor! The whole stadium erupts into cheers, chanting Pi-pi-tza, Pi-pi-tza! Probably in the huff, Migu has started rubbing out all the chalk fairies with the soles of his trainers. The contest is over. Those stupid girls Miruna and Tatiana are going to be frothing at the mouth. As if I care. Let them so much as squeak and they'll be in trouble. The fairies are now disfigured. They have turned into a coloured smudge. You'd think it was puke. Listen to that! Pukey fairies, pukey fairies. We all burst out laughing. That's what it's like being friends: you have a laugh, you tell jokes, you don't just play and nothing else, like the wimps and that lot who don't know anything except football and hide-and-seek. The dimwits.

Bebe's spotted us. Bebe's the fourth. Let's wait, 'cause he'll come over here. And come he does. Bebe's got big ideas. Let's build a fort. Let's not hang around doing nothing. To build a fort you have to go into the garden around the back of the block, snap some leafy branches off the trees, hang them from the fence, pile them up one on top of another. Bebe explains what to do and we carry out his orders. Six branches from the tree by Beardy Lame-man's window, six from the tree by Mrs Constantinescu's window. They'll throw a fit if they catch us. They'd be ready to chase us until next Tuesday, to ring our doorbells and grass on us. But those are the breaks. Every occupation has its hazards. The fort is ready. It's even got a roof. Bebe's pleased with it. Pipitza's a bit wary. What if they catch us? We won't even be able to see them coming from inside the fort. Migu gives him a kick in the backside. Offside. Pipitza's blubbering. He's going to tell his gran. Just you wait until you get home. Migu couldn't care less. Kindergarten tots have no business in a fort. I keep mum. I don't want to give myself away. I'm in the big group at nursery school. But I don't see why I shouldn't stay with them in the fort. I mean, I built it. Bebe remembers. What about him: he's still in kindergarten, too. For me to stay with them I have to prove I'm not. Bebe knows a test. Come on, inside the fort, let's see how clever you are. Bebe grins. I go inside the fort. It's a bit manky. You have to crouch and you can't move around too much, otherwise the roof will cave in. A twig is poking me. Anyway, at least I'm in the fort. Bebe has got something in his pocket. He rummages and pulls out some matches and a cigarette butt, with a filter, a BulgarTabak, 'zee best,' foreign, from Bulgaria, top-notch fags. I pinched it from the garbage pail. Let's see if you've got any guts. On my word, I don't really want to. I might die of poisoning. Even if I gave up the fort, Bebe still wouldn't let me go. He's too gleeful at forcing me to smoke. I was forced, Mother, I give you my word of honour. If I had been able to flee, I would have fled. They were pinning me down, Bebe and Migu. They'd twigged that I didn't want to die of poisoning. Bebe lights the match and takes a drag on the cigarette. Now let's see whether you're a kindergarten boy or not. The cigarette is between my lips. They were threatening me, I swear. Inhale, inhale deeply, inhale deeply! O, Lord, what a revolting, choking, stinky nastiness immediately filled my lungs. I'm going to die of poisoning, hallelujah, I never expected to start coughing so badly, for minutes on end, as if I had a coffee-mill in my windpipe, you could have put me on a ventilator and the smoke still wouldn't have come out of me. Bebe was splitting his sides. That's the way to do it, bravo, you're a big lad now, but stop bleating like a goat, or else you'll give us away. I carried on giving them away, however much I wanted the coughing to abate. Have another drag, go on, hey, no, that's enough already. Migu's grip had loosened somewhat. I burst outside. All I had time to see was the fort roof collapsing. I caught Bebe cursing my name and saying something rude involving my mother, but that was all. Adieu, Rahan. O, Lord, let me slam the door shut behind me, so that no one will ever ask me anything again.

Yes, well, they'll ask me now, won't they? As for all the stuff about spitting, swearing and smoking, you can give whatever excuse enters your head – that you were threatened, that they forced you, that who the hell knows what else – you can stand on your head and fiddle for all the good it will do. It just won't wash. That's my opinion. Even if Filip was able to rid himself of that nightmare about Steaua, and I have no doubt he was quite able, it doesn't mean that the same thing applies to me. In case I have forgotten, I have an itch in my noggin that insists on reminding me.

And I don't think it will be enough for me to describe to you the gentleness of Uca, her smile that used to light up any downcast morning, afternoon or evening, those caresses that used to erase in an instant any torturous complication as if it had never existed, as long as into my memories there always creeps that cursed bookshop, whether, like an unscrupulous emotional blackmailer, I used almost to drag her, knowing, oh-ho-ho, all too well that she could never refuse me anything, that all I had to do was throw myself on the floor and bawl at the top of my voice, thrash my legs up and down and foam at the mouth, and she would spend the last of her pension on some remote-control toy car that would, the very same day, end up wheeless under the bed or behind the bookcase.

No, I felt no remorse. The same as I felt no remorse that time when I played, if you can call it that, with Monica one rainy afternoon on Lunca Siretului Street, D 40 (also in Camp Road), Uca's four-storey block, teeming with pensioners, both nice (Mrs Buzescu, Mrs Sandu) and nasty (Mr Buzescu, Mr Sandu), in which her bedsit with all its mirrors housed so many wonders: a kitchen where the games were solitaire and tabinet[12] (I don't know how, but I always used to win); a bathroom with glass cabinets and a cup with a picture of Castle Peleş in which rested a toothbrush, a comb and a tube of pineapple-flavoured 'Cristal'[13] toothpaste, which I periodically used to sample; a dark cupboard full of goodies: jam, syrup, tomato juice, *zakuska* and pickles; a room with green curtains perfect for hiding behind for hours; an armchair (like a king's throne) on which Uca would knit me bobble-hats and gloves; a chair that turned into the goal in which Augustin Oneaţă scored goal after goal until Duckadam and Stîngaciu covered themselves in shame and vanished; another marvellous chair carved with an eagle chained to an Indian, who had been out gathering firewood, supposed to represent Prometheus, and another wooden figure, a curly-headed cherub, who was meant to be rapacious Zeus; a vitrine where there was an iron bear holding a lamp post, which, for some reason, always used to be knocking the head off the nearby Arab seated on a flying carpet; a stumpy, curly-headed doll (I won't say anything about it; I think you can imagine it for yourselves); a bed the size of the *Titanic* on which I lost myself in the sweetest luxury that has ever existed; a huge wardrobe full of sheets and blankets beneath which lay a jewel-like bar of Fa[14] soap, with a sticky, icky taste, although I never got out of the habit of nibbling it; another cupboard in which resided the great Manitu, the Indian god, otherwise an ordinary candle with the face of a hideous man; and a gigantic Russian radio set, on which I used to listen to plays directed by Rome Ochelaru and, in the evenings, without fail, the crackling, mysterious voice of Neculai Constantin Munteanu on Radio Free Europe.

Monica was the daughter of the secret policeman from the second floor, the only person in the block, apart from his wife, who was not yet a pensioner. Monica was small, ugly and stupid. Monica always used to get on my nerves, but that didn't prevent me, whenever I grew bored of gods and football, of tabinet and toothpaste, from inviting her up to the third floor to play with me, the devil knows why. I would quickly get bored. She was stupid, as I have told you. She was also snot-nosed. What I can't understand now is why she kept coming every time I invited her, even though (I think it must have entered her head in the end) she would be slapped and have her hair pulled only five minutes after coming through the door. Maybe that was what she liked. I don't know. But if that was the way it was, then at least she should have shut her mouth and not snivelled like a mental case at the first kick in the behind she received. Most of the time I would promise her that I wasn't going to do anything to her, just so I could beat her up even more when she stopped whining.

She was a phenomenon that girl, because, however hard I try, I cannot recall ever in my life having beaten anyone so systematically and relentlessly as I did her. Anyway, that afternoon, it had started raining and maybe the close, stale air or the gloomy, sullen sky was enough for me to start laying into her harder than ever before. It was as if I was possessed. I tripped her up as she ran for the front door. And when she got up I managed – bravo, Pușița, encore – to bang her head against the door. She was wailing like a banshee, the devil take her. It did not for an instant matter that Uca shouted at me to stop and even tried to restrain me. I saw red. And now I shall pause, like a coward, no, like the vilest of cowards, as if nothing else happened: nothing about the hand that hit her, not the little girl, but her, Uca, nothing about her tears, the tears of a kindly, small, frightened grandmother, nothing about the long hours I then spent hiding under the quilt, nothing about the kiss she later gave me on the forehead, that's enough Pușița, don't be sad, it doesn't matter, it's in the past, in the past, nothing about the apple pies, the 'Pufarin' rice puffs, the Mentosan lozenges, the boiled sweets and the squash she offered me (oh, the irony!) to placate me, nothing, absolutely nothing else about that rainy afternoon.

No, I have decided: the best thing would be for me to tell you the story about Bogdan, and let that be an end to it, come what may, whether I get rid of the itch or not, it's enough already, full stop, because I feel as if I have been overburdening you with all my villainies, vile deeds and outrages, and you will, I am sure, want to rest for a little, cleanse your thoughts and go to bed. I've no idea. Each to his own.

I, for example, knew Bogdan from a hide-and-seek game. He was six at the time, and I was three. In any case, it was the first time in my life I had ever played that game. It was night, pitch black, but there was not at all any whiff of cheese. Bogdan was 'it'. His brow was resting against a tree trunk and his arm on a litter bin and he was counting up to a hundred. And obviously whoever wasn't ready would get bonked with a spade and guzzle lemonade, which all seemed very strange to me. And nor did Bogdan want to walk his bear, and the bear's chain was getting rusty, in any case all it took was for him to look in the wrong direction and I rushed up behind him and spat on him. Bogdan threw his hands up in despair. He calmly explained to me that you weren't really meant to do it. It was just what you said, understand? I understood vaguely that the spade, the lemonade and the bear didn't exist, but at the same time they did. I was also happy, and the reason was embarrassingly simple: when in the history of the world has a three-year-old boy ever been able to get away with spitting on a six-year-old?

So, Bogdan, as you will already have guessed, was a decent lad. He used to call me outside to play toy soldiers. This was unhealthy, because, however many varieties of toy soldiers there might be, they're not polytheists, they need a single God who will know all. With many people you get into all kinds of arguments and the battles lose their magic. But he liked to play like that. And he didn't like loneliness. How about you come to my house. I'm bored. I'm on my own. Mum and Dad are at work. Granddad's gone shopping. He lived in D 14, on the ground floor. He had a broken microscope. He wanted to play mummies and daddies, he the daddy, I the mummy, and to do that, apparently, we had to take all our clothes off and get into bed stark naked, he would jump on top of me and then we would roll around. The rolling around wasn't that bad, but when he lay on top of me it was nasty, he was heavy, bony, he was smothering me, I told him this, what a stupid game, but he was dead set on going on with it, he was dying to be his dad, then I heard his granddad at the door, ringing the bell like a madman, he must have been weighed down with heavy bags, he was a bad'un that granddad, I could see it from the desperation of Bogdan, who jumped up and started getting dressed, get dressed will you, hurry, hurry, don't let him catch us, I got dressed and before his granddad could come into the bedroom Bogdan shoved me onto the balcony and told me to jump, and so I jumped, you'll never have seen a mammy like me in your life, it was a good job he lived on the ground floor and I wasn't left stark naked.

Bogdan wasn't a good husband. He pretended I was invisible until we moved to the Dristor district. In his mind he must have filed for a divorce (like my parents). Adieu, Father, you'll find yourself another mother. Never mind. That's the way things were meant to be. Each to his own.

Two clarifications:

1. 'It's pitch black with a whiff of cheese' is what Filip used to say to me on the summer nights when there was thunder and lighting and we pretended to be frightened and huddled under the blanket.
2. I don't know why, but that itch isn't niggling me as much now.

VIII

Father wasn't at the Tractor Wheel

If Father shaved on Sunday morning, it meant we were going to the cinema or a match. Father loved pinstriped trousers (which he ordered from a tailor), shirts in pastel colours (with the top buttons undone) and velour or suede jackets. We used to stroll up and down the Republic Boulevard and every time it seemed to me that in that one-hundred-metre stretch between the Gambrinus Restaurant and the Army Club were gathered together all the cinemas in the world and all the happy people. We would walk for ages, like two bewildered ants in a vast anthill, until a poster, a title or an actor's name caught our fancy. Then Father would leave me to wait in a sheltered spot and plunge into the crowd. I think he must have breathed flames through his nostrils or turned somersaults. I don't know what he did, but it must have been something out of the ordinary, because he would always return holding his arm up, so that I could understand from a distance that he had succeeded, so that I could see the tickets fluttering in his hand. But it sometimes used to happen that the hour when the film started did not coincide with the hour indicated by his Russian watch, and so we would go in anyhow and pray we hadn't missed much.

When darkness enveloped the auditorium, when the world outside ceased to exist and in its place was bodied forth that other world with its colours, music, dialogue, plots and characters (and, you can be sure, the cardinal rule there divided things into the good and the bad), when the projector began to purr like Fifi, our cat, and when the stale, sour air began to freeze (because of a bloodthirsty bandit, a cruel German, a power-hungry cardinal, an elegant and dissembling woman, an avalanche, a Sioux chieftain or a devastating explosion), well, in those moments, I felt that Father's aftershave smelled like cinnamon and his hand was very warm. When we went outside, it was Sunday lunchtime and the daylight (even on cloudy days) dazzled us and forced us to wipe our spectacles. Before taking the trolleybus home, we would stop off at a little café next to the Beer Dray Restaurant, where he would drink a large vodka and buy me a Pepsi and a few cheese sandwiches. I don't know why, but Father, sipping from his glass, always used to gaze out of the window at the deserted street and the grey plaster of the sidewall of the National History Museum.

In the stadium it was different, even though it was also called 'Republic', like the boulevard with all the cinemas. As it was Sunday morning, we used to go to the matinee matches. And who plays in the matinee matches? Rapid F.C. No one else. Fifty thousand people would cram into the stands bringing with them their sardines and smoked sprats (and the stands themselves resembled a sardine can), they would sit on the steps, hang from the fences, climb up the loud speaker poles, and clamber on top of the huge billboard inscribed in red letters, 'Long Live the Socialist Republic of Romania!' And the fifty thousand (minus two: Father and me) would go into a hypnotic trance as soon as the players left the dressing rooms. That was when a long plum-red snake would appear at the mouth of the tunnel, look around to get the lay of the land, hastily cross the running track, slither over the cropped grass, come to a halt in the middle of the pitch and twist from side to side, saluting the crowd, before breaking into pieces, 11 players and five or six reserves, depending on how many vertebrae there were.

What erupted around us was not a choir, or a hubbub, or a roar: it was 49,998 simultaneous declarations of love. Rapid were playing. That was all. The opponents didn't exist, given that the second-division teams were weedy and green, like frogs, and everybody expected them to be swallowed up by the snake. After the referee blew his whistle and the ball began to roll, all that counted was how the orchestra on the pitch handled their instruments. If Nae Ionescu felt like plucking the fiddle on the left flank, if the titchy Paraschiv had a mind to tap the zither in midfield, or if that brindled ox Damaschin was pumping away at the accordion in the eighteen-yard box, it would turn into a real party, with whoops and cheers. Sometimes, however, the musicians would be tired, because they were young men, and Sunday morning follows Saturday night, when they used to get plastered, bladdered or blotto at all kinds of wedding receptions, christenings, stag nights and birthday parties. Then it would be lamentable. Really lamentable. Thousands of men, most of them swarthy (swarthier than that brindled ox Damaschin, who had cacao-coloured skin), would all of a sudden feel swindled by their mistress with the boyish name, Rapid, and start to whistle, swear, boo, threaten and curse, so that I (but not Father) would be afraid lest they catch fire, immolate themselves, lay their hands on crowbars. And I was not afraid for nothing. One sunny, joyful Sunday morning, not the one when an old, ruffled up gander (Dobrin, who had ended up playing for Tîrgoviște Steelworks F.C.) picked up the plum-coloured snake by the scruff of the neck and dashed it to the ground, but another morning, when Father had a slight cold, one of those swarthy men, betrayed by his mistress (in a miserable match against Slatina Aluminium F.C.), hurled a crowbar at the pitch. He didn't hit any of the players, but rather one of the 49,999, who had paid for his ticket and was sitting munching pumpkin seeds. And that man, who never even saw the crowbar flying towards him, because he didn't have eyes in the back of his head, like an ogre, and who was suffering just as much because of the girl with the boyish name, fell down in a pool of blood and died. It was in the paper, that Monday. In *Bucharest Information*. In the column 'The Capital's Militia Inform Us'. It was in the afternoon. Father had left to go to one of his construction sites (maybe he would be coming back in a week, maybe in two weeks). Mother was dozing. Matei had not been born yet. I had built myself a den under the desk, using blankets. I lit a candle (not for the man who had been munching pumpkin seeds, but because it was dark inside the den) and I realised that I would never be going to matches at the Republic Stadium again. And I didn't.

Today, I wonder what we were doing there in the first place. I supported Dynamo, Father Red Flag. We didn't have any business with those second-division clodhoppers. Things have their own logic, however, and mysteries (sometimes) unravel of themselves one fine day. First of all, in the family's prehistory, a slender brown-haired girl had whispered a question to a jug-lugged boy during a university entrance examination, to enter the Philology Faculty, to be precise. He will have detected an audacious naturalness in her expression. He hesitated a little, raised his fountain pen from his answer sheet and, out of pride, if not other motives, gave her the answer. But he did it clumsily, with too much aplomb, and he was observed by a supervisor. His answer paper was cancelled and he was made to leave the hall. He waited for her at the entrance, not with reproaches and tearful tales, not with a scandal or with flowers, but to invite her to an athletics competition. And they went, because she was remorseful (for all the audacious naturalness of her expression), and that boy (who smoked continuously and didn't lift his eyes off the ground very much) had been limping for a few days after spilling sulphuric acid on his left foot.

In the sports stadium, at the start of a middle-distance running test, she had a fright and screamed loudly, very loudly, because she couldn't understand who was shooting a pistol or why. Everyone around them guffawed, and the first episode in the serial (not a soap opera or a sitcom) came to an abrupt end, against a period soundtrack of, let's say, a song by Gianni Morandi or Pompilia Stoian. From the closing credits we can see that the role of the slender brunette was played by Mother, 18 at the time, and the short bloke with jug lugs was Father, who had quarrelled with my grandfather and, not having anywhere else to sleep, was spending his nights in a tobacconist's, on a mattress crammed under the counter. Another significant detail: the athletics context was being held in the Republic Stadium. Finally, also in the murky, far-off period before my birth, another (not at all negligible) episode closely connected with that stadium took place. Father was obliged to shave his head after betting with a friend, at a life-and-death match, that Red Flag would beat C.C.A.[15] and take the champions' jerseys back to Brașov for the first time ever. It didn't turn out that way. For, on a cannonball shot from Tătaru, because of an evil spell, or something like that, the ball wedged in the corner of the goalposts (literally – it remained jammed between the post and the net), the likes of which you see only once every two decades. With his head gleaming like a light bulb, that pint-sized supporter, whose identity card gave Săcele under the heading *Place of Birth*, must have looked more jug-lugged and mortified than ever.

Cigarette break. And, given that I'm not going to light up a cigarette while Father is watching, I shall step out of the story for a short while and go in search of Matei. We, the brothers Florian, have a number of matters to clear up:

Matter 1 – Lord, how nasty internal itches can be!

Matter 2 – I feel sorry for all those warriors who fell during the battles behind closed doors, in the endless tundra of little Matei's bedroom, where nocturnal darkness steals from behind the curtains at two o'clock on Sunday afternoon, where there is a huge rock that is the spitting image of a book and a hill that is like a wrinkle in the pillow case, where the dawn presently appears as the curtains are drawn back and where the soldiers' guts (according to a voice from the upper reaches of the universe) have no taste. May God rest the souls of Bill, the nameless grenade-thrower, Frank, and the general's radio operator. And may the Great Spirit receive with open arms the Indian riddled with Bob's bullets!

Matter 3 – Had it not been a question of 'minuscule plastic corpses, on which a pack of invisible coyotes is feeding', had the prairie not been an expanse of tundra and had the general not been accompanied by a radio operator long before the invention of the radio, I would have felt even sorrier. And another question would have arisen. The smell. The dreadful smell in Matei's room. Think only of the malodorous puttees of the Yankees, their breath stinking of gutrot whiskey and chewing tobacco, the sweating horses and what must have happened inside that cowardly Frank's trousers when he found himself grappled to the ground by the wounded knife-wielding Indian.

Matter 4 – Such is the history of the U.S.A., as my brother puts it so well, referring to another historical period (that of D 13): 'carnage bedecked with terror and blood, with fear and agony'. And I am proud of little Matei, of what he did in there, behind the closed door, because he was a free and just spirit (the Little Spirit, a pre-school Amerindian god), capable of resurrecting Joe Lemonade and imbuing him with tenfold strength. I am happy to discover that, in Flat 40, the pale-faced soldiers did not kill children and old people, they did not rape women, girls and goats, they did not shoot the wolves that danced with Kevin Costner, they did not burn down wigwams and they did not massacre bison (and not because they couldn't even if they wanted, but because the divine fingers always thrust them into complicated situations, into misty chasms, into passes, onto screes, where the Red Skins would manage to finish them off, rejoicing in the countless victories of the war they would ultimately lose.)

Matter 5 – It's obvious that I was Rahan, too, but most of all I was Tarzan, because I liked his war cry more (not to mention Jane). I never stabbed those bovine-eyed dollies, Transylvanian Miss, Oana, Luana and Sînziana. In fact, I never even knew their names or what they were doing in our flat. It was a good job Matei laid hands on the nail file (when you are Rahan, having a dagger is the number one rule) and turned them into sieves. What ugly, stupid dolls!

Matter 6 – The world of Rahan and *Rahan* comics (socialist publishers and all) existed even before Matei was born. Likewise, the poisoned arrow that felled the blond savage existed before the poisonous mushrooms that caused his dream about death, and the rain that washed the venom from his wound (miraculously healing him) fell from the sky, or from some grey clouds, to be exact, long before he ate the toxic fungi. Sceptics may consult the dog-eared collection of *Rahan* that stand as witness in libraries.

Matter 7 – When big Matei left the door to little Matei's room wide open, my eyes did not darken. Lucky for him, for the co-author (who suspected or feared that my eyes would darken), that he has got rid of that internal itch.

… I've smoked three cigarettes by now, not just one. And Father must be sick of waiting for me and peering into the mists of time all by himself, imagining how his life (and ours, everyone's) might have turned out if Tǎtaru's cannonball shot hadn't stopped where it did, but rather bounced off the goalpost.

In the very beginning, when we moved to Camp Road, D 13 looked like a ship anchored in an almost deserted port. In the distance you could make out other ships, and between them, ruffled water, caressed not by a sea breeze but by a wind off the plain: an expanse of sticky mud and garbage. In the mornings, when he set off to work, Mother would wrap his feet in one-leu carrier bags (of different colours) which she tied with string below the knee. It would take him half an hour to reach the asphalt, at the Moghioroș Market, where he could finally take off the mud-caked carrier bags (finally both the same colour: brown) and board the bus in his shoes. Later, causeways began to appear in the port, and D 13 came to be moored by thick hawsers to the wharf baptised Bǎiuț Alley. And it was precisely then, in the spring when it became clear where the streets, pavements and green spaces were going to be, that the block committee held a legendary meeting, which Father was persuaded to attend, although to this very day it is not known how. And Father floored them, he enraptured them and left them dreaming sweetly. He promised them beeches, willows, oaks, red maples, silver firs, planes, grey pines, walnut trees, robinias, lilac and jasmine bushes, rhododendrons, junipers, and white cedars, in fact whole rows of white cedars, a lawn and flowers, bulbs and flowerbeds, roses and ivy. The weather was warm and dusty. The mud had been transformed into beaten earth. They were walking round and round the block, Father in front and the block committee a few steps behind him. They were nodding and saying, yes mister engineer sir, that's right mister engineer sir, and he was tracing imaginary lines, circles, rhombuses and ovals with his right hand. He was talking excitedly, jotting things down in a notebook, laughing, drawing diagrams. He was short in stature, domineering and very well disposed. When Mother asked him that evening, 'What harm did you do those people, Aurel?' he sighed heavily, like an all-knowing tomcat, and answered, 'Wait and see.' And he went off to read on his bed in the study, not in the bedroom.

In any case, two weeks after the legendary meeting, the tenants of entrances A, B, C, and D were living with the conviction that Mr Florian the engineer, with his know-how and connections with nurseries, greenhouses, forestry ranges and horticultural institutes, was going to transform the waste ground which surrounded the block (and which surrounded us, one and all) into a peerless botanical garden. I could see for myself how convinced they were, because Naghy and Florea kept giving me sweets, Mrs Constantinescu kept giving me pancakes, Beardy Lame-man gave me a ping-pong ball and a biro pen, and Matilda, alone as she was in the world, plump, coquettish and with a kiss-curl on her brow, one day gave me a peck on the cheek. Afterwards, they started knocking on the door, looking for mister engineer sir, asking when the first truckload of saplings would be arriving. Mother had no idea, nor did I, and Father would make desperate hand-signals for us to tell them he wasn't at home.

When the time for planting had passed and the season for bulbs, saplings and seeds had come to nought, in other words, when summer was on its way, Naghy clipped my lugs for calling his daughter 'fatso', Florea tried to wallop me for wiping my feet on his doormat (after I had stepped in some dog shit), Mrs Constantinescu from the ground floor resumed her shrieks and threats when I thundered down the stairs from the fourth floor (I used to descend seven stairs at a time, while making the banister rattle and boom), Beardy Lame-man went sour, and Matilda seemed sadder and more withdrawn than ever. In the end, Father, having been cornered, told them that he was an electrical engineer and to stop pestering him so much, because he wasn't an authority on plants. Someone suggested that, given that his expertise was in that area, he should at least repair his doorbell.

But as far as repairs were concerned, Father was an illusionist. With a solemn mien and learned explanations, he would straight away convince you that nothing could be repaired. With regard to the plug socket in the hall, next to the bathroom door, he claimed that it didn't receive any electrical current, that there must be a severed wire somewhere in the wall. In order to use the washing machine in the bathroom, Mother had to struggle with an extension cable that stretched all the way to the kitchen, where she would have to pull the refrigerator out of the socket. In the end, one afternoon, when he had need of it, Father replaced the broken socket in five minutes.

His actions were, to tell the truth, unpredictable. When we had guests (which was quite often), either he would become expansive, crack jokes and sit chatting until dawn the next day, or he would be grumpy, speak monosyllabically and shut himself up in his study. And this way of being did not depend on the circumstances, on the people, on personal likes and dislikes, but quite simply one day he was all honey and the next more like quinine. He often quarrelled with his father. Sometimes they would not speak to each other for years, because the vampires and werewolves of the past would always rise to the surface, no matter how deep they buried them. My grandfather had divorced at the end of the War. He had divided up the children with his ex-wife, keeping the four-year-old boy (Father), and started roaming the length and breadth of the land, going wherever he could find well-paid work. The boy no sooner settled into one school than he had to go to another, and so he finished each school year in a different town and made no friends anywhere. Moreover, whenever the leaden-grey clouds of resentment and frustration clashed in Grandfather's firmament, it was the boy who attracted the electrical discharges like a lightning rod. And those bolts of lightning (beatings, punishments and a multitude of mean tricks) did not abate even after there appeared in their lives a kindly, warm Hungarian woman, whom Father, from the bottom of his 1950s heart, for a long while used to call Comrade Irina, as he had heard them call her in the upholstery section of the Autobuzul.[16] And even if Grandmother was kindly and as warm as a fresh loaf (so kind and so warm that every morning Pişta the tomcat used to conduct her to the factory gates, walking along the fence tops, a journey of about three kilometres), Father still used to run away from home, primarily to Braşov, where his real mother lived. But that whining woman would give him a bowl of soup, comb his hair in a parting and send him to the train station, saying each time, 'Auraş, darling, mummy doesn't have any room for you here, because, look, I've got a husband and children.' Once, at the age of 14, Father alighted from the train at Hunedoara and got a job at the steel works. He had escaped from electrical discharges, at least most of the time. In later life, I think he must have preserved the early habit of roaming the length and breadth of the land and the reflex of running away from home. Otherwise I can't explain why he kept leaving home for the construction sites. He said it was for the money, but no one believed him. Sometimes, after interminable arguments, Mother would convince him to remain in Bucharest in a nice cosy office job. There were periods when I had a father on Băiuț Alley, a flesh and blood father, not just one on paper and at weekends. If in those periods there had been installed in Flat 40 a love-meter, the needle would have been off the scale, it would have been glowing and wagging its tail. Theoretically, in those months there was someone to protect me (from Naghy, from Florea, from the lanky louts that pick on little kids). On the other hand, in many respects, it put a damper on things. I would hear unwanted words, uttered curtly: 'Don't get up from the table until you finish what's on your plate!' 'You're not going outside until you finish your homework!' 'You're not going to any football match unless you tidy up this mess!' And a war of nerves would commence, which sometimes he won, sometimes I. Regardless of the outcome, I used to waste a lot of time on those silent conflicts, and time meant friends and play. My unbounded freedom was seriously dented whenever Father was in Camp Road day after day, although he still abided by his construction-site rituals. He still played dice against himself. He filled all kinds of notebooks with probabilistic calculations connected with the lottery and football pools. At his bedside he kept a large, A4 photograph of the love of his life (Ioana Domșa, who had dumped him long ago). He kept the radio on even when he slept. He read a lot. He smoked industrial quantities and drank at home, preferably bitters or vodka. On the Sunday mornings when he didn't shave, meaning we weren't going to the cinema or a match, I would get out of bed, pad along the hall and snuggle up to Father under the blanket. We would listen to the children's radio theatre together. Have you ever listened to *Emil and the Detectives*? Or *The Adventures of Tom Sawyer*? Or *Treasure Island*? If not, then you missed out!

As for Grandma, you ought to know that she often baked scovergi,[17] which were terribly hot and hard as stones when they cooled. After I was born, as she couldn't remember the name Filip (which must have seemed like something from another planet to her[18]), she used to boast left and right that she had a grandson who was called Anton. I don't think she visited us more than twice in Camp Road in the whole of 12 years. I only used to see her when we went to the Ferentari district, where I, pleading not to be left there for days, said aloud (and with precocious impertinence) that they had an ugly house because there weren't any paintings on the walls. Grandpa, on the other hand, must have visited Băiuț Alley about 10 times. Aged, ailing and on foreign soil, he no longer fulminated. He used to give me a three-lei coin or a five-lei banknote and tell me to buy myself some doughnuts. He would repair the doorknobs, add putty to the window frames, change the washers on the taps, and keep hoping that there would be a permanent armistice between Father and himself, not just sporadic ceasefires. But Father would not, for the life of him, abandon his position as belligerent, in spite of all my mother's insistence and mediation skills. He wasn't impressed even when Grandpa picked cherries for me using a bill and hook, or when he took me fishing (to the brickworks pond in the Pantelimon district), or when he complained of the unbearable pains in his knees (caused by arthritis, which in the end he passed on to his son, like a delayed-effect lightning bolt). The war between them kept re-erupting, and the weapon of mass destruction that Father had discovered was to abandon the battlefield, not in retreat, not as a capitulation, but as a means of condemning the enemy to loneliness and yearning. Categorically refusing to hoist the white flag, I think Grandpa suffered like a dog. And his stubbornness was immeasurable. I tried to measure it one summer, on his first visit to Băiuț Alley, but I didn't succeed. He was holding me by the hand (just as he probably used to hold the little boy he had ended up with after the divorce) and I was pointing at our window on the fourth floor of D 13, in the kitchen the light was even on, but he kept telling me irritably that we didn't live there but in the block across the street, also on the fourth floor, also on the northern corner. He dragged me up to the last floor of D 14 and he wasn't budged even by the fact that the nameplate on the door said Eretescu. He kept ringing the bell (as if he were announcing an inundation) and he asked the bloke who opened the door what he was doing there and where was the family of engineer Aurel Florian. In the end, he went back down the stairs grumbling and when we reached our flat he scolded Father for not being able to draw an accurate map.

And given that sometimes I felt that Father could protect me from Naghy, Florea and the lanky louts that pick on little kids, I thought that he would also be capable of quelling my hysterical lady teachers. And so I asked him to come to my school, after the physics teacher (whose name I wouldn't be able to remember today even under torture) slapped me out of the blue in the laboratory, just as I was stroking Nicoleta Neagoe's thigh. Her ring (with a green stone) caught my upper lip and I bled like a stuck piglet. Lord, how I dreamed my Father would punish her! And come Father did, on a war footing. He promised me he would resolve everything. He went straight to the staffroom and asked where he could find the physics teacher. She was right there, in the staffroom. She soon emerged, with her wavy chestnut hair, a beige jacket and a pleated skirt, which was green (like the ring), with her high-heeled shoes, against the mosaic of echoes and voices. Her right hand was raised, not to strike once more, but rather floating gently, languorously. I had imagined that I was going to see and hear many things, but what I saw and heard left me gasping for air. Father bowed gallantly and kissed the hand that had walloped me. He kept apologising for the incident (as if I had bitten her finger and cut my lip on the ring) and was overjoyed to learn that I was quite a good pupil, but that a little more diligence wouldn't do me any harm. All of a sudden, the physics teacher seemed to me to resemble that other woman (Ioana Domșa) who always used to gaze at us from the photograph at Father's bedside and always listened to the children's radio theatre hour along with us. As I have said, with him it wasn't hard to be left dumbstruck, open-mouthed, agape. In the Danube Delta, for example, at the Murighiol campsite, he spent a whole evening in the beer garden (with an acquaintance, Sandu, a sub-engineer who called him boss and had a Fiat 800 and a wife called Sanda). He made me look under all the lamp posts for stag beetles (to use the next day as bait for the catfish) and, very late, he sent me back to our cabin for a packet of cigarettes. He told me to enter as quick as I could and shut the door, so that the mosquitoes wouldn't swarm inside. The mosquitoes didn't swarm in, but instead there was something under the cupboard, a small animal that was whining, squealing, squeaking, scrabbling. I don't know what other sounds it was making, but it scared the life out of me. I climbed onto the table and for almost a minute I stared at the floor. I thought it might be a rat or a polecat, until a puppy the size of a jam jar came out, a little darker than honey and just as scared as me. It was the puppy I had been playing with for three days, head over heels, madly in love (because at that age you don't fall in love with girls, but with dogs). It was the Alsatian puppy that belonged to some French people who were caravanning and had left that afternoon. I couldn't grasp what was going on. My chest grew warm, like after a cup of hot tea. I picked it up in my arms and ran to Father. Father laughed and took me in his arms (I'm sure that, in spite of all the cold beer, his chest grew warm, too, like after a mug of mulled wine) and he whispered that he had stolen it for me. His friend

Sandu, the sub-engineer with the Fiat 800 and the wife called Sanda, gave me a complicit wink.

Then, setting out from that point, two curved lines began to protract slowly, impalpably, lengthening with each passing week and month, until one after the other they closed to form two circles. The first circle was a construction-site tale: a fire had been kindled in Father's heels by a hussy from Constanța, whom he had hired to look after some paperwork; the hussy, whose complexion was indiscernible beneath her make-up, but whose low-cut blouses and miniskirts made her breasts and thighs all too discernible, had a hankering to profit from Father's sizzling heels and to make herself a tidy sum. Sub-engineer Sandu, like the crafty servant boy in the fairy tale, had set his eyes on both the hussy and the tidy sum; when Father was least expecting it, the hussy and sub-engineer Sandu fled with the tidy sum in the Fiat 800; the militia caught them, and the legal system of the Socialist Republic of Romania convicted them of theft of public property; seething, Father returned from Sinaia, where his sons (baby Matei and I) had been taking the mountain air and, to the last detail, told the whole story to his wife (Mother); as she listened to him, Mother became as stony as the crullers from Ferentari when they cooled; Mother was unspeakably beautiful when she was stony; Sanda, the wife of sub-engineer Sandu, who also had a baby at the time (not one like Matei, because no baby could ever have compared with him), later showed up at Flat 40, block D 13, and wailed until her nose ran. The second circle described a dog's life (literally), not a very long one, up until the last breath and the last spasm: Kita proved to be a mongrel more wonderful than all the Alsatians in the world put together; she chewed all the shoes in the house, all the spines of the books on the bottom shelf of the bookcase, the arm of an armchair and a shelf in the vitrine; Florea hated her; Naghy would bend down to stroke her; in the summer, at Father's construction site in Agigea, Kita barked at the waves and tried to catch the seagulls; after she was poisoned by an old woman from C 37, she languished for a day and a night, but she heard the way I was crying, she saw the way I slept next to her on the carpet, and she strove to come back to life; Kita was capable of miracles, like a fairy godmother. Perhaps you will not have forgotten Miracle C, in chapter 4 ('I was sitting on a sledge. I was holding the rein and whispering, 'go, Kita, go!' And she heaved with her elongated little body, a body slightly darker than honey, until the sledge began to budge. That was the hard part. After that she ran like mad, with her mouth open and her tongue lolling to one side in the breeze. I could hear our hearts ticking, like two kitchen clocks. I could sense how they gradually merged until they ticked in unison. Between the Ialomitza and the Argeș Valley, who has ever possessed such a dog? No one, I tell you, no one'). Once, after Easter, she found a lamb's skull in the grass and carried it all the way up to the fourth floor, where she guarded it proudly on the doormat, as if she had been out hunting and brought back a rabbit, and not a stinky discarded soup bone; she went off with Father one autumn, to one of his construction sites, when he was suffering from loneliness; because of all that loneliness, Father forgot to vaccinate her on time; after she fell ill, Kita grew sad, she used to lick my hands more often than she slurped water, and after she went into a coma, she opened her huge, glassy eyes one last time; we met pupil to pupil when the vet planted the syringe with strychnine in her heart and when her heart ceased to tick like a kitchen clock.

Father collected three-lei coins in a milk bottle. But he was also saving up money we didn't know anything about, because he wasn't overjoyed when a strange little stork stopped off in Mother's belly and set about hatching. It was then I found out that Father desperately wanted a car. I don't think it was a Fiat 800 he wanted. I suppose it must have been a Skoda or a Lada. However, the important thing is that, after the stork finished its work, the baby that came out of the egg surpassed all the technical specifications of a Rolls Royce or a Maserati. Recently, when we (the authors of this book) were climbing down a rocky slope in the Bucegi Mountains, I can swear that I heard Matei Florian doing a perfect imitation with his lips of the latest model of Porsche. Looking at Mother over the course of nine months, Father never for a moment suspected what a luxury limousine was growing in her womb. Later, looking at Matei over the course of so many years, he gradually understood.

As an engineer, Father liked to be the boss of as many people as possible, but as a photographer he was a reclusive artist, who did not require an audience. His black-and-white photographs would have won plenty of prizes and found their place in magazines if he had cared about such things. All that interested him were contrasts, contours and light, with which he conducted alchemical experiments in his dark room (installed in the reserve toilet of Flat 40). And often, after Father had stayed shut up in that one-metre-square room, in the dark, I used to see how the photographs became visible like auriferous sand or even gold nuggets. He would sometimes take me into his enchanted workshop, hold me up, explain each move in detail, he would let me adjust the levers of the enlarger and immerse the exposures (9/13, 10/15 etc. Orwo, Azomureş etc.) in the developing fluid. Together we would discover familiar faces and places on the freshly developed films. We would talk about all and sundry (or everything under the moon and sun). We didn't listen to the *children's radio theatre hour*, but it was if we did. When we emerged from the darkroom it was like on those Sunday mornings coming out of the cinemas on Republic Boulevard: the light of day, or the bulb in the hall, would dazzle us both and force us to wipe our spectacles.

In the long periods when Father was away at the construction sites (claiming that without people like him the country would go to wrack and ruin), I used to open the door of the darkroom and explore it. It smelled nasty, of stale, rancid air. In Father's absence the mirage of the camera obscura melted away and the other face of that Lilliputian space revealed itself: a disused reserve toilet. One day, at the time when Matei was approaching at the pace of a marathon runner the age of two, in the trays with fixative liquid there appeared a host of new photographs. Mother and I thought they must be pictures of the baby, because Father was always photographing him, but hadn't been working on the films. It was not the case. They were pictures of an unknown brunette, in whose eyes could be read familiarity, loyalty and patience. With the nonchalant air that conceals embarrassment, Father started rattling on about a female colleague from work who had moved into a new flat and hadn't found anyone to help her carry the furniture and bring a camera. Mother, I noticed, was exquisitely beautiful. She no longer seemed as stony as the crullers from Ferentari when they cooled. Nor was she turned to stone by the telephone calls she received from a driver Father had sacked (a vindictive sort), from whom she found out that mister engineer visited Bucharest regularly, not every two to three weeks, but for four to five days at a time, not going home, but staying somewhere on Griviţa Avenue, with an unmarried woman.

Later, when Matei had passed the three-and-a-half-year mark of the marathon race, on the Thursday when Mother returned from her Uncle Didi's (she had gone to cook him something, because his wife had just died), Father asked her for some sandwiches. Mother didn't want to make him sandwiches, because it was no longer her task. Father, who had drained a bottle of vodka all by himself and could have gone to Griviţa Avenue whenever he liked to eat a thousand steaks, decided that a thrashing would be heaven-sent and struck Mother for the first and only time in their two-decades-long marriage. He punched her, giving her a black eye, and pushed her on top of an electric radiator, which was normally used for keeping Matei warm. I was screaming at the top of my voice. I tried to hold him back, to hit him, but he shoved me away and pinned me to a wall. Then he slammed the bedroom door and continued to use Mother as a punchbag.

In the *ABC* it says: 'Father's at the tractor wheel, / Mother's cooking us a meal, / And at school we increase / Our knowledge when there's peace.' What a lie!

IX

The Homeland is a Plate of Pigweed Borsht

They are a kind of mist. The light of the lamp, the stairwell of the block, the image of Filip. The gloomy mist that appears all of a sudden in a mountain hollow, creeping softly at first, still delicate, still translucent, then, unawares, burgeoning, rising, cold, glassy and opaque, until it completely envelops you (a kind of living, silent, menacing breath), until the things around cease to be things, shed their certainty, restfulness and meaning, becoming vulnerable, on the brink of vanishing forever. In order to rediscover them, for nothing can be done without them, you have to grope, to fumble, to tread mindfully, to take care not to wake up the Bogeyman or the other spirits that make their nest there in the mist (spirits not so much frightening as much as unknown, and precisely for that reason all the more frightening), to accustom your eyes to the diffuse, milky, heavy light, to recite a verse from a poem about the Hawks of the Homeland for encouragement: 'We are the nation's future bright, / Like fearless hawks in soaring flight, / And in the world we're going to build, / Our tomorrow will be fulfilled.'

Strange. Perhaps in that moment some mysterious incantation caused the spirit of the hawk to nestle inside me, like a budding shoot from the ancestral trunk, but I didn't spread my wings towards the light, even less so towards the Homeland (the Homeland was fat, had permed hair and was the spitting image of Comrade Stănescu from kindergarten), but rather I began to float above chairs and cupboards through Flat 40. Down below there was a stagnant, evil mist, perhaps from the cigarettes Father used to smoke, perhaps it had materialised all of a sudden from some unknown corner of the bookcase or perhaps it was merely an illusion (the light of the lamp? the frozen image of Filip? a light bulb flickering ever dimmer in the stairwell of the block?). I recall that I could barely make myself out in that suffocating fog. From somewhere at the height of the ceiling I could see only the top of my head. I was breathing. All of a sudden I was twain: one above, floating, the other below, lost, frightened, overwhelmed, groping through the mist, unable to understand a multitude of things (Father's fury, the explosion of curses, the fists), a useless shell abandoned on a red armchair. Up above it was much better. I could turn my head when I wanted, look at only what I felt like looking at, peek for an instant with my hawk-eye at Mother in front of the bathroom mirror trying to wash her face, her yellow sweater with the flower pattern which was stained a violent red (blood? maybe it's just oil paint, tempera, watercolour?). 'Go away, Matei darling, go away.' Had the other Matei, the one down below, entered the bathroom and was he looking at Mother motionlessly? Was she trembling? (But who has ever heard of a trembling block of stone?) Mother was very beautiful, the most beautiful mother in the world, the only one. Mother was washing her face. Mother had to change her sweater. It was Filip who pulled Matei out of the bathroom, isn't that right, Filip? Wasn't it you who tugged Matei by the hand? I can't remember it very well, I was floating quietly up above it all, my nose was touching the patches of mould and the spiders' webs on the ceiling, it may even be that I wasn't there, it was Father who was there (if Father ever comes again he will turn on the light he will ask for sandwiches he will go away), and Father was a bit angry, all fathers get angry sometimes, even the best father, my father, who used to call me *spoiled as muck* and ask Uca not to keep buying me so many toys, he probably wanted to buy them himself. Fathers need to be forgiven when they get angry, they have their reasons, they're tired, they're lonely, they're sad, and even if they don't sit behind a tractor wheel, they know a thousand other things, how to make paper aeroplanes and what you have to do to make polenta look like a cake. For me it was always enough, I didn't need fathers like the others had, fathers who could drive tanks down Băiuț Alley and destroy everything in an instant, fathers who had buttons at home that if they pressed them the whole of Europe would disappear in smoke, and the whole of the sky and the moon and the sun and Asia, fathers who were friends with Ceaușescu and who played backgammon, fathers who could come with all the militias and the armies and the rockets in the world, fathers who brought their children kangaroos and Cuban sweets (sometimes there would be some sweets left over, but never kangaroos), fathers who sat around on Sundays in their vests listening to *Football, Minute by Minute*, fathers who were there all the time, not like mine, who rarely was, as I have told you, it doesn't matter, Father is Father, I can't find any better definition (and nor am I going to try) and I was a hawk and I was flying above the mist, I didn't have any business with the Homeland back then, the mist had somehow seeped under our door, it was in the stairwell of our block, it didn't let me see whether Filip was crying, whether he was holding the Matei down below by the hand or whether the warmth I felt was coming from somewhere else, where in the Lord's name could it be coming from? The stairs boomed under their feet, Filip's and Matei's, and then, I don't know, maybe the night outside, maybe the street lamps, maybe warm or maybe cold, the hawk vanished, Matei asked me to come back and we both vanished, swallowed by the mist.

I became a hawk once more (which is synonymous with the future) when it came to my awareness (thanks to our Comrade Teachers) that the red tongue with the pointed tip, like an elephant's, was not tied around our necks merely for decoration, that it was called a cravat, and that that cravat had been put on earth to make some bizarre connections between children, hawks, the Homeland and the Party, in the sense that the children with the cravats were hawks that the Homeland had given birth to, so that they could fly and thank the Party for having sent them to kindergarten. I have to admit that there was something rotten in the whole set-up. In fact, a number of things were rotten.

Number one: if some children turn into hawks, they don't do so because they want to, so that they can pretend to be doing something important or bronze their wings unhindered in the sun. The reasons are generally different, the flight is short and chaotic, and the memories sad.

Number two: in this metamorphosis the cravat is not worth even a frozen onion. However much you beg it, it will never become more than a wee rag with a tricolour hem.

Number three: let us suppose that you had a tribute of happiness and you didn't know what to do with it. Would you give it away free? Would you keep it in a wardrobe with mothballs until the day when someone succeeded in explaining to you what a 'tribute' was and what it was used for? Would you give it, like the comrades say, to the Party? And why, pray tell? Because the Party sent you to kindergarten so that you could grow up and learn? What if the kindergarten is horrible? Why should you give the Party a tribute of happiness if it sends you somewhere you don't want to go?

There's also a number four: whereas I knew a thing or too about the Homeland, about how she dressed or when she lost her temper, I was unable to picture the Party at all.

Apart from that, I had nothing against the Homeland giving birth to herds of hawks (like little winged cows) which it then sent to graze the light on a plateau like a garden. That was the Homeland's business and there's no point bothering your head about it too much. What seems a little bit weird to me is that at kindergarten they never said anything about Cristos, who, if the statistics are to be believed, was the first flying creature in this novel. Maybe they hadn't made him, Cristos, into a hawk (Coshutza always neglected to tell me whether he was wearing a red cravat when he was flying) or maybe he flew over the blocks with his gang of loons for completely different reasons, reasons unknown to comrade Stănescu. It is my honest opinion (take this as a parenthesis) that in the absence of any other evidence, Cristos was the first hawk of this homeland. Not that it has any importance, and don't think I'm telling you this just to contradict the comrade. I'd be well and truly bonkers (batty, bananas) if I were to venture any such thing. As everybody knows – you can even ask Coshutza – it is not wise to contradict comrade Stănescu. As if anybody could be so out of his mind as to want his lugs to turn red from all that tweaking, or his fingers to swell from all those thirty-centimetre ruler-blows raining down on them. Not to mention the slaps across the face, the hair yanking, the standing in the corner or on tiptoes with your arms in the air. And so all these rotten somethings (one, two, three, even four) have remained little question marks which only in the safety of my room do I have the courage to raise. Anyway (another parenthesis): this thing about raising question marks sounds so false that it sets me thinking seriously. As if I didn't have anything better to do. Anyway.

The Homeland was Comrade Stănescu, because she was the only one who had the honour of cramming it into our heads. It's very simple if you stop to think: we were children. Children have cravats. Children with cravats are called Hawks of the Homeland. Hawks have duties to the Homeland. To be well behaved, to stand in a row, to hold their hands behind their backs, to eat anything (not just stew, boiled rice and blanquette, but even pigweed borsht, which, for someone like Paul, was cause for tears, struggling and eternal revolt), to recite poems, to sing the little song, to give their heart to mummy on 8th March (besides all kinds of snowdrops pasted onto bits of cardboard), to count one, two, three, four, five, six, we're standing to attention, to snitch on each other (declarations... declarations to the comrade...) about what they did when the comrade wasn't looking, not to hear a pin drop, to keep everything squeaky clean, to construct the future, to applaud the Five-Year Plan, to learn by heart the picture books with all the wonders of the Homeland (the mountains, the lake, the concrete block, the crane, the Dîmbovitza River, the Sphinx Crag), to say where they've been and what they saw (cranes, mountains, lakes, seas, the zoo), to behave decorously at home and on the street (I kiss your hand and good day), to give up their seat to old people on the bus, the trolleybus, and the tram, to help them cross the street, not to call them old geezers and grannies, to cross only when the green man lights up, to do the household chores, to plant flowers in the garden, to water the pot plants, not to pick the flowers in the park, to do the dusting, to help with the baking, repairing the plug sockets and, in general, to help Mother and Father, who can't cope with all the work, to help with constructing socialism, to keep clean and not do like Scruffy (a stinker who doesn't know the meaning of soap, toothbrush, toothpaste and handkerchiefs, an idler who's always got dirt under his fingernails and a snotty nose), not to kick sparrows, pussy cats and doggies (because some of them only have three legs and can barely move – hop, hop), to throw rubbish only in the bin, not to light fires in the woods, to develop a talk (Filip, for example, will tell a story, and one of the hawks will elaborate on it). In conclusion: duties are what Comrade Stănescu decrees. If you don't fulfil your duties, it is Comrade Stănescu, not the Homeland, who flies into a terrible rage. Given that it doesn't get angry, the Homeland doesn't exist. Given that the Homeland doesn't exist, although everyone is convinced that it does, the Homeland can be none other than Comrade Stănescu. Q.E.D. More broadly, *quod erat demonstrandum* (because in the meantime I went to school, where I learned all kinds of strange stuff, such as mathematics and Latin).

In her good moments, when her face turned velvety with a smile that was a harbinger of fictive sweets, Comrade Stănescu would string us along saying that we were her children. Which is to say, she was a kind of spiritual stork which, in the absence of anything else, had set about hatching hawks with cravats. The bad part was that those eggs had either not been kept warm enough or they were too different from each other, because some chicks were dreadfully disobedient and boss-eyed. A minute of inattention was enough for the hawks of the Homeland to turn into little fiends, unwashed beasts, soul-devouring animals. And of all the nooks and crannies of the nursery, the sandpit seemed to exist for the sole purpose of wiping any smile off the comrade's face. It was the kind of jungle that is fenced off with halved tyres, in which various tribes (small, medium or large groups) have been abandoned by their gods, who withdraw to knit in a sacred place (a bench in the shade) so secluded that you would swear it did not exist. In the absence of the divinities, that square of sand would then be transformed into a miniature homeland, with wars of independence, magnificent achievements, and rapacious fascists. The fascists would always arrive from the neighbouring sand pits, fling words of abuse and insult the working class – all those brave diggers of galleries and tunnels, who toiled by the strength of their arms and in the sweat of their brows for the advancement, prosperity and pride of the collective. Any gesture (for instance that of crossing the rubber border) was regarded as imperialist aggression, an infringement of peace treaties, a glove flung in the face of the warriors, for whom there was nothing left to do but lay hold of their weapons and repel the invading horde. I for one was a warrior.

As a warrior, one of the important attributes that devolved upon me was that of detecting spies and suspect behaviour, which were almost always camouflaged beneath cunning and hypocritical words of the 'lend us a bucket' kind or the 'aha, so you're building a castle' variety. It was self-evident that a country with solid moral principles, such as ours, would never lend intruders so much as the handle of a bucket. And a matter such as the construction of a castle was already something that acquired the dimensions of a state secret. In those times, the competition was so ruthless that any wretch who dared to divulge to the neighbouring and enemy countries (tribes) any detail of a multi-storey building would automatically be regarded as a traitor and would have to suffer accordingly. I was the one who used to see to that. After brief deliberation, the council of elders (those over the age of six) would pronounce, in accordance with the gravity of the deed, how many kicks up the bottom were required in order for sins to be expiated. The punishment varied, not so much in the number (as one might expect), but above all in the force and technique employed in the act of kicking. To be more explicit, I ought to tell you that a serious offence was equivalent to a bomb-kick with the toe-tips, whereas a misdemeanour translated into multiple formal whacks with the side of the foot.

Wars, on the other hand, were short and chaotic. Not because the fighters didn't know how to trip up the enemy or put him in a neck hold, but because some frightened little girl would always flee to that territory with the shade and the bench; she would return with a cohort of cursing lady comrades. It would be the end of the war, of freedom, of the day. The gods had returned.

The most memorable battle in the turbulent history of the sand pit (the one which signalled a lengthy period of peace and just governance) occurred only by a fluke of fate. Who could ever have imagined that the cook could have a son? And how did it happen that she brought him to the nursery on precisely that day? We shall never know. What should be borne in mind is that that creature, who kept hanging around the sand pit and casting the stealthy glances of a beast of prey, was not like us. It was, if you will, as though Mircea the Old had been cornered by the tanks and machine guns of the USSR. A threatening and puffed-up USSR, a wild beast looming from the mists and horror of the future. With a whoop that chilled our hearts, our borders were breached, as though they had been nothing more than a few pitiful halves of tyres. In less than an instant, the wall that enclosed two mountain bases sank beneath his pitiless plimsolls. Then a fortress. Our entire civilisation, the fruit of so many sacrifices, collapsed just like a sand castle. And his grin, his grin and his sneer seemed to say it all: 'I'm in the fourth form, you're still at nursery; I'm in the fourth form, you're still at nursery.' It was then I understood for the first time that a homeland cannot be built without dignity and courage. Then, on seeing the terrified and powerless faces of my hawk citizens, I felt flowing through my veins something of the grimness of the freemen led by Stephen the Great (or was it Michael the Brave?) when they clashed with the Germans at Oituz and Posada. With implacable hatred I then whispered to myself: 'They shall not pass!' Then too, a mighty urge, a pounding heart, an arm of iron and a hand of steel made me push him over. And, as though in a dream, in an explosion of pride and the triumph of my lately oppressed people, I saw the haughty smile wiped off his face, I saw his heels touch the half tyre, and his giant frame, that of a fourth-form pioneer, come toppling to the ground. In short: I cracked his nut, because his invader's head proved too fragile in contact with the asphalt beyond the sand pit. Needless to say he took to his heels. It was not until that moment, in that all too real life of a hawk at nursery school, and not in that other, less certain life as Rahan's double, that I truly understood what the destiny of a hero means: to be embraced, adulated, borne on the shoulders, loved… A hero prepared to be slaughtered by the rolling pin of a cook, but such things already have very little importance.

I hereby consign to this page of history that the Homeland itself, that is, Comrade Stănescu, took my side and explained to the unhappy mother that I had done nothing more than to defend my manor and amenities and people. Comrade Stănescu, the mother of us all, always vehemently upheld that an oppressor should suffer no other fate than to be locked up in a kitchen for the rest of his days.

Justice was done. And without overly pausing to think, I wholeheartedly embraced the most beautiful of all the world's trades. That of living legend. That of Alldomineering and Allpowerful in the decisions, affairs and actions of a kingdom. You can't even imagine how many there could be. To make fun of snot-nose Angelica. To be given the best toys. Always to get a share of the crusty part of the loaf. Not to admit you're in love with Roxana, Diana and Ana Maria, because otherwise you'll be in for it. Never to tell the three girls that they are loved in secret, because no greater shame can exist. To eat only with the embossed spoon and fork, the unmistakable sign of the chosen. To sit only on the throne (stool) in the immediate vicinity of the drawing of a football on the tablecloth. To wield with dignity the sceptre of power (a red ring which was normally used for throwing onto the neck of a plastic duck). Not to support Steaua. Not to be snitched on to the comrade. To give the orders in *Simon Says*. To sing *The Little Nut Tree* only if forced to. Not to touch dolls. Only to tear off their heads. Not to hit the girls. To have pictures with cats and flowers painted for those who don't know how (in this case, me). To avoid enemies. To love Red Indians. To be silent when you are told to be silent. And lots, lots more: a mound of duties and problems with which I permanently had to deal.

A lucky thing with God. Who, from up there, from that heaven thronged with angels and cherubs and shiny stars, must have seen how much I was suffering for my subjects. And, presumably in order to deliver me from all my bitter toil and torture, he sent me a great big divine sign during my afternoon nap. That sign, for sign it was, took the form and content of a ferocious bout of diarrhoea. It is true, at lunch I had scoffed a plate of rancid peas, but, if this and nothing else was the cause of what then occurred, then why, of all the hawks of the Homeland, was it precisely me who was designated to bear witness to the doubtful quality of a meal? It may well be – nothing can be excluded – that behind it the curse of the cook may have been at work. What is certain is that, when I awoke – and believe me, I did so almost simultaneous to that distressing phenomenon – I experienced moments that were by no means pleasant. Because a sign from God is one thing, but it is something else entirely to sit on a stool when in the hidden intimacy of those short trousers there lurked such a monster of rebellious peas. Not to mention Comrade Stănescu, who, her senses honed in the detection of excrements, uttered with cruel force the rhetorical question 'who's shit himself?' and then, as an implacable consequence, 'it's stinking out my nostrils.' The question was, naturally, rhetorical, because the comrade was not expecting anyone to reply. And so, already bearing the cross on my shoulder and the evidence squashed by the stool, and amid the hare-brained cries of my subjects, who were claiming Angelica as the sure culprit, the comrade pulled our trousers down one by one, mercilessly uncovering about 20 sincere confessions (i.e. hawk bottoms) until, well, the wing of destiny came to a fluttering stop by me and that was about all. I must tell you that I would never have imagined that a silence could speak such volumes. And, yes, silence can be the same thing as consternation, except that I would have preferred never to learn this philosophy. Above all their heads something hovered, I might call it an unuttered question, if a question could be so damnable as to hover, anyway, I'm telling you, hover it did, and might approximately be translated in the following form: what did I do to deserve this?

I know, I know, what I did in the days that followed was pitiful: to explain to people who believed in you that it wasn't exactly your fault, that it was the curse of the cook, that the peas were under par, that, just like a line in a film I hadn't seen, 'no one's perfect,' that I was poisoned by an enemy of mine, a certain Cristos, and all the rest of it. Only God I passed over in silence. It's somehow understandable on my part. In the end, becoming a living legend is not all that bad.

Back then, when my good renown still went around the whole kindergarten and reached even the ears of the bloodthirsty twins Horia and Dragoș from the neighbouring big group, who showed their respect by keeping a regulation distance even from the most insignificant shield-bearer in our camp, when the other big group, ours, was still dwelling on the lofty peaks of prosperity and maximum development, the Homeland ceased to be comrade Stănescu. Purely and simply, and not just purely, but above all simply, this idea of duty was replaced (vanquished, shattered) by something much more powerful, less palpable, but genuinely rousing. To be precise, it was a great big symbol plonked on our coat rack. A crest. And the crest was in very close cahoots (so close that I never managed to prise it off) with an almost mystical object, which awakened in me all kinds of contradictory emotions, from the highest veneration to the blackest scorn. That object was called a peaked cap. Connected to it, somewhere in the dining room or often in the kitchen, with a bottle of something in front of him, maybe vodka, there was a bloke. The peaked cap was his. The bloke was an officer. And he served the Homeland, which is to say that crest with the red star, mountains, pine trees and wheat fields hanging from our coat rack. That was his job. To wear a crest. Which is to say, to walk around with the Homeland on his head. At last I had clear, essential and shocking proof that the Homeland existed. Comrade Stănescu was thus condemned to a cruel fate: to revert to being a simple comrade. It was just like in the proverb with Mohammed and the mountain: given that I hadn't managed to find it in the flesh and blood, the Homeland indulged my whim and came to me. It was simple. As simple as could be. What I couldn't understand was what that short, plump, bald bloke had done to deserve such an elevating distinction. For, decidedly, he didn't particularly look like he was worthy to carry out such a mission.

In the first place, and here I shall let you be the judge, his automatic gesture whenever he came through the door was to disburden himself of the Homeland and hang it on a hook. As if he could hardly wait to do it. As if it was a burden far too heavy for his sweating pate and the curls at his temples. Then, and let this remain between ourselves, his attitude lacked grandeur. In fact, his attitude was lacking, full stop. He had business with Mother. And he called me 'Maten'. I shall have you know that there is nothing in the world I dislike more than being called 'Maten'. Maten is a dope's name. Mother and Father christened me Matei. Only when you want to butter me up, let's say, or if, as it were, I'm dear to you, do you call me 'Mateiaş'. 'Motă' and 'Puşiţa' are, likewise, absolutely forbidden. 'Puşiţa' is what Uca always called me, and 'Motă' is what Mother calls me. And that's all there is to say about it. Because in the big group you are big and you get terribly annoyed by such affectations. 'Maten'. Have you ever heard the like? Not to mention the fact that when the bloke showed up, 'Maten' had to skidaddle outside. I'm talking about me, if you still haven't twigged whom I'm talking about. And I really have no idea whatsoever as to why, whenever he showed up, I would want to stay at home, purely and simply to be with Mother. It was not possible. And what was even worse was that Mother used to think like him. While I was putting my shoes on, the Homeland would chortle at me from the coat rack. In those moments I used to hate the Homeland. I would call it a stupid, a moron, a cow, and lots more. And let me not be misunderstood, but it was also the Homeland's fault.

If I had been a homeland, I wouldn't have let myself be worn like that, by just anyone. I would have chosen a man like Old Shatterhand, someone strong, handsome, noble, to serve me and defend me all day, from dawn to dusk. And, in fact, all night long. I mean, how can you entrust yourself to the hands of the first person who comes along? And there was something else: that bloke even had a son, Florin. And let anyone say whatever he likes, but I am convinced that it is impossible to serve the Homeland when you have a child. Because that's why a father has a child: to look after it. And so, whatever the bloke might have done, it still wasn't right. If he served the Homeland, it meant that he was a bad father, and if he didn't serve it, then in vain did he walk around in a peaked cap. Two in one. No? Florin came to our house three times. A big mistake. Because he got on my nerves, very badly. Which is to say, he didn't understand that I couldn't be bothered to take any notice of him. But he insisted. Far too much. Inexcusably much. For example, once he started explaining to me what you could use my wooden building blocks for. The wooden building blocks were mine. And other than 'Maten', nothing gets on my nerves more than someone telling me what you can use my things for. I wouldn't have cared if he had come up with something radical. But no, Florin, with incredible calmness, started showing me how to build a tower. This was beyond my powers of comprehension. How can the idea enter your big fat head, even for a second, that a boy who has had wooden blocks since the age of three wouldn't know how to build a tower? Even a rooster could do it: you put one block on top of the other, and there you have your tower. It was clearer than ever to me that there was something not quite right with that lad. In the sense that he was a bit daft. I told him this, as evenly as possible, and what do you think he did? Absolutely nothing. He went on building the tower. Back then, the same as today, in fact, my patience had its limits. And once those limits have been crossed, you can be impelled to do all sorts of things. For example, without pausing to think about it too long, you can demolish his marvellous handiwork with a single swipe and, to make yourself quite clear, you can aim a block at his head. And hit it. And feel good about it. On that occasion, one in principle reprehensible, I did discover something good, however:

THE BĂIUŢ ALLEY LADS

that you can have a father who serves the Homeland and that it is still no great shakes. Florin, also in the big group at nursery school, didn't have any stamina and he collapsed like a soufflé at the slightest impediment. Not even when he told on me to his father did anything happen. Because it was my house. And they were my blocks. So there. And the bloke resembled his son a lot. As I told you, it took three visits for him to realise that there was no point bringing Florin along. Each time it ended the same way, because, after a person understands whom he is dealing with, he feels an especial pleasure in demonstrating to the other that he is a milksop. Afterwards, I didn't go as far as to throw a wooden building block at his head, but a slap or a kick would suffice for him to start crying. No, Florin didn't visit us any more, but one fine day someone much nicer and much more loveable arrived. At the same time, someone who was a much bigger cry-baby. For a baby it was. His name was Mircea. And he was my brother.

My brother Mircea, baby as he was, finally vindicated the bloke. Whereas up until then he had not condescended to demostrate to me that he had any purpose being in our Flat 40 with four rooms on the fourth floor, all of a sudden he became a personage with full entitlements. He was the father of my brother. And, as if that involved some kind of shamanic powers (as a guide, teacher, sage or who knows what), as if my real father were no longer my father, in his mind there occurred a kind of short circuit that must have given the feeling that he needed to devote a little time to me. Whereas up until yesterday (a rather pallid and indefinite yesterday) we had not got past that stage of consummate candour, of the 'How are you, Maten?' 'Hello, all right' kind, the short circuit redirected him towards my humble drawings (C minus, if you can believe it), towards my hands and face (which were grubby, obviously), towards my knowledge of the natural world (invariably less than Florin's). In a word, because sometimes a word has the gift of saying everything, he became insufferable. But as for suffering, it was the Homeland that suffered the most. The Homeland ceased to be a homeland in itself and, through the miracle of binary fission, reduplication or some other scientific process, it became a kind of extension of that bloke. An appendage of him on the coat rack. That it represented something terribly grandiose I do not deny, but for me all this increasingly resembled the unmistakable symptoms of a pain in the rectum. It is true that there were still moments when I rejoiced in the Homeland's existence: when the peaked cap vanished from the coat rack and settled itself back on the bloke's head. It meant that his peace-keeping mission had come to an end and that the business of serving the Homeland was about to unfold elsewhere and with other mothers. I don't know what her reasons could have been, but Mother did not rejoice as greatly as me. And nor did Mircea, I think. In his way, he obstinately tried to demonstrate it to us. With frightening strength and energy (it was obvious even then that he would grow up to be a great mountaineer), he would scale the metal mesh of his cot, grasp the bar at the top and jump up and down for hours on end, bouncing on the mattress, until the cot became a kind of vehicle, a walking bed, which would move, slowly but surely, across the room. Even a man riding a bison wouldn't have thudded so loudly. Mrs Hîncu from the third floor, terrified by the thumps coming from the ceiling, refused to believe that such a thing was possible. She was so adamant that Mother had to call her to witness the naked truth. Or rather the cotton-nappy-clad truth. I recall that Mrs Hîncu (who was one and the same person as Remus's mother) boggled her eyes. They were not as big as onions, but rather watermelons. She made the sign of the cross and said: 'I've never seen anything like it in my life.' And then she left, somewhat reassured. At least now she was convinced.

Out of respect for history and in conformity with the truth, it is fitting that I should make a precise note of the year that marked Mircea's debut as a mountaineer. The route, otherwise an absolute first, presented in its middle section a surprising zero-degree incline, which, in layman's terms, might be translated using the word horizontal. What should not be overlooked is the decisive aspect of the age my brother had reached. I suspect that 'tender' is the adjective that resonates the most closely with that age, which occurs, approximately, between the seventh and eighth month after birth. This detail, mentioned in the lines above in the form of its synonym, the noun 'aspect', causes the terms of comparison no longer to function within their normal parameters. What seems at first sight (a trifle, a bagatelle) an act of the utmost ordinariness – the fact of climbing out of a cot – acquires a wholly different significance.

I might even write, and here I go, as you can see, that that descent from his cot, equivalent to the start of a mountaineering expedition, has all the necessary data to be compared with a flight landing. And for such a flight you need nerves of steel, heightened stamina, exemplary stoicism (what else other than pain can you feel when you land on a carpet with a dull thud?), and a pre-established plan combined with a hefty dose of that imponderable alloy with which all the world's great adventurers are endowed: courage. Without it, all that snaking on all fours over the bedroom floor, over jingling obstacles, wooden horses, fallen soldiers and sharp-edged blocks, all that journey towards the light (and in the present context the light should not be taken for a cheap metaphor, because it denotes precisely the goal towards which Mircea was heading), would have been worth less than frozen onion. That light was not small and twinkling and nor was it at the end of a tunnel. No. It was lolling on the balcony. And unfortunately, the door to the balcony was open. I won't enter into specialised details. I have the vague intuition that they can be tedious. I can, however, testify that my brother finally made it to that strange and laundry filled summit, our fourth-floor balcony. Besides various patches of blue sky, the view (comparable only with the wild splendour of Mount Ceahlău at sunset) included the majestic, bristling crags of the antennas of block C 37 and the milky mists of the garden at the back of block D 13, a gleaming stretch of Parva Alley, sundry blocks, trees and bushes, and somewhere, lost on an accessible horizon, the square and jolly outline of School No. 57. It is quite likely that Mircea wished to abandon himself completely to that light which bathed so many wonders. It is quite likely that he thought with sadness of the balcony that seemed not to offer him it all. And then, his intrepid explorer's heart must have made a decision. Without having any pegs or pitons hammered into the rock (understandable given that he was the first to venture by that route, and of the rock face it can be said that it looked a lot like a block of flats) without thinking even for an instant of the usefulness of a rope (indispensible when abseiling), without being equipped with a harness or girth, but only a nappy and the braces of his little duckling-emblazoned shirt, my younger brother, just like a baby of seven or eight months, began slowly but surely to insert himself feet first between that narrow gap between the parapet and the floor of the balcony. He had managed to push his legs through, then his botty and a little of his tummy when everything came to an end, at the shrieks of a woman from the block opposite, whose emotions, were I to list them, must have begun with stupefaction and ended with hysteria. Mother, who was ironing in the kitchen, understood whereabouts her baby must have vanished and, without pausing overly long to think, put a stop to that adventure, one glorious for mountaineering, but terrifying for us, the others, in the most logical way possible. She grabbed him by the shoulders and yanked him before he could slip into the void. And trembling, she put him back in his cot.

The bloke was not up to date with any of this. He would come by infrequently. He would bless me with a 'Maten' (I was, it seems, growing bigger by the day). Lately, Mircea had also acquired a pet name: 'Piciric'. He would stay for a little while. He would smoke. My real father no longer came by at all, however. He had somehow entered a strange zone with a lot of mist. I didn't like to seek him there. It was cold and Mother wore a yellow sweater. The Homeland didn't know anything about these things. I don't know why, but from the way it sat there, abandoned on the coat rack, I had the feeling that it couldn't care less about Mother's sweater.

One fine day, I lurked until the bloke wasn't nearby. Like the Rahan of old I stole up to the coat rack, seized his cap by its stiff peak and, with great circumspection, piddled in it. Just a few drops, so that no one would suspect. Then I thought about having a poo in it, but that would have been going too far, and, to be honest, I didn't need to go. It was then that I understood, without the need for complicated demonstrations, that of all the things in the world the Homeland was, most of all, a potty.

X

Mysterious are the Ways of the Lords

When Mother, with her prow-like womb and her frigate-like figure, hurried off to weigh anchor in the bustling port of the Municipal Hospital and, before lunchtime, disembarked a little baby named Mircea on the quay, there already existed another Mircea.

As chance would have it, on that day in late April, a day of buzzing gnats, sunshine, a gentle breeze and girls who had shed their winter boots and woollen stockings, both these Mirceas were deathly pale. The first, the baby, because of the umbilical cord in which he had become entangled during his disembarkation, the second, our grandfather, because of the pulmonary cancer he would later be diagnosed as having, at the beginning of June.

I was so happy! For the time being. I rushed into the maternity ward like streak of lightning wrapped in a lycée uniform. The doorman, porters, doctors and nurses dared not bar my way. Mother had polished off a jar of chocolate spread and was fidgeting in bed rather than sleeping. We hugged each other, a hug so long and so tight that I started seeing stars. Those stars were green, unlike the gold ones on the epaulettes of the newborn's father.

About a week later, after completion of customs and medical formalities, the new Mircea left that insipid port and set off, not over the waves, but dry land, for Băiuț Alley (to take possession of a metal cot, a multitude of nappies, a blue tub, and the notion of home). Uca gazed at him at length, with her hand to her mouth, and whispered wonderingly: 'What a gnarled child! Will it live?' Mother did not laugh, but nor did she come down with mastitis. As the mother of a newborn, she had heard something similar 16 years previously, when the old Mircea, her father, had said about me (examining my perfectly bald head, which had led a midwife to nickname me Genghis Khan) that I looked like an abortion. I am convinced that from the bed in which he was coughing, sweating, regularly taking his temperature, plotting on graph paper the course of a strange fever (usually 37 point something, but sometimes, out of the blue, over 39), listening to Beethoven, Mahler and the Voice of America, re-reading in late spring and then at the height of summer (coughing, sweating) books about the Himalayas, Tyan

Shan, the Cordilleras, Alps and South Pole, my grandfather must have transmitted to that metal cot seven kilometres distant the seductive dream of snowy peaks, the mysteries of alpine alchemy, the language of the clouds and winds, and the frisson of redemptive ascents. A minuscule, gossamer-like fleck (but which can't have been gossamer because autumn was nowhere on the horizon) must have taken flight from the centre of Bucharest, from no. 21 Crăciun Street to be precise, it must have risen high in the air and floated over the rooftops, boulevards, trees, spires and vacant lots, before finally reaching the blocks of Camp Road, and there, not at all disoriented, knowing exactly its destination and purpose, it must have wended its way towards D 13 (towards the northern corner of the block), flown through one of the open windows of Flat 40, sought and discovered the room of the newborn babe and, while he, the infant, was fast asleep (imbued with intra-uterine memories and fresh extra-uterine sensations), it must have glided up one of his nostrils, where it will have been inhaled like smoke and flitted through his veins and capillaries until it located his soul in a hidden recess of the tiny body, where it will have nestled like a magical seed, from which would sprout in its purest, most crystalline form a love of the mountains.

For all that distance (seven kilometres, as I have said), the minuscule fleck was not borne through the air by the soft breezes of the dog-day weather, or by summer storms, or by angels, or by the unseen powers of telepathy, or by the fates, or by enchantment, but by the gift of homonymy. In the hot months when one Mircea was growing stronger by the day, the other Mircea was melting away, when Mother was caught as if in a vice between the two, between her son and her father, the former cadging milk from the breast (with the insistence of one newly arrived in the world), the latter filling her cheeks with tears (with the abandon and world-weary disgust of one terminally ill), the duality of that forename caused the mountaineering passion of the one to seep into the other, so that their shared love might live on.

However, there is also an older circumstance, a kind of gentle historical truth, that cannot be passed over. Before that frigate with the outline of a pregnant woman, with its womb-like prow, cast its anchor and allowed my youngest brother to disembark (after nine months on board), a strange little stork made its nest in Mother's womb and hatched a huge egg, from which (also after nine months) my middle brother emerged. And so, for a long time, a very long time, for almost 11 years after I first appeared in the city of Bucharest, completely bald and with my umbilical ready to be snipped, our grandfather (Mircea Kiril according to his baptismal certificate, simply Mircea in his official birth certificate) was my grandfather alone. He was mine and none other's. Since he was mine alone and I was his only grandchild, since he, as a father, had had two girls and I was a boy, you can imagine what thick ropes, like mooring lines, invisibly bound us together. As a sign of our friendship, I called him by his first name from the time I started making articulate sounds. I didn't quite hit on the right sounds and, perhaps for that reason, the time when I cried out at the top of my voice at a family get-together, no one could understand what was wrong. When no one was looking, I had taken a sip from a little glass I found on the edge of a desk, and then I had run into the room where they were all gathered. In fear and amazement, I was convinced that I had swallowed fire, stammering between my sobs, 'water Mitza'. They required patience and perspicacity (and here they were aided by my index finger, which pointed at the little glass) before they could understand what had happened. The water was strong schnapps, and Mitza was Mircea.

Later, after I learned my letters, not just the sounds, we scaled wheezing slopes and descended dizzying valleys, we hiked across saddles, escarpments, and crests, through ravines and forests, over plateaus and screes, past cataracts, and among juniper and raspberry thickets and expanses of nettles. The first imposing peak he showed me was in the Retezat Massif, not in the lofty region of grey crags and sparse grass, but in the Pietrele Cabin, where he emptied his rucksack and on the tatty mattress a mountain of cigarette packets heaped up, all Snagov brand, an astounding sight for a little boy still in nursery school. Also around this time, in the August (I think) days when plenty of people on the ridges and in the glacial valleys asked me, 'How old are you, sonny?' and I, puffed up like a cockerel, answered, 'Five', I climbed Peleaga, Păpușa, Judele and Slăveiu and I threw a host of stones into Galeșu and Bucura tarns.

One morning, on a hiking trail marked with a red triangle, I remember Mircea (whom, I swear, I never once called Grandfather, Grandpa or the like) stopping all of a sudden and explaining to me that he had to water an old ash tree. Rays of sun were filtering through the foliage and droplets of light were pattering onto the earth, the burdock, the mushrooms, the lichens and the mossy stones. Fairies and gnomes might well have poked their heads out of the hollows (although they didn't) and I was thinking about how good he was, tall, bronzed, with his thermos flask of hot coffee for him and pocketful of sweets for me, about how much he cared about the big old tree, sprinkling it with a gleaming yellow jet, like lemonade.

Little by little, climb after climb, hike after hike, season after season, discovery after discovery, I became accustomed to his mountain rituals. I became a gifted disciple. On muddy or frozen slopes, we would slip and tumble one after the other, singing at the top of our lungs (*Here we go, here we go, / Bumping on our arses, / Oh no! / Oh no!*); on heights where the horizon could be touched, stroked or held in the palm of the hand, he would start a duet (*Oh, Mrs Sima, where have you been, / I'm really dying to use the latrine, / I do not like this, not one tiny bit, / Because I really need to take a ... walk*) and I would round it off (*Yonder over the Carpathians, / Left a bit, then right a bit, / There's the place you need to go / If you want to take a ... hike*); ...; in glades or in long walks through the forest, we would recite countless poems about Arthur, all of them with funny rhymes. With my hand on my heart, I declare that all these things (which may upset many people, given that it's a matter of manners, upbringing, and the way a grandfather behaves with his grandson) were the very fountain of joy. Up in the mountains, the difference in age between us was shattered by the wind, the 48 years were blown away like pollen or dust into deep ravines. And as I was unable to move mountains and become an adult, he would become a child again, not only in the ditties and jokes from his real childhood, but also in hundreds of gestures, words and signs. Once, in the cabin on Mount Omu, after we had finished eating our bean broth, I found by chance, under the grubby tablecloth, on the edge of the table, an inscription carved in the wood. And this is what it said: Mircea and Didi, 1935. His chin quivered, his voice also quivered, many things inside him quivered (you could see it from the sparkle in his eyes) as he recognised the inscription from almost half a century ago, when he and his brother, one aged 15, the other 14, had played with a penknife in that same cramped room, perhaps after also eating bean broth. Well, it was with that kid, with that lycée pupil who had just carved his name on the table of an alpine cabin and who happened to have replaced his brother (as his hiking partner) with his first grandson, that I roamed the mountains.

The evenings were different. We would turn out the light. The door to the balcony would remain ajar (however cold it might be outside), the rustling of the trees would often blend with the crackling of the fire in the stove, the shadows of the branches would fuse on the wall with the shadows of objects in the room, and the darkness would fill with stories, but not about ogres, princesses, puss in boots, crystal palaces and wicked witches. Tucked up in the blanket I would listen to a different kind of fairy story, about Alexander the Great, Ulysses, Domitian, Mucius Scaevola and Pompey, about Magellan and Vasco da Gama, about Edmund Hillary and Tenzing Norgay, about Robert Falcon Scott's ponies and Roald Amundsen's dogs, about terrible blizzards and avalanches, about bears and wolves, about Mozart and Salieri, about the countless sons of Johann Sebastian Bach, about Richard the Lionheart, Henry V and Bonaparte, about the Vikings and the constellations. Those nocturnal monologues used to merge like gentle streams into one blessed river, gleaming like bronze, not in the rays of the moon, but in my grandfather's halo of light.

Mircea Kiril had been top of his year at the Saint Sava College (where in games of tipcat[19] he had been nicknamed Mircea the Centaur), he had been awarded the highest mark in the country for his baccalaureate (when he had in public astonished Gheorghe Țițeica, Professor of Mathematics at Bucharest University, by demonstrating that the statement of a problem was wrong), he had graduated top of his year at university (even though he had, in his second year, wed a superb woman, who, with her honey-coloured wavy locks used to melt the ice of the Oteteleșanu skating rink), he knew perfect Latin (being capable at any time of reciting whole passages of Cicero, Horace, Tacitus or Juvenal), the poet he loved best was George Bacovia[20] (whose work, incredibly, he used to read in the pulmonary diseases hospital after he had been diagnosed with lung cancer), as an engineer he had built and designed more or less everything that could possibly be built or designed (collecting dozens of patents in a blue file, which he kept among his mothballed clothes, he was fascinated by the Wars of the Roses (unravelling with his eyes closed the tangled chronologies of the York and Lancaster dynasties), he admired Scipio Africanus and Seneca in equal measure (esteeming their courage and stoicism), he saw the Soviet invasion of Afghanistan as merely a step towards the Persian Gulf (in the Kremlin's attempt to control the oil market), he wasn't a football supporter (and because my Dynamo mania saddened him, he used to praise Jesse Owens and Emil Zátopek to me), and he ascribed the queues at the food shops to a perverse idea on the part of the communists (that of keeping people busy, so that they wouldn't think about freedom, their rights or other such nonsense).

Before any meal with Mircea, the scent of toasted bread would spread enticingly through the house. In the mountains, that scent didn't follow us, but toasted bread would always appear from his rucksack when we stopped to eat. One summer, I wrote a miniature novel, in four parts, which I called *The Culinary Passions of My Grandfather*. It went like this:

1. Aunt Frosya, Truffles and Sherbet

With puffy cheeks, a dimple in her chin, her chest powdered above her décolletage, which revealed a mole, just above her brooch (this is the way I know her from a small portrait in oils with an oval, gilded frame), Aunt Frosya used to go to play rummy on Thursdays. In the morning, she would always take care to order a carton of confectionaries from Nestor's, nicely wrapped in waxed paper, and then, before lunch, with her white hair and her haughty gaze (from the same painting), she would secrete the parcel in the wardrobe and lock the door to the bedroom. An aged aunt, not the kind with a woollen cardigan, but with parasols and hats with veils, Eufrosina had a keen sense for danger. She knew very well what it meant to have children in the house and often exclaimed 'les barbares!'

Back then, bizarrely, my grandfather was a little boy. And little boys have always been endowed with a special (albeit not olfactory) sense whenever chocolates, cakes or biscuits appear in secret under their own roof. Mircea Kiril, oblivious to the blossoming of the generation of '27 and the budding of the economic crisis of the '30s, would enter his great aunt's room as soon as she went into town. He would hide behind the drapes, under the bed, in the linen chest or among the mothballed clothes. He would hear her footsteps when she returned. He would detect by the rustling, divine by the sounds, where the gleaming parcel was hidden, and wait for her to lock the door and depart. Then he would emerge from his hiding place and silently seek it out, untie the ribbons and unwrap the waxed paper, stuff his mouth with two or three truffles at once, run his fingers through the cream of the charlottes and lick them one by one. The cacao powder made him want to cough, but he did not cough. And finally, like a sated, lazy tomcat, he strove to tie the coloured ribbons back up so that the package would appear untouched. Lord, how Aunt Frosya blushed on Thursday evenings, at the rummy games, when they served her confectionaries!

Once, not on a Thursday, but on another day (there were, after all, six others to choose from every week), the little boy who would later become my grandfather discovered on the top shelf of the wardrobe a jar of sherbet, wrapped in a petticoat. He emptied it at leisure, lolling on the huge, ship-like bed of his septuagenarian aunt, and finally, overwhelmed by boredom, he caught a few flies, which were tapping their heads against the windowpanes, and shut them up inside the jar. Aunt Frosya burst into the drawing room that afternoon, exclaiming: 'Fulvia, the cursed creatures ate it all up! And then they died…' Fulvia (her niece and Mircea Kiril's mother) smiled with one eye and gave the child who was drawing a cockerel a sharp look with the other.

2. Military Service with the Artillery

They were times of war. Hard times. But not as hard as they might have been, because my grandfather (having, according to the law of nature, become a man) had married soon after the fall of Odessa and then, instead of being sent to the Russian front (thanks to the intervention of a general's wife, an aunt of my grandmother's, from Jassy), he had gone to a school for artillery officers. During manoeuvres east of Turnu Severin, he was visited by his young wife (who caused more heads to turn than if she had been a deluxe automobile) and received permission to spend a weekend with her, in a village near the military camp. Like two doves, they dreamed of pancakes, they cooed together in that country kitchen, they fluttered their wings and, with moil and toil, they put something on the stove. The liquid in the frying pan spat and smoked, but it would bind or brown, until the old woman with whom they were lodging took pity on them and said: 'Put some flour in that milk, dear.'

3. The Summer Miracle of the Işalniţa Combine

In the years before communism, the clock of my grandfather's personal history ticked slowly and softly, so as not to interfere with the loud ticking of collective history. As the brother of a political prisoner and the son-in-law of an industrialist, engineer Mircea Kiril (the former little boy) worked on isolated construction sites, whither it was hard for cadre files to find their way because of the clouds of dust, the sketchy maps and the impracticable roads. During the construction of the radio transmitter on Mount Coştila, he ate nothing but jam and maize porridge for months, and on his way through the snowstorms or mists to the Jepi funicular in Mălin Valley or the Albă Valley, he would share out cigarettes to men with beards and rifles, men not wearing communist uniforms, who did not unclench their jaws to say anything, but saluted him and thanked him with a nod of the head.

Later, when the ticking of the clock became faster, when my grandfather's two daughters were gambolling through schools in central Bucharest and he was away working on construction sites connected with some highway or railway or other, the meals became different. In Săvineşti, where a notice in the entrance hall of the block said 'The rearing of pigs in the bathroom is strictly forbidden!' he received lots of fresh eggs – not farmyard eggs, but balcony eggs. In Işalniţa, returning from Bucharest one Monday in July, his room mate filled his plate with broth. 'Mr Engineer sir,' he asked my grandfather, 'do you remember that chicken soup from last week? It had gone really sour, but I stewed it and it made a lovely broth. Did you like it?'

4. The Salami in the Stove

In the times when his timepiece was sounding more and more cracked, and my grandfather had long since become a grandfather (because I had been born, gurgled, learned to walk, talk and kiss the girls, to recite patriotic poems and even solve equations), he was no longer working on the construction sites, but in a design institute on Griviţa Avenue. And he got the idea of renting an attic room to a woman who worked at the sausage factory. He didn't ask her for any money, because money was becoming increasingly pointless, and sausages, because of the pensioners who stockpiled them in cellars, caves and pits dug under cover of darkness behind the blocks, were becoming abstract notions. The lady paid the rent in salami, six per month, which she fearfully used to sneak out of the factory thrust inside her diaphanous, perspiring viscose blouse. In summer, when he didn't light the fire, my grandfather used to store the salami in the stove.

On the day of my ninth birthday, in Flat 40 of block D13, three troubling natural phenomena occurred. First of all, shortly before it started to get dark, using Father's camera I photographed four legs, two in white stockings, two without, two belonging to Alexandra Ştefănescu, two to Magdalena Dina. They, the girls, were sitting pressed up against one another on the edge of my bed, and I, asking them to smile and pretending to snap their faces, immortalised everything from the waist down, in particular what could be glimpsed beneath their skirts. Later, at sunset, when all three of us were playing hide and seek, I happened to be it, and I was searching and searching for Alexandra Ştefănescu, in my own house, where I knew every nook, cupboard, curtain, niche, cranny and so on. I kept searching and searching, but I couldn't find her. Alexandra Ştefănescu, with her snub, slightly turned-up nose, had had the fantastic (and daring) idea of hiding under my mother's skirt, a long one, which reached to the floor. And Mother, continuing to bustle around the kitchen, arranging olive halves, slices of pickled cucumber and cubes of cheese on the spam sandwiches, allowed her to crouch there until I gave up, shouting as loud as I could for her to come out wherever she was. Later, but not very late, shortly after Mr Dina and Mr Ştefănescu took their daughters home, someone else knocked at our door (the bell was out of order, as usual). It was Mircea. He was panting slightly. He had brought me a green Pegasus bicycle, the most expensive model, with gears and the seat adjusted to just my height. In order not to get the wheels dusty, he had carried the bike all the way from the bus stop on Argeş Valley Street. For two or three hours, until almost midnight, he jogged along behind me, in between the blocks – reverse order compared with our hikes in the mountains. Mother claimed that as a final consequence of the three natural phenomena that occurred that evening, I kept pedalling continuously in my sleep, hitting her with my knees in her stomach until the break of day, when she was forced to move to the empty bed in my room.

***

The taste of peace is sweet. Like halva. And there comes a day, in the tumult of the war with the grown-ups, when every child discovers it, by chance, after dozens and hundreds of weeks spent in the trenches and on the battlefield, after charges, ambushes, retreats, marches, encirclements and regroupings, which are all, absolutely all, as sour as lemons or apricots. From that moment, tenacity and courage begin to falter, the spirit of belligerence is mollified, the bridges to the enemy extend more often and more lastingly, and things fumble into the zone of armistice and goodwill. All of a sudden, Matilda's vases of flowers are no longer tied to the door handle with string (so as to fly off their cast iron stand and break into pieces), Beardy Lame-man's motorcycle no longer has leaves stuffed in the petrol tank (to clog up the carburettor so it won't start), the Ciocan family no longer tread in cat turds left on their mat (having renounced the confiscation of footballs and the interruption of memorable matches on Băiuţ Alley), old man More can wait for his mail in peace (because his letterbox is no longer stuffed with mud and worms). At first, the equilibrium is fragile. It can shatter at any moment. At the first thoughtless gesture the adults make, the enmity can flare up once more and the counter-strikes are ruthless. Matilda, for example, if she lets slip vinegary words or tugs someone by the ear, is lost, utterly lost, no matter how much she might guard her plant pots on the third-floor landing. On Monday morning, at dawn, the tubby bloke with the little beige Skoda, the agronomic engineer who has spent the night with her on Saturday and Sunday, will become drenched in sweat (and a bundle of nerves) as he pumps away, for an hour, an hour and a half, after finding his tyres have been let down, the air caps removed. Beardy Lame-Man will also have to behave nicely to the kids, otherwise he will bear the consequences, regardless of whether his motorcycle is locked up in a garage far away. In winter, after salvoes of snowballs aimed at his living room and bedroom windows, he will discover how hard the frost can be, as he sweeps up the shards and looks for a glazier. Many, very many things can happen, especially given that when the slumbering conflict reawakens it is not like the flame of a candle but a roaring blaze. That sweet taste, like halva, is perverse and beguiling, however. It leads to a kind of addiction, and so the lulls that precede the final, lasting peace become longer and more frequent. The exceptions (slowly but surely) become the rule. Among other things, it is highly pleasant to enter Stair D of Block D13 without a care, not to have to sneak, not to have to walk on tiptoes with your eyes peeled and your ears skinned, to be confident that no threat is lurking anywhere, to ascend calmly and with normal steps, not to be miserly with your good days or your affable replies to neighbours. And at such tranquil moments, when arms have been hung up on their hooks, when military strategies are gathering dust, and the redoubts have been temporarily abandoned by the combatants, gestures and actions that would have been unimaginable in the past now become feasible. For example, I, Filip, who had provoked Mrs Constantinescu to so many outbursts of fury, who had driven her to the verge of a nervous breakdown with my clomping down the stairs five steps at a time, with my clanking of the metal banister, with my insufferable talking back, and with all my guerrilla actions, I, who had heard from her lips so many rebukes and curses, who had garnered slaps, lashes and stinging bottoms, well, one serene spring day I asked her to lend me a hammer, a screwdriver and a chisel. It was shortly after lunch. I had just got back from school at the beginning of the third term. I was on the verge of peeing myself. I felt as though my bladder was about to explode, but I couldn't manage to unlock the door with the key on the string around my neck. I knocked on the door for ages, loudly, with my fingers and my fist, then, with no intention of resuming hostilities with the grown-ups, I piddled in a chipped red enamel pot, in which the Cristache family were cultivating some gillyflowers. No one saw me, and so, after eating an apple I'd found in my satchel and loitering on the stairs, I got the bright idea of forcing the lock. To be a burglar, to break into your own house, is a stirring thing. It is rather like a pickled cucumber, for which you get a craving in times that are sweet beyond compare, like halva. When I asked her, Mrs Constantinescu didn't enquire me why I needed the tools, and nor did I have any intention of returning them. She quite simply gave me them, munificently (because peace ultimately has its price) and I took them, swiftly climbed to the fourth floor and set about hammering at the door frame, in the spot where I assumed the latch bolt must be. I was absorbed. I had planted the chisel in the wood and I was hitting it with the hammer. The noise was deafening, the stairwell was booming like a factory, when, all of a sudden, in the midst of my efforts to make the lock give way, something unexpected happened: I heard a slightly astonished woman's voice from within, asking 'is there anyone there?' and I saw Mother appear in the doorway, with the most innocent face in the world. Behind her, a short stocky bloke immediately appeared, in an under-vest and khaki trousers, who gave me a wave and smiled at me.

At that time of the afternoon (and of spring) when I was rather hungry, I came to understand that war has unsuspected faces, that a new front could open where I least expected (i.e. in our kitchen) and that the enemy parachuted there from fictive clouds (there was a clear sky, after all) was not a fighter who played it by ear, but was well trained. Looking at Mother, who had put on a calico skirt and a brick-red blouse, and at that bloke, who was now shod and clad in military uniform, with three pips on his epaulettes, I gave a dry gulp. And I was astonished to discover that the taste of war was not necessarily bitter, like lemons or apricots. It could be as bitter as aspirin. All three of us were in the kitchen (Matei, thank God, was at nursery school; I think he must have been taking his afternoon nap, and no one, absolutely no one, not even the 'bloodthirsty twins Horia and Dragoș', as per chapter nine, dared to disturb his slumber). Mother was frying potatoes and, unusually for her, was asking me something about school. The officer was cautiously surveying the terrain, attempting to find out what I was like, scouting, reconnoitring, seeking to gain a precise picture of my troops, fortifications, heavy armaments and munitions. Munching fried potatoes one by one, in a leisurely way (after all, no one was rushing me to finish and leave, and in any case I wouldn't have left no matter how much anyone rushed me), I tried to throw him false leads, to spread a thick smokescreen, not to give him any clue as to my forces and their position on the map. At one point, he started talking about aeroplanes, imagining that he would enthral me according to a recipe that few boys can resist. I let him chunter on. I pretended to be interested in his aeronautical knowledge (Mother boggled her eyes, because she knew very well that the young Filip didn't want to be an aviator, but rather an *argitect* or a *gebul*). I imagine the bloke must have wanted to rub his hands together in glee, but he refrained, for strategic reasons. He felt as though he was on a high horse, that he was galloping. He thought that I was caught in his khaki spider's web. He delayed dealing me the *coup de grâce* for the sake of indulging his oratory, until I interrupted him, offhandedly, chewing a mouthful of bread, and asked him what happens if the pilot and the co-pilot come down with diarrhoea.

After the hot war on Băiuţ Alley, which, because of its high temperature, was in the end touched by a breath of affection between the combatants, a cold war commenced in our kitchen. A war of attrition. A complicated, dirty war. And what mattered was not merely the fact that kids, pining for lemonade and gooseberries, can't stand aspirins; all kinds of other deeds, creatures and principles weighed like lead. The officer – whom Matei had christened *the bloke*, whom Uca (among us, the Resistance fighters) called *the General*, whom our grandfather would not even deign to name, and to whom our Uncle Didi referred as *that man* – tried to entice the Florian brothers, to weaken their vigilance in their own barracks, Flat 40. And, being boys, and thus rather like young turkeys, with our wattles, feathers and instincts, we would not leave Mother alone with him as long as we were in the house and for as long as we did not succumb to slumber. Consequently, we would all be stuck in the kitchen, where it was cold, dreadfully cold. We were engaged in a cold war, after all. As far as I was concerned, I always addressed him with the formal *vous*, but not as a sign of respect, but so that he would understand that, whatever he might do (and he really would have stood on his head and swallowed glass beads to get me to use the informal *tu*), I regarded him as an odious alien, an aggressor. He, in his turn, without having the slightest interest in my life, but just to plonk me at an imaginary school desk, let's say the fourth in the row from the window, would question me from time to time in connection with mathematics and literature, fields in which he was convinced that he shone. And after he had shone, he would light a cigarette, shine for a little longer, then go greenish-white in the face and toss back his glass, observing that she, Mother, never made broth or fed her children multivitamins.

The officer was always at odds with the lower- and upper-middle-class residues of Flat 40 and, in a broader sense, those of my mother's family, but I suspect that sometimes, when he shut himself up in the bathroom for a long time, he used to inject Pelikan ink into his veins, so that his blood too would turn blue, at least just a little. It is nonetheless unclear what used to go on in the bathroom – suspicion is suspicion, and truth is truth – and all that I can describe with hand on heart is that when I used to go in after him (and I was obliged to do so, in the morning, because otherwise I would be late for school) there used to be a very composite odour inside. In the air floated dense deodorant vapours, because in this way he imagined that certain deeds might be concealed or rectified. Otherwise, he was nice. Once, he evaded from the kitchen of Flat 40 together with Mother and the two of them went off to sunbathe and paddle in the Argeș River, and he waded into the deep water up to his hips and caught a roach or a perch in his hands. To be honest, I think Mother is convinced even today that that small fry was the biggest and most beautiful fish in the whole world. And, in her way, she is right.

A cold war, as recent history has proven, is not won by bayonet charges, but by tenacity, cunning and, as in chess, apparently innocuous moves made today with the aim of confusing the enemy tomorrow. Such a register, I do admit, was not really at the disposal of us, the Florian brothers. Caught up in so many whirlwinds (I, for instance, after signing the peace treaty with the adults of Băiuț Alley, had discovered the discreet charm of the bench outside Stair A, where a chubby chestnut-haired girl named Monica used to practise a kind of pedagogy of the kiss; Matei, still in nursery school, in that astounding phase of living legend, was also busy with 'a mound of duties and problems'), we did not wrack our brains with perfidious stratagems, with the long-term struggle. My brother piddled in the officer's cap (arriving at the unprecedented conclusion that the Homeland is a potty), while I limited myself to trifles. When he telephoned, I would pretend that I couldn't hear anything or, disguising my voice, I would tell him it was the wrong number, sometimes I would trip as I was carrying a cup of cocoa, which, obviously, would spill over his trousers or shoes. In the evenings, when the moon set out for a stroll over the huge collective antennae and over the host of receptor dishes pointing at Bulgaria, in our kitchen there would begin to be heard a crackling, hissing, buzzing and droning. I knew for a fact that these sounds weren't coming through the walls, because D 13 was a sturdy block (albeit one with rising damp), built from pre-fabricated slabs of concrete. And I also had another reason not to puzzle over the provenance of those bizarre noises: for, I was the one who used to turn on the radio. On the short-wave frequency. I would gently turn the dial, watching the green line slowly travel along the scale, passing over all kinds of Arabic music and Slavic, Prussian or Anglophone stations, as opera arias, exclamations in French and pop hits fleetingly resounded. I would keep turning and turning until, in the area of one of the best-known frequencies, a voice in Romanian could be distinguished, sometimes clearly, sometimes faintly. The crackling, hissing, buzzing and droning would then intensify, as though they had become terribly enraged and, like wasps, wanted to sting the gentleman at the microphone. It was also then that the officer's pallor would intensify. He would toss back another glass and fix me with his grey eyes, in which something nevertheless gleamed – I think it was the reflected tip of his burning cigarette. He would say nothing, merely emitting a 'hmm' after the final salutation: '… this is Neculai Constantin Munteanu at Radio Free Europe, wishing you farewell.'

As I sat at the table and munched fried potatoes, drew pictures or erected towers of matchsticks, the way in which that man spoke used to make me melt. He was our ally, the ally of the Florian brothers in the kitchen cold war. Once, however, something unexpected happened. On the dial of the Glory radio set, beneath the small square pane, a red beetle was scampering. I screamed and jumped up from my chair, offering the officer, who also had his allies, the occasion to give a scornful laugh. Trembling powerlessly, I prayed that the hand of Neculai Constantin Munteanu would arise from beneath the casing of the radio set and, gently but authoritatively, flick the bloke's nose. The hand did not rise up.

One rainy afternoon, I realised that we had lost the cold war. Mother came into my room (formerly Father's room) as I was sprawled on the rug reading. She sat down on the bed and we talked for a while about a novel by some Russian writer and about how black the sky was. She asked me whether I wanted milk and rice and I told her that I had just polished off two bowls. Then she said, all of a sudden, that I was going to have another brother. Defeat was so beautiful! Like Mother.

***

It was the way it had to be and no one is to blame. Mother left at around three to breastfeed the new Mircea. My Uncle Ionică, the doctor, said that he would be gone about half an hour, maybe two, so that he could rest and fetch a urinary catheter. My grandmother Veronica had shut herself up in her altar-like room and was praying ceaselessly. My Uncle Didi, whose name is carved on the edge of a table in the cabin on Mount Omu (next to that of his brother and the year 1935), was crying softly in the kitchen next to a bottle of palinka.[21] Matei was little and he was at Uca's. And I, having just arrived home from lycée, this time not like a lightning bolt, wrapped in a school uniform, but like a whipped dog, kept stroking the brow of my old and beloved Mircea. I kissed his hands and promised him that we would climb to the Cross on the top of Mount Caraiman. My tears were choking me and I had a lump in my throat. And he, Mircea Kiril, who everyone said was in a deep coma, lifted one finger slightly and wagged it to say that we wouldn't, then he breathed ever more shallowly, until he breathed no more. I think he is at the Cross now.

XI

Resistance, Peace and Cadence

It may be that no map in the world, no matter how detailed – with latitudes and longitudes displaying that nonchalance of irrefutable imaginary things, with jumbled throngs of sinuous or squiggly brown lines to mark contours, with esoteric altitude triangles to let you discover high and low ground, with those continuous or punctuated blue veins, which reveal to you not a region's aristocratic breeding, but only its hydrographic network, with the green blotches of forests and the pale yellow blotches of grazing land, with all the puny white squares whereby science swiftly and irrevocably demonstrates to you that man not only exists but has also built villages and towns for himself, with the straight or jagged, rarely curved, lines of paths and roads, with rigorous toponymy (of the Argeş Valley, Ialomitza Valley, Parva, Băiuţ variety) – no map in the world will ever mention the cross that was carved into the bark of that tree. In fact, I can be sure of it. Not because dense, luxuriant, liana-draped vegetation will have blotted out its existence, like an ancient idol overlooked by explorers in search of pagan curiosities, not because its significance in the secret purpose and course of the world will have borne a striking resemblance to the fate of a vegetable (let's say an onion abandoned outside in the frost), not even because of the otherwise well-considered and pertinent reason that maps have not hitherto been concerned with the mysteries harboured by the dark gardens of four-storey blocks, but merely because, in certain cases, only the memory can plot the boundaries of a particular place, in order to reveal and decode at its very heart the axis around which everything else revolves. And as the memory, like any other thing devoid of the cold assurance of a well-constructed map, can sometimes become so clouded that even the image of Grandfather Mircea is reduced to nothing but the grave reverberation of a voice and the almost fantastical recollection of huge striding steps, what is required is for something else to slip its way inside the brain's remotest recesses, a kind of strange nameless gleam. And when this gleam comes into contact with the hornets buzzing around in there, it will produce a kind of beneficial short circuit, which will enable you, let's say, to see Coshutza in the middle of the road, dragging his right foot through the dust until the asphalt shows through.

Not based on any commonsensical argument, but rather on diffuse intuitions, I am almost convinced that there exists a bizarre attraction (or at least a permissive sympathy) between such strange nameless gleams and the trolleybuses of Bucharest. Without there being any fire handy, I might even burn my fingers a little to demonstrate to you that although the R.A.T.B. (Bucharest Public Transport) does not have any contract with the invisible world, there is a route, perhaps an aerial one, from which, especially in one of those demented moments when all you can say is that you're riding in a trolleybus hanging on the bar, it is possible to glimpse, like a shining cut-out, that rectangular, block-thronged territory flanked to the north by Camp Road and bordered to the west by Ialomitza Valley Street and to the east by Argeș Valley Street. It is then that the plain which stretches to the south is revealed. And it is possible that, just as the gift of homonymy made a 'minuscule, gossamer-like fleck … [rise] high in the air and [float] over the rooftops, boulevards, trees, spires and vacant lots, before finally reaching the blocks of Camp Road,' this mysterious trolleybus may be more permissive than any aeroplane (it is a well known fact that the aeroplane won't take you flying because you're too little) and let you view or remember (it's the same thing) how, concealed within the cut-out, hidden from maps and scientific understanding, there pulsates, strange and imperceptible, a cross carved in the bark.

It is hard to say who had the courage, patience, lunacy or, quite simply, impulse, one night – after the din of the shooting had long since died down and the pistoleers, both the quick and the dead, had left their makeshift hideaways and quietly gone home, after the light bulbs in bedrooms and kitchens had one by one been extinguished, leaving the streets to the dim and flickering care of the street lights – to have stolen (most probably like a cat, or a lynx) up to that tree in Camp Road, hidden away among identical trees in the garden behind D 13, and to have carved, perhaps with the aid of a knife, a screwdriver or a hatchet blade, that apparently ordinary cross, a cross which, however, turned red whenever something important was about to occur. It may even be that it was no one (and from here to the improbable apparition of wee creatures in a mustard jar it is but one step). The cross may have sprung into being all by itself, without there being any need of people with knives, screwdrivers or hatchets. Whichever of these possibilities is the real one, and not discounting a third, compromise solution, in which the person, preferably while sleepwalking, was merely the instrument of unknown spirits, it is clear that not only its enchanted glow (like the russet sky at sunset), but also its very presence on an otherwise nondescript tree in Camp Road was sufficient to captivate us, to mesmerise us, to certify to us that what we had taken to be merely a garden had become, overnight, a sanctuary in the fullest sense.

Radu was standing next to me. And if, in the decades-long history of the neighbourhood, there was ever anyone disposed to be enthralled and mesmerised quicker than the blink of an eye, then that person can only be Radu. If I take account of his theory (or rather his certified revelation) which held that the Indian god Manitou had appeared behind block D 13, then the possibility that a garden could be transformed into a great big sanctuary, all of a sudden, acquired the certainty of a natural fact. In his presence, ordinary words would grow flustered, they would bashfully hide behind the likes of a Migu or a Doru, they would try to riposte from the cover of a football match, before vanishing altogether, weighed down by the unstoppable *gravitas* of expressions like 'this precarious defence is doomed to failure' or 'the strikers make no contribution to verticalising the ball'.

Radu was gifted with that rare ability of being able to ferret out the truth – cartoon strips and stories of cowboys-and-Indians – from the dusty and discouraging stack of old almanacs. He could pick his way along the rocky trails of the Apache warriors with his eyes closed. He could have elaborated an entire thesis entitled *The Life and Adventures of Dr Justice* by consulting his complete set of *Pif* comics.[22] With the greatest of ease he could reel off a list of all the baddies Rahan had ever done battle with during the course of his turbulent existence. He would give lectures on the meaning of human sacrifice in the consolidation and glory of empires known only to him. He would have been capable of laying down his life in order to promulgate the offside position in the rules of street football. He was intransigent and tenacious in fending off any objection on the part of his parents when it came to arming his fictive armies with knives, swords, bows and arrows, pistols, rifles and machine guns. He proved to be extremely attentive with regard to the numbers and accoutrements of his cohorts of toy soldiers. He was obdurate with any plebs desirous to enter his house and ransack his treasures. He was always ready to press his ear to the asphalt and announce to us the impending arrival of Winnetou. He didn't give tuppence for records with fairy stories about *Celandine* and *White Blackamoor.* On the other hand, he was ready to swear eternal fealty to whomever was worthy to be his blood brother. And, in one way or another, I was worthy.

It is true that the offside position left me cold, and, what's more, it seemed completely pointless to me. I also had reservations about listening with your ear pressed to the asphalt, not necessarily because I was nonplussed about Winnetou's working schedule, but merely because that dusty asphalt never inspired me with confidence. And it is equally true that somewhere deep down, in a secret place inaccessible even to blood brothers, I felt a warm and guilty liking for that little wimp Celandine and even for that great big milksop White Blackamoor. If I had any reason not to confide any of this to him, and, believe me, I had, then it cannot be explained by the almost magnetic attraction I felt around his marvellous toy soldiers, or by the petty argument that he used to let me come up to his flat on the first floor, entrance B, to shoot his bow and arrows, but only because such a confession would have been an act of betrayal in his eyes, and I can testify that those same eyes would have filled with tears and fury, and this was the last thing I wanted. Beyond his refined tastes when it came to fairy stories and records, his mystical worship of Rahan, and his profound scholarly knowledge of Apache civilisation, Radu was capable of a fraternal and passionate sincerity that made you melt. At least, it made me melt. I know that it seems hard to believe, but there were days when I forgot to play football, merely because during our journeys to the borders of the kingdom, namely to the bend in Camp Road, his stories used to become vividly real. We would be spied on from the tops of the ten-storey blocks by all kinds of individuals wearing war paint. We would be attacked by packs of starving coyotes, in other words two or three stray dogs, otherwise disposed at any moment to stop barking and let themselves be petted. We would watch the endless herds of bison thundering past and then stopping at the Ialomitza Square station. Fearlessly, we would leave civilisation behind and gaze for hours at the black vultures (as we used to call the crows) wheeling above the corpses of the palefaces which, we were convinced, dotted that field at the edge of Bucharest. And we would imagine that beyond Argeș Valley Street, where the grown-ups used to say that the no. 368 bus made its final stop, there extended a land of shadows whence no mortal, perhaps with the exception of Rahan, had ever returned alive.

It was one of those days. The leaves were turning yellow and littering the ground, perhaps because it was autumn, perhaps because they had grown bored of dangling from the trees. The morning was damp, dank. Radu was chattering away about the canary he was going to buy. The sky was gloomy and overcast. The sun was probably idling somewhere above the Grand Canyon, stubbornly determined to remain hidden, not deigning to illuminate the garden. It was a kind of nocturnal morning. It was the kind of weather when time is too disgusted to flow. And then, in the space of just a few seconds, long enough for you to be drawn by a strange light, you discover that never have you been more mistaken, that everything has changed, and a mere garden has become a sanctuary over night. Neither Radu nor I sullied the miracle by touching it with our fingers. It was enough that it was there before us, pulsating, a living proof that the stories had always been true and that the trolleybuses really could change into bison. The significance of that sanctuary, which Radu strongly believed signalled the presence, perhaps in some tumulus or unknown hollow, of Manitou, we learned a little later, after we had come round from our enthralment and mesmeric trance. Afterwards, our hearts racing wildly we discovered the snails and the cavity with the ants.

We had always believed that ants were unworthy of the slightest attention and that they would never be anything more than a pepper-like condiment for an absurd stew (consisting of worms and flower petals) cooked by the girls. It was obvious that we had been mistaken. What was happening in the former garden, the current sanctuary, had something of the solemnity of a sacred ritual, in which the snails (not just two or three, but nine or ten) were overrun by the ants (which were in the thousands) in a frenzied sacrifice that culminated in a disturbing metamorphosis, namely: once they had feasted on the slobbery and undoubtedly magical flesh of the snails, the ants hurried to ascend to the minuscule cavity in the trunk of the tree carved with the cross, they cautiously entered the protective pitch blackness. Unseen and unknown, having sloughed off their boring former lives, they emerged once more, tentatively and timidly at first, into the pale morning light. What we were privileged to witness no longer resembled a boring old story about ants. Those insects, the former ants, had acquired wings. No, they had not learned how to talk and they did not preach to us about the second descent to earth of Cristos, who had long since become Cristi and, at that hour, was probably sitting bored to death in his carpeted flat. And nor did they have any intention of bringing the rain. They merely spread their tiny, translucent wings and began to swarm helter-skelter around our heads and then through the garden. It was perhaps the first time that not even Radu was capable of finding any explanation. The cross in the tree bark had turned completely red and its colour gave us the sensation, I don't know why, of an ogre standing on a block balcony holding an enormous bucket, a snarling ogre that was the spitting image of Beardy Lame-man, an ogre lurking in wait for two children. And what puzzled me was that something in that sensation told me that we were those children, bowed over the snails and the ants as we were. And as we crouched there looking at the snails and the ants, it was not until we felt the icy cold water seep through our clothes and soak us to the skin, it was not until we saw on the first-floor balcony the snarling ogre's face of Beardy Lame-man and our ears rang with the words 'damned hooligans' that we understood that what we had ascribed to a sensation, was in fact the naked truth: the cross was a kind of monitory mirror in which the future could sometimes be glimpsed bright red. On that day, because Radu was sopping wet and, unlike me, had seen fit to cry his eyes out, I did not have a chance to communicate that astonishing discovery.

It had to wait until Sunday. I know for a fact that it was Sunday, because the light was leavening on the other side of the windowpane, gentle, calm and immovable. Filip was pretending to growl like a tiger, and I, perched on his chest, was trying with all my might to mimic his ferocity. A scent of tea and toast was wafting over us. The radio set was also imbued with the feel of a Sunday, and it was purring like a huge cat, playing a Tchaikovsky piano concerto. The music curled up cosily in every corner and nook, it lazily tumbled out into the street and even snuggled inside the placid clip-clop of the horses' hooves, in the asphalt of Băiuț Alley, in the gypsies' cart, in their long and tremulous cry, which gradually shed its meaning and transformed into a reassuring 'a-a-a-any-old-i-i-i-i-i-iron!' I could have sworn that as long as Filip believed he could growl like a tiger and tickle his brother at the same time, nothing would ever change, that the world would remain the way it was, eternally frozen in a Sunday like a lambent globe, that any amazing discovery was not worth much compared with the certainty that you had nothing else to do except wait for the cartoons and the five minutes of Laurel and Hardy and that, in fact, not even the cartoons or Laurel and Hardy are capable of giving you a greater joy than that paltry symphonic music and toast during which an older brother, after playing dead, has been resurrected and is pursuing you under the blanket. If there was still a future

– and a glowing red cross to announce it – it would have to wait. Until the afternoon, when a plump woman would appear and poke her head around the corner, yawning and rubbing her eyes, sapped from immobility and the futility of *The Sunday Albu'* on the telly, sending older brothers outside to play football in the school yard and middle brothers to the first floor of entrance B, to knock on the door of a lad called Radu.

As for this lad called Radu, it might be said that in the absence of an older brother (whatever you might say, a sister doesn't count), the miracle of a Sunday did not touch him at all. In any case, there was no worthwhile explanation for the way he agitatedly waved his arms and tried to convince me that there was no betrayal more dreadful than that of abandoning your sanctuary. It goes without saying that he believed me about the cross. What was incomprehensible was his stubborn insistence that not I, but he, discovered the truth first. There was no point in me reminding him that in the moments when the Beardy Lame-man ogre could be dimly distinguished in the carving on the tree bark, Radu had been absorbed (fascinated, enchanted, enthralled) by the wings of the ants. It was likewise clear that, having set off down the irksome slope of gainsaying, Radu would have denied to the bitter end even the much more obvious matter of him not having withstood the bucket of cold water and having burst into tears that verged on the hysterical. Given how set on a quarrel he was, I wouldn't have been surprised to hear him saying that a warrior such as himself is alien to the dishonour of tears. Anyway, even if it was pointless, I nonetheless reminded him of it. And what shocked me was not the icy silence with which he reacted to my words, but the incandescent cast of his, up until then, pale and freckled face. Radu was smouldering. We descended the few stairs to the entrance on to the street without saying another word to each other. Then, without looking at each other, we headed to the garden behind the block. It was as if the cross had been waiting for us. The ants and the snails had vanished without trace, however. It was quiet; it was Sunday.

The season had started. In Vîlcea, Nicolae Secoşan was announcing the first goal. It was the third minute and Chemical Works Rîmnicu Vîlcea were already beating Corvinus Hunedoara. Nicolae Secoşan was commenting live. Apart from that, nothing. We were standing there in a kind of surly silence and watching how the cross, up until then quiet, docile and even ordinary, slowly began to turn red. But this had nothing to do with Dynamo. Orac had scored from a free kick. And if there were any doubts, the match was taking place in the stadium on Stephen the Great Boulevard, Bucharest. Bihor F.C. against the semi-finalist in the Champions' Cup. The fate was sealed. That's what Radu told me. Not about the team from Oradea, but with reference to me. I was going to get a thrashing. On behalf of all the liars and traitors in the world. He had warned me. "En guarde, pussycat!" Or something like that. I ran for it. I didn't want to sully the sanctuary. Radu was saying something. Panting. Running. Accursed, peerless rascal, miserable coward, paleface (pale? he was much paler than I was, maybe not right at that moment, but in general), drinker of firewater, pitiful insect, mouse with a human face, crossbreed of an envier and a fly, bespectacled cobra, babirusa, warthog, gibbon, maggot, rattlesnake, tuatara, congenital imbecile, doll-lover that you are. At that point I stopped. I saw him coming and without thinking too long I hit him. He toppled like a log. He picked himself up and with tears in his eyes he looked at me with hatred, yelling through clenched teeth, 'You'll pay for this!' That was all. Then he vanished back inside the block. I was smiling and I felt like crying. I had hit my blood brother. I had hit the one with whom I had taken an oath, with whom I had discovered the sanctuary, with whom I had watched the herds of bison. The borders. The cactuses of the prairie. The treasure of the silver lake. I think that what I wanted to do most of all was to cry. And not because, as she was hoping, Aura Brontos-Aura tweaked my ears out of the blue thinking it would teach me a lesson. It didn't. And it didn't even hurt. It was easy for me to wrest myself from her ugly four-eyes grip. Her and her silly, sissy brontosaurus eyes. It was easy for me to stick my tongue out at her. Just like that. So that she wouldn't stick her nose in ever again. So that she would learn to stay out of quarrels between blood brothers. She had no idea that there existed a cross in which I had seen her tweaking my ear and all the rest. And nor will she ever know.

As soon as I got home, I locked myself in the bathroom. I cried my eyes out. I swore that I would never gaze into the red mirror of the cross again. Carefully, slowly, I tasted those salty little droplets. I rubbed myself with a towel. I calmed down. I went into the living room, turned on the television and started watching a match from Bulgaria. Levski Spartak vs. Lokomotiv Plovdiv. It ended 2-1. Sundays were dreary. Like matches from Bulgaria.

Obviously, in the end, I succumbed to the temptation. It wasn't every day that Dynamo played in the semi-finals of the European Champions Cup. I had to know – I mean, it was a matter of life and death – whether the lads had any chance of knocking out that team with such a phantasmagorical and terrifying name: Liverpool. And for that, it was enough for me to forget the promise I had made, to run to the cross, instead of passing by haughtily and defiantly (the way I had during all those months when I felt I had a vow to keep) and to remain there until it condescended to turn red, or not, as the case might be. It was no big deal. Ultimately, once I found out how things stood, I could always apologise afterwards. No, there was no doubt about it: this was no time for qualms or pangs of conscience. Night was falling. Dynamo were about to play at Anfield Road.

I can't say I saw the moustache of Ian Rush bristling in a changing room, or Kenny Dalglish's eyes sizzling and sparkling like hot coals, or Whelan snuffling softly, and another phenomenon that eluded me was the palms of Țețe Moraru, in the other changing room, expanding before his very eyes, and nor did I glimpse the Mosquito's thatch of hair or Gigi Mulțescu's craving to do the victory samba. On the other hand, what I can confirm is that the buzzing silence, which crackled like an electric transformer and which was first heard at the end of chapter four, held sway over not only Filip's heart (having become, after a complex series of metamorphoses, the size of a flea), but also over that life-form hidden away between the blocks, which Radu and I had lately christened the sanctuary. And since in order to survive every life form, be it a garden or a sanctuary, needs perhaps not chambers with atria and ventricles but at least an organ resembling a heart, the cross had taken over that function and was pulsating slowly in the bark of the tree, to the rhythm of invisible globules of deafening silence. It might be said that I was swallowed by a translucent whale, through which, if I looked carefully, I was able to glimpse burning light bulbs, the shadows of people gliding softly through their flats and even a dark splotch of sky. It might be said that there remained nothing else for me to do, if I wanted to escape at any cost, except pray to that heart-like cross in the hope that the monster would take pity on me and drop me off, just like the frigate dropped off the baby Mircea, in any port in this world, no matter how choppy it might be. I remember that the heart was glowing madly and there was no question of seeing in it Augustin hitting the goalpost or Graham Souness's insipid goal. I woke up in the house. I had been asleep.

On the night when Mother left the bedside lamp with the green light burning, and the Bogeymanman (a kind of man with phosphorescent eyes who floated inside a black, invisible sack, a shifting chunk of darkness) stalked me from the shadowy corner of Father's room, waiting for my ears to start ringing from the pitch blackness and silence so that he could peel himself away from his hiding place, I dreamed of big Matei. It so happened that he was sitting at a writing table, unshaven, holding a pen, with which he was scrawling something difficult to understand about time, jumbling up flying storks with a missed goal by Oneaţă Augustin, confusing the living room with flood lights, he was telling me about Father and some sandwiches or other, he seemed exceedingly agitated, he kept going on about how it would be better for both of us if it weren't for the Bogeymanman, I didn't try to contradict him, especially given that I was of the same opinion, but I would have liked to tell him to refrain, to give it a rest with the Bogeymanman (he kept calling him a grimacing beast, an idiot, a vile monster), it could occur at any moment, he knew it, too, and apparently he was ready for it, it didn't take long, and out of that buzzing silence, to be more exact from the shadowy corner of Father's room, there peeled away a chunk of darkness that rushed at us, the words had vanished as usual (however much they tried to remain written, they were being erased letter by letter), somehow, I don't know how, because I couldn't shake off the terror, Matei drew it towards the light in the kitchen, the monster fell into the trap, it was too late for him, however grimly determined to reach Matei he seemed, to hypnotise him, to petrify him, I managed to peek from the corner of my eye, to see him blinded, beginning to unravel, bellowing ferociously, almost stupidly, realising that in but one footstep, in but one instant, big Matei would grasp him by the hood and thrust him out of the window, wipe him from the face of the earth, like a big black beetle, the Bogeymanman was struggling, but already there was no escape, in the clear glare of the light bulb he no longer seemed so terrifying, he could be defeated, he could be tossed out of the window, he could be punched in the snout, that instant seemed to have passed, because all of a sudden Matei sat down beside me in the diffuse, soothing green light of the bedside lamp, he was asking me to forgive him for all kinds of strange things, a book and a chapter five, he was trying, I don't know why, to mollify me, he talked to me writing about my dear Filip (who also seemed to be his brother and whom, no matter how much he contradicted him, it was clear he loved enormously), about Uca, about Ştim and Ştam, about his need to remember that the most beautiful little house in the world is underneath the quilt, about lots of things to do with me (some of which I didn't even want to know, like Dynamo losing the return match against Liverpool F.C, for example), anyway, I would have liked to tell him to calm down, to show him that the Bogeymanman had long since perished, that when I grow up I want to be like him, the great vanquisher of the Bogeymanman, but the words stubbornly refused to let themselves be uttered, it was a strange dream, in which I couldn't speak, I couldn't do anything, it was as if it wasn't I who dreamed him but he who dreamed me, with the greatest difficulty I managed to stop him writing long enough for me to hug him tightly, very tightly and whimper softly, in a whisper, Matei.

XII

To Tudor Vladimirescu,[23] with Astonishment and Suppositions

If the school uniform trousers are lying scrunched up on the radiator and the blazer is hanging from the window handle, if one slipper is in the hall of Flat 40 and the other is hidden behind an armchair in the living room, if a vanilla ice cream is melting on the desk of schoolboy Filip and trickling over books, exercise books, scrawled paper and photographs, if under the bed there are jumbled a red sock, a tennis ball, a ruler, apple peel, peanut shells, a pioneer's badge, a blunt pencil and a chest expander (between whose chords the spiders are weaving as though on a loom), if all these things are the way they are, it does not mean that all is at sixes and sevens. Messiness is one thing, chaos quite another. Examples:

1. Elena Ceauşescu was in fact called Ramona. But in order for this to be revealed, what was required was a lorry with a white cab, which entered the yard of the nursery school and tipped four tonnes of coal under a poplar, so that a hundred children in short trousers could gather around the heap and imagine that the presidential aeroplane had landed, and so that Ramona and I, after clambering to the summit, could slowly descend the steps of the aeroplane, waving happily to the wildly cheering crowd.

2. Lab ware, no matter how sophisticated, can be smashed to pieces in the blink of an eye. One August evening, down in the box room of Loopy, whose father was a chemist and the director of an institute, we opened dozens of brown, green and beige boxes, with German and French labels. We removed wonderful objects made of glass, large, fragile, queerly shaped bowls that tapered into slender, spiralling tubes, through which, we believed, might gush polymers. Loopy arranged the vessels on the shelves. We all armed ourselves with the rocks we had brought in a tartan bag. He roared like a warrior about to attack. He took careful aim, and urged us to do likewise. The barrage was annihilating in its force. Those delicate objects shattered, without groaning, without screaming, splattering not polymers, but myriad shards of glass. Loopy's parents had just divorced, and his father had gone off to the seaside with a curly-haired young researcher, who was at the beginning of her career.

3. When there are lots of heads bowed over you, when you can hear worried voices and feel the chill from the floor all along your back, more than ever before you become aware of the flickering light bulb on the ceiling. You don't know who they are, the people looking at you, you cannot make out what they are saying, you don't understand why you are stretched out on the frozen mosaic floor, but you take note, with amazement, that the filament of the light bulb is changing colour every fraction of a second. Against the backdrop of this enchanting discovery, which you cannot wait to share with the others, you are gripped by another astonishing thing. All of a sudden you recognise the people, their words acquire meaning, you understand that you have fainted and that you are covered in blood. Their fear is contagious. You forget the flickering light bulb and hastily return to the real world. Someone is wiping your forehead and hair with a wet handkerchief. Someone else is bandaging you with a scarf above your right eye. Then the generic you, *through which the story has been flowing, becomes an* I, *the second person singular dilutes and disappears, giving way to the first person. And it didn't even hurt when the nurse stitched my orbital arch.*

I was at the Forest Glade camp, for the winter holidays, in the sixth form, mad on a secret game we played in the dorms after lights out, when we would light a fire in the stove using bits of foam ripped out of the pillows. In turn, one of us would inhale very deeply, 12 times, and then another would grip him by the plexus, until we lost consciousness. In the space of less than a minute, I dreamed fantastical things, with incredible intensity and clarity. On waking, one by one we described in detail what we had seen in that parallel world, which we had christened the cosmos.

Once, I was launched into orbit in the corridor outside the canteen. We were all waiting to go in for lunch. A girl with a snub nose, by the name of Daniela, didn't believe one jot of my descriptions about being a cosmonaut, and so a boy who was a rugby player, by the name of Gutzanu, volunteered to propel me into outer space and hold me up for as long as I floated through the meteor-streaked heavens. Afterwards, he explained that during my flight I kept struggling, and so he was sure that I had come back to earth. He let me go. I flopped like a limp rag. The wall was knobbly, with large grains of calcio-vecchio. *My face scraped down it until I reached the floor. A girl with a snub nose was wiping my face and hair with a wet handkerchief.*

4. It is no easy matter to win two eclairs with whipped cream. But after you have been to the cemetery with Cerasela and her sister, after you have played mummies, daddies and babies and had to attach a twig between each of their little legs, out of pity, you can safely lay a bet with Ionutz Costov when he says that girls must have willies because otherwise they wouldn't be able to pee. We argued about it on the way from D 13 to the pastry shop at C 7. Dodan Sorin, nicknamed The Rat, Ratty to his friends, crossed the bet. And it was Despina Tudorache from IV F, on her way back after refilling bottles of soda water at the shop, who cleared up the issue. Ionutz, Ratty and I were in the third year, in parallel classes, I, B and D respectively.

5. Marionettes are lifeless, painted wooden people who from time to time become animated and make children happy. For a long time no one believed me, especially when we were on our way to the theatre on a school trip, travelling to the centre of town on a long, chugging bus that didn't make any stops. On the stage we saw frenetic beings that looked anything but like they had just emerged from coffins. In vain did I tell them that Mother worked at the Wee Spelk Puppet Theatre. Some of them imagined that all puppets had souls, like Pinocchio. Others ascribed to the opinion of Gigi Monkey, who, given his uncle worked as a scene shifter at the circus, had seen how the animals move around, breath and snuffle not only during performances but also in the menagerie. I had to organise a little excursion. There were five or six lads from Băiuţ Alley, and Mother showed us around the empty auditorium, the puppeteers' booths, the woodwork shop, the scenery crammed wings behind the stage, and the office of the set designer, who was picking out materials for Gretel's dress. Then we went down a narrow corridor, at the end of which, in a windowless room lit by neon lights there were countless metal stands, like coat racks, from which were hanging hundreds of puppets on strings. I was as quiet as a mouse. And Nicu the Shoe stroked Petre the Little Tiger, he pinched him to wake him up, he shook him, softly at first, then vigorously. And he began to cry. The Shoe, that is, not Petre the Little Tiger.

Five examples are the same thing as five experiments and in the best empirical tradition they can bind together to form a *Philosophical Moment* (somewhat akin to the *Philosophical Moment* broadcast on the radio back then). In conclusion, nothing in Camp Road was at the will of chance. Perhaps even in the past, in the mists of history, it was no accident that Tudor Vladimirescu's *pandours*[24] broke their march and pitched their tents in such a place. With his mind heated by the flame of freedom and his legs cooking inside his top boots, Vladimirescu must have scented a kind of celestial order that dwelled on those plains full of thistles, henbane and yarrow, from where the dogs of Bucharest could be heard barking until dawn. I am sure that he felt something of this sort, even if nowadays, one and a half centuries later, beyond the Răzoare (Baulks) neighbourhood the only weeds that grow are between the blocks, in the cracks in the pavement and in the three major valleys: Argeş Valley Street (where the 68, 108 and 118 buses turn around), Olt Valley Street (the terminus of the 105 bus route) and Ialomitza Valley Street (the end of the line for trolleybuses nos. 84 and 93).

One fine day, let's say a Friday, the boxing epoch arrived. And the dawn of the boxing epoch coincided with the start of the period of major nosebleeds. Not because of punches, as you might expect, but for a completely different reason. On that day, Gianni Pascu set about chucking all the junk out of his basement, with the blessing of his father and grandfather, the one a headwaiter at the Lido, the other a manager at the Wayfarer. We helped him, especially given that we knew what he was planning, and his plans smiled on us all. We carted everything, down to the last tin tack, to the rubbish bins. We swept the floor and washed the walls down with a hose. It wasn't hard to clean up down there, because the Pascu family, whose refrigerator was full of cutlets, cheese, ham and whiskey, did not stuff their basement box room with sacks of potatoes, barrels of cabbage, jars of jam and pickles, and demijohns of wine from the country. In any case, the project was based on a linguistic affinity, transforming a box room into a boxing room.

Messrs Pascu, Father and Grandfather, removed their wallets from their trouser pockets, moistened their fingertips, counted out as many banknotes as were required, ran to and fro making purchases for the length of a week, paid for vans, draymen, painters and a workman with a drill, and then, patting Gianni on the head, gazed in enchantment at how they had done up their entrance D box room. In one corner, fixed to the ceiling by three thick chains, was a huge punch bag covered in brown leather, like a section from a tree trunk. In another corner there was a punch ball, clad in black polyvinyl. On the wall that faced block C 37 had appeared an espalier and a large mirror, as tall as the freshly whitewashed room. On the floor was a rubber mat and dumbells of various weights. And on a shelf were waiting two pairs of brand new boxing gloves. They did not have to wait long.

At first we were overwhelmed. It was as if there was not enough air for all those boyish lungs. We touched the punch bag, the punch ball and the boxing gloves as if they were made of crystal and might shatter into pieces. And then we commenced the assiduous training sessions, in which hierarchies and glory were reversed: Boniek (that was Ică) did not shine in the art of pugilism the same as he did in ball dribbling; Platini (that was me) pummelled the sack but avoided sparring with flesh-and-blood opponents; Ratty, a clodhopper who always played in defence, a caveman-like full back, knew how to take his punches and had a ferocious jab. In a few short weeks, the boxing top 10 looked completely different to the football top 10. Gianni alone was to be found in both: in the first he was a featherweight fighter with good footwork, strong lungs, a good, high guard and a harrying hook; in the second, he was self-christened Paolo Rossi, as a new leaf on a crooked family tree, whereby he tried to convince us that he was the descendent of an Italian family.

The fiercest bouts brought together in the same ring (located in the southernmost extremity of D 13, under the metal bar for carpet beating in the garden outside) Gigi Monkey, who was 2.03 metres tall and played inside left in handball for the Steaua juniors, and the thickset Ratty, who was thick rather than fat, with hands like shovels, the index finger of his right hand permanently crooked at a 60 degree angle after he had poked a nail in a plug socket years before. Gigi, with his long arms and a lunge that any champion would have died for, would keep his distance from his opponent and repeatedly hit him on the crown of his head, not delivering any decisive blow, but rather to avoid provoking any memorable events. Sorin Dodan, nicknamed The Rat, Ratty to his friends, would puff and pant like a steam engine. He would circle the huge ox in front of him, throwing lots of punches into mid-air, as if he were catching flies. He would endure the niggling punches raining on the top of his head and sometimes he would get in an uppercut to the liver, which would bend Gigi double, so that his face descended to a reasonable distance from the floor, enough to make it accessible to a direct hit, delivered full force, which would finish him off. They were the most beautiful boxing matches I have ever seen in my life, especially when dozens of spectators gathered, not to make bets, but to kibitz with all their soul.

Apart from that, one Sunday, when the Pascu family was away at the seaside, and the other residents of D 13 were at home, gawping out of their windows, there was an inundation coming from the Pascus' second floor flat, with devastating torrents of water. All the efforts of Naghy, More and Florea to break the door down came to nought (no one had ever seen a Yale lock like it!). And Mrs Constantinescu from the ground floor, who was also being flooded, found the telephone number of some of the Pascus' relatives in the telephone book. That afternoon, on Băiuț Alley seven motorcars arrived, including a beige Mercedes, from which alighted, coming to the rescue, not macaroni eaters, but some 20 women wearing floral gypsy skirts and headscarves and 10 men who looked as if they had left behind violins, accordions and zithers in order to come running. They were Gianni's aunts and uncles, there to salvage whatever could still be salvaged. Afterwards, Gianni still used to hum melodies by Toto Cutugno and Adriano Celentano, and my nose still used to bleed, out of the blue.

I would get nosebleeds on the bus, in the street, and when I was reading or sleeping. Once, it bled while I was dozing in the bathtub, and when I opened my eyes and saw the red water I screamed at the top of my voice. For weeks at a time, I used to walk around with cotton wool up my left nostril. In my pocket I used to carry a medicament which was like a sponge that would dissolve and sometimes stop the haemorrhage. I always had shirts, sweaters and T-shirts with large, blackish stains on the chest, left out to soak. After dozens of cauterisations, the doctors declared that it was no longer possible to seal the vein with silver nitrate, and Mother took me to the Fundeni and Colțea Hospitals, where a surgeon wanted to vulcanise my nose with a piece of skin excised from my back or my bottom, and an ear, nose and throat man suggested a treatment using X-rays. Matei, who had seen me so many times pounding the punch bag, but had never seen me box, suffered greatly. What made him suffer all the more was the fact that his friends Migu and Pipitza were Gianni's younger brothers and they had filled his head with definitions of manhood and pugilistic tricks. A wee little lad lost among the seething crowd gathered at the southernmost extremity of D 13, he used to look on Ratty, Loopy, Gigi Monkey, Gianni, Dan Apostol, Botty, Nicu the Shoe and Luigi as though they were comrades of Rahan. They would ply their fists galore, with real boxing gloves, while I watched from the corner of the ring, timing the rounds with a stop-watch. It was also back then, during the epoch of boxing and nosebleeds, also in the basement of entrance D, that another significant event took place, likewise in accordance with the rule laid down by *Philosophical Moment*, viz. nothing in Camp Road was left to the will of chance.

A few months after our grandfather had breathed his last and, I believe, set off for the Cross atop Mount Caraiman (where his soul would haunt the rocky trails, crags, gulleys, brooks, and glacial cirques), our grandmother Veronica sold her Florentine dining room furniture and with the money bought a bedsit. And because she wanted to get rid of them, but was ashamed to throw them away, she brought us a heap of parcels containing the old Mircea's personal effects. While the new Mircea, who now had three milk teeth, was crawling on all fours around Flat 40 upstairs, I spent 11 days down in the box room, which now both did and did not belong to the Florian family, because Mother had reverted to her maiden name after the divorce. All by myself, I opened package after package. I examined file after file, envelope after envelope, document after document. All jumbled together, there were letters, postcards, engineering designs, photographs, patents, articles cut out of newspapers, diplomas, technical reports, invoices, rigorous graphs plotting a moderate fever, construction site schedules, private jottings, lung X-rays, sketches of two little girls named Cristina and Ioana, three typed copies of an unpublished book with the title *Boundless Horizons*, hundreds of pressed edelweisses and gentians, a standard and devastating letter of dry refusal from the Sport and Tourism Publishing House, a badly spelled postcard from a little boy named Filip, medical prescriptions, the guarantee certificate for a radio set, and a greetings card without a message, only a drawing of a little house flanked by a flower and the signature of Matei. My grandfather's life was in those packages. With care, curiosity and a strange love, which sometimes prevented me from hearing the hubbub from the boxing room through the walls, I arranged that life in order. In the last package, not quite in the last envelope, but in any case one of the last, I found a thin wad of banknotes. There were ten one-hundred-lei notes, wired from the summit of Mount Caraiman, when the angels had taken advantage of a snowfall and a northerly wind blowing towards Bucharest.

In fact, everything took place with a purpose, each thing in its own time. If Matei had not been born (and 'the baby that came out of the egg surpassed all the technical specifications of a Rolls Royce or a Maserati,' cf. chapter eight), Father would have bought himself a car. What good would it have done him? Later, after he remarried, his wife had a Dacia 1300 and he failed his driving test three times. Moreover, in chapter six, 'Auntie Lucica said that, without Matei, she would have died without knowing what love was,' and, you can be sure of it, Știm and Știam would have been bored to tears. To tell the truth, if my parents had not separated, a) Father would still not have enjoyed domestic warmth, no matter how torrid the radiators in D 13, b) Mother would not have been 'convinced even today that that small fry was the biggest and most beautiful fish in the whole world,' the fish in question being a roach caught in the Argeș River by an officer using his hands, c) I would not have broken the door to Flat 40 using a hammer and chisel and I would not have seen Mother 'with her prow-like womb and her frigate-like figure' bringing Mircea into the world, and d) it would not have been possible to tell the tale of how Grandfather 'transmitted to that metal cot seven kilometres distant the seductive dream of snowy peaks, the mysteries of alpine alchemy, the language of the clouds and winds, and the frisson of redemptive ascents.' Likewise, in the logic of the purpose and basis of any occurrence, one spring holiday, when I was in lycée, I went to Sinaia with little Matei and two friends. And not only did we go to Sinaia, but one afternoon, at the insistence of one of them, we went to the swimming pool (where I hadn't set foot for a good few years). And not only did we go to the swimming pool, but also, as we were going in and she was going out, I found myself face to face with a lithe brown-haired girl. She was like a doe. And not only was she like a doe, but also, because of the way her eyes sparkled, the way she blinked and held her head slightly to one side, she was so beautiful that it made me dizzy.

End no. 1

I couldn't be bothered to draw hooks for handwriting practice. And as if that wasn't enough, in the middle of the white sheet of paper there was a huge splurge of ink. There was nothing to be done about it. Except maybe to invent a blotter. And I wasn't capable even of doing that. Without doubt, Radu was also drawing hooks. And Cristi. And Pipitza. An entire alley condemned to draw hooks. Even Migu, Doru and Bebe had been through it. It hadn't killed them, it is true, but nor do I think it did them any good. It had stultified them. All those hooks. I went out. I mean, how can a boy do his homework when his fountain pen is leaking? The cross had grown bored. Apart from me, no one else took any notice of it. Because of school, probably. Anyway.

I happened to be wandering lost in a labyrinth of convoluted, identical, monotonous Băiuț alleys, I was trying to stay calm, to find Block D 13, night was falling, pitch black, there was a whiff of cheese, around me the streets were beginning slowly to dissolve, I kept whispering 'resistance, peace and cadence, whoever cannot go on, a hand to help them along,' somewhere there had to be an entrance, a stairwell, a fourth floor, a teddy bear, what you give you can't take back, a kind of cardboard sun had appeared, it was struggling to shed light, to show me the block and the entrance, my limbs were leaden, eventually I broke through and found it, everything had run to seed, the people had vanished or perhaps they had never existed, Mrs Constantinescu, Florea, Naghy, Hîncu, in the letterbox there were thousands of envelopes, I was trying to get to them, but the metal lid remained stubbornly locked, there was a smell of staleness and spider webs, in the windows of the blocks around about the curtains were fluttering (after all, in that eerie silence it was impossible for the wind not to be blowing), I climbed the stairs cautiously, one by one, the landings looked as forsaken and empty as the labyrinth of Băiuţ alleys, behind the door of the Pascu family not a thud, not a voice, was to be heard, I could swear that Migu and Pipitza no longer lived there, the fourth floor had turned into a kind of mouldy attic, I couldn't understand why I had to knock, I knew that no one would answer, I went inside Flat 40, it was hard to accustom my eyes to the even, motionless, rancid light, there was someone else there now, someone unseen, all our things had been replaced with bizarre, unfamiliar objects, wardrobes and carpets, plastic fruit and jars of pickles, I was trying to make sense of it, to call for Mother, so that she could cast a magic spell and everything would go back to the way it was before, but even my words had vanished, then I found myself in front of Radu's door, I was hammering on the door with my fists and my feet, the door did not open, Radu had gone away, or maybe he was in the garden, but in the garden there was no one, there was nothing but darkness and the same impenetrable silence, there was not a trace of the cross or the trees, nothing but seemingly interminable night, I would have remained there for all eternity, if Filip had not smiled at me, if he had not called me over to him, so that we could leave those ghostly blocks, silently, together.

The next day, Comrade Jeanne the Can tweaked my lugs for not doing my homework. Little did I care. I had heard that the summer holidays were on the way and everyone would be going out to play. What I had not yet found out was that in the holidays I would be crossing Ialomitza Valley for good, arriving in Siret Floodplain and staying with Uca for a time. The time had come for me to learn a new expression: we're moving.

End no. 2

...the roar of the engine, vrrroooommmmm, the first roar, causing the furniture, the sacks of books and clothes, the boxes of crockery and the carpets rolled like pancakes all to judder. On the first roar, the panes of the vitrine started rattling. Then, I don't know why, the roaring grew louder (maybe because furniture vans roar louder than other vans). Slowly, we set off. When the van moved off the kerb, a bag of toys fell on my head. It slid off a cupboard. The tarpaulin at the back began to flap, and as we turned the corner at the end of Băiuț Alley it flew aside long enough for me to see that, at the southernmost extremity of D 13, at lunchtime, in the pellucid April air, no one was flying...

The Author

Filip Florian (born 1968) is a prize-winning novelist, whose early career was spent in journalism and broadcasting, including work as a radio correspondent for Deutsche Welle. A native of Bucharest, Florian left the city to spend a five-year period in the Romanian mountains. He emerged with his first novel, Little Fingers, now widely published and in eight languages. *The Băiuț Alley Lads* is a collaboration with his brother, Matei Florian. In the style of a first-hand account, the reader is invited into the life of two brothers growing up in Băuțeii Alley, Bucharest. Compelling and curious, the novel is published here in English for the first time.

The Translator

Alistair Ian Blyth was born in Sunderland in 1970 and educated at Bede School, Cambridge University (BA), and Durham University (MA). From Romanian he has translated a number of works, including *An Intellectual History of Cannibalism* by Cătălin Avramescu (Princeton University Press), the novel *Little Fingers* by Filip Florian (Houghton-Mifflin Harcourt), the novel *Our Circus Presents...* by Lucian Dan Teodorovici (Dalkey Archive Press) and two books by Constantin Noica; *Six Maladies of the Contemporay Spirit* (University of Plymouth Press) and *The Becoming within Being* (Marquette UP). His most recent translation is Stelian Tănase's *Auntie Varvara's Clients* (University of Plymouth Press). He lives in Bucharest.

Hardback edition first published in the United Kingdom in 2010 by University of Plymouth Press, Scott Building, Drake Circus, Plymouth, Devon, PL4 8AA, United Kingdom.

ISBN 978-1-84102-267-3

A CIP catalogue record of this book is available from the British Library

Translation: Alistair Ian Blyth
Publisher: Paul Honeywill
Publishing Assistants: Charlotte Carey, Victoria Halliday and Emily Wilson
Series Art Director: Sarah Chapman
Consulting Editor: Liz Wells

Typeset by University of Plymouth in Janson 10/14pt
Printed and bound by R. Booth Limited, Penryn, Cornwall

Visit www.uppress.co.uk/romanian.htm to learn more about this series

Published with the support of the Romanian Cultural Institute

Reference

[1] The nickname of F.C. Dinamo București (founded 1948) is 'The Red Dogs'.

[2] I.T.B. (Întreprinderea de Transport București – Bucharest Transport Company): during the communist period, the name of what is now the R.A.T.B. (Regia Autonomă de Transport București – Autonomous Bucharest Transport Administration).

[3] Leonida was a cake shop in Romană Square, one of the few such places in Bucharest during the communist period.

[4] Refrigerator and electronics factory on Timișoara Boulevard in the Camp Road (Drumul Taberei) district of Bucharest. Now defunct.

[5] Rahan – French comic strip written by Roger Lécureux and illustrated by André Chéret, first published in Pif Gadget (see note 22, below) in 1969. Rahan is a prehistoric hero and inventor (he discovers that the earth is round, for example, and uses his ingenuity to construct devices that anticipate modern inventions), who wanders the earth, championing the downtrodden, battling for justice and tolerance, and imparting his proto-communist principles of liberty, equality and fraternity to the primitive tribes he meets along the way.

[6] Linking hands, two equal rows of children stand facing each other. One row chants, 'Land, o, land, we want soldiers!' and the second replies, 'Who?' The first row calls out the name of someone from the second. The person called out has to charge the first row, and if he manages to break through, he can choose one of its members to join his row. The game proceeds like this, with each row taking it in turns to call out a 'soldier' from the other, until the ranks of one of the armies have been reduced to just one or two.

[7] The trainers manufactured at the Finca rubber products factory (now defunct) in the town of Drăgășani were a famous 'brand' of the Ceaușescu period. Nicknamed 'gumari' (gumsters), they were cheap and durable, but their quality deteriorated as the 1980s wore on and economic austerity, shortages and mass deprivation reached their apogee.

[8] Dan Spătaru (1939-2004), prolific songster of the easy listening genre.

[9] B.P.T. – Biblioteca Pentru Toți (The Library for All). Famous Romanian publishing series founded in 1895. During the communist period, B.P.T. published in paperback hundreds of classics of Romanian and world literature in print runs aimed to reach the masses. Small in format (16.5cm tall and 11-12cm wide), with uniformly red covers during the Dej period and individually coloured covers during the Ceaușescu period, B.P.T. books could be found in virtually every home in Romania during the communist era.

[10] The communist bloc version of the Tic Tac, complete with a shoddily made and unreliable dispenser.

[11] In the Socialist Republic of Romania, little girls' dolls, uncontaminated by the influence of the capitalist-imperialist Barbie, had such traditional names as these.

[12] Card game, from the French table nette.

[13] Another famous 'brand' of the communist period. 'Pasta de dinți Cristal / face dinții ca de cal' (Cristal toothpaste gives you horse teeth), as the rhyme used to go.

[14] Brand of toiletries from West Germany, much sought after on the black market in Romania during the communist period.

[15] C.C.A. – Casa Centrală a Armatei (Central Club of the Army), the name of C.S.A. Steaua București (Steaua Bucharest Army Sports Club) in the 1950s. The club adopted the name Steaua (the Star) in 1961. Steaua F.C. separated from the C.S.A. in 1998. Steagul Roșu Brașov (Red Flag) changed its name to F.C. Brașov in 1990.

[16] Uzina Autobuzul București – The Bucharest Bus Factory. Privatised and renamed 'Rocar' in 1990. The company went into liquidation in 2004.

[17] Scovergi are made from bread dough, usually with a cheese filling, and fried in a pan.

[18] The name is not common in Romanian, and even less so in Hungarian.

[19] In Romanian, țurcă. A game in which a piece of wood tapered at both ends is struck at one end with a stick so as to spring up and is then knocked away by the same player.

[20] George Bacovia (1881–1957) is widely regarded as having been one of the most important Romanian poets of the 20th century. The mood that is evoked in Bacovia's work is one of isolation, neurosis, lovelessness, despair, and existential anguish. It is a subjective state that simultaneously permeates and is exuded by his poetry's décor of muddy, provincial streets, pluvial autumn weather, deserted municipal parks, claustrophobic salons, railway sidings, abattoirs, ramshackle slum dwellings, cemeteries, and insalubrious taverns. The boards of this eerie, expressionist stage set are trodden by a cast of consumptives, suicides, alcoholics, madmen, funeral processions, the sniggering ghosts of Poe and Rollinat, and the alienated, anguished persona of the poet himself, assailed by disembodied voices boding imminent self-annihilation.

[21] A kind of brandy made from plums or other fruit.

[22] Pif Gadget was a children's comic that ran from 1969 to 1983. The comic was an organ of the French Communist Party, originally created in 1945, with the title Le Jeune Patriot, changed to Vailant in 1946, before finally becoming Pif Gadget. 'Pif' was the name of a comic-strip character (Pif le Chien), while the 'gadget' was a free gift that came with each issue (for example, 'Pifises' – sea monkeys). Thanks to its ideological credentials, Pif Gadget was one of the few western publications of its kind to be available in the communist bloc.

[23] Tudor Vladimirescu (1780-1821) – Wallachian revolutionary who led an uprising against the corrupt and oppressive Ottoman Turks and their Phanariote puppets in the Romanian principalities. The fields outside Bucharest where Tudor Vladimirescu and his pandurs (see note 24) camped during the Revolution of 1821 were the site of what would later be the Camp Road district.

[24] Pandurs – In the 18th and 19th centuries, irregular troops of various nationalities (Croats, Serbs, Romanians) who fought against the Ottoman Turkish imperialist oppressors in the Balkans using guerilla tactics.